SPOTLIGHT ON POPPY

MYSTIC FALLS
BOOK TWO

MARY WARREN

To all the dreamers, never forget dreams grow and change. Don't be afraid to change with them.

FOREWORD

Dear Reader,

I am so thrilled to share this story with you, but we all need to protect out mental health. Please be sure to check the content warning. If you are good to go, I hope you enjoy this lovely romance between these two wonderful characters.

Content Warning: Sexual explicit content, Mild Violence, Past parental death (cancer and car accident) Childhood neglect and abandonment, Parental alcoholism.

CHAPTER 1

Poppy

"Poppy, I think I'm going to be sick," Josie groaned as they pulled up to the farmhouse where all the bridesmaids were getting ready. Poppy could just see the look on Hannah's face if she walked in there with a puking bridesmaid. It was not happening.

Poppy put her hands on Josie's face and looked into her eyes.

"No. You're not. It is your sister's wedding day and you're going to pull yourself together."

"I know," she said, as she took a slow deliberate breath. "I'm so fucking hungover." Josie pulled down her oversized sunglasses and appeared to steel herself for the day as they stepped out of the car. Poppy's best friend, Hannah, was getting married today. Hannah had lived in the city when they were kids, but would always come back to her family's farm during the summer. They spent their summer days running back and forth between each other's houses and splashing in the creek that separated them. Then last year

Hannah moved to the Glenn family farm permanently. Today was her wedding day. Poppy was happy for her best friend.

Happy.

Yes, happy and not at all jealous.

"Hey Han, we're here. Where are you?" Poppy called out as Josie winced and covered her ears.

"I'm upstairs," Hannah called down.

They made their way upstairs to Hannah's room where they found her sitting on a chair getting her hair done. She looked beautiful and she didn't even have her dress on yet. Hannah was curvy and blonde and beautiful. She was sitting doing her make-up in front of the large vanity that led into the lavish master bath. Poppy had always known this room to belong to Hannah's parents, but after Hannah moved into the farmhouse permanently, she and Graham had taken over this room, and it showed. From the reading nook with a giant shelf of romance novels, to the framed picture of Hannah and Graham on the wall, it was much homier than it was before.

Hannah's sister had flown in yesterday from LA for the wedding and proceeded to get shitfaced at the rehearsal dinner. Poppy tried to keep her under wraps so Hannah wouldn't worry. But it's kind of hard to hide a bridesmaid dancing on the bar, having to be wrangled into a car, and showing up the next morning in sunglasses still reeking of booze. Hannah was a bit of a planner, and a bridesmaid puking was definitely not in the plan. Meaning it was up to Poppy, as maid of honor, to babysit her.

Poppy's family owned Smith's orchard on the property next to the Glenn's farmhouse. It was a staple of the community. Her brother had taken over operations after their grandfather passed away four years ago and was working to make improvements. Poppy, however, was still just trying to figure it all out, and with everyone around her settling down, she felt like she was running out of time.

Getting out of Mystic Falls was something Poppy had always wanted. She'd left for college, and even lived in the city for a while doing the whole starving artist thing. But she came back when her grandfather got sick and just never seemed to get enough steam to get anywhere after that.

But today was not a day to dwell on that, it was a day to celebrate Hannah and Graham's love, plus it was time to get ready. Poppy curled her long brown hair and braided two pieces on the side to pull back out of her face, then pinned some flowers into her hair. She then worked on Josie's hair while she sipped her Gatorade. Hannah didn't even ask, which Poppy was thankful for.

"I need to go to the bathroom," Josie said, standing abruptly. She left quickly and shut the door behind her.

"How drunk was my sister last night?" asked Hannah.

Poppy had to laugh to herself. She should have known there would be no keeping a detail like a hungover bridesmaid from Hannah.

"She was 'dancing on the bar' wasted. Sam and Josh both had to wrangle her into the car. Then she slept on Sam's couch, but don't worry. I got it all under control," Poppy said in her most reassuring tone.

"I know you do. Best maid of honor ever."

"And don't you forget it." She put her hand up and Hannah slapped it a five.

"Not even a chance. I wanted to tell you." Hannah turned from the mirror to face her. "Yesterday Graham and I made a little trip to the Ren Faire in town."

"Oh yeah?" This piqued Poppy's interest.

Hannah and Graham had a very interesting love story. Last year at the Renaissance Fair Hannah had bought a love spell from a vendor at the fair. Later that night, she performed the spell, not thinking it would work in any way, but the next morning when she awoke to Graham in her barn... from 1745. It had been quite a year for them, but they were a match. Poppy had never seen two people more in love or more suited for each other. It was like they both brought out the best in each other and they shared such a deep love. It was palpable to anyone who was around them.

Poppy would give anything to have a love like that. And if this was going where she thought it was going, she might just make her move to find a love like theirs.

"Yeah, we stopped by the tent of the Scottish witch and invited her to the wedding," Hannah continued.

"Is she coming?" Poppy tried to sound calm, but she was screaming on the inside. She had wanted to make it to the fair to see if the witch was there to get a spell of her own, but on the weekend of her best friend's wedding, there just hadn't been time. But if the witch was indeed in attendance, Poppy was going to see if she could get a spell of her own. She wanted her own magical boyfriend. Maybe then she could finally start living her life, find a way out of Mystic Falls and stop feeling like there was something just out of her reach here in this small town.

"She said she would try," Hannah said. "I still can't believe our own story sometimes. However it happened I'm just grateful. I love him so much." The last couple of words caught in her throat and her eyes got a little glassy.

Poppy reached out and gave her hand a reassuring squeeze. "I know you do, and so does everyone who sees you two together."

"That sounds like some good speech stuff right there, maid of honor," she said trying to collect herself.

"Oh trust me, I got the speech in the bag."

The door opened and Josie slipped back in. Even though

her eyes looked watery and her breath smelled minty fresh, they all proceeded to get ready as nothing had happened.

Poppy slipped into her knee-length, emerald green dress. It hugged her curves and showed off her large chest. She fixed the daisy that was nestled in her hair and gave herself an appreciative once-over in the mirror. She looked good, and she knew it. Poppy was fat and was once self-conscious about her body. She had a big butt and a belly, but she also had a very large chest. Sometimes it was too large if she were being honest, but she learned to work with what she had been given. And with a best friend like Hannah, who you could share clothes with, it all seemed to work out.

There was a soft knock on the door. Hannah's mother came in carrying the bride's dress. Hannah slipped it on, and all three women turned and looked at her, all of them with tears in their eyes. It was a white knee-length gown, the top fitted and the bottom flowy with lots of sheer layers. She wore a beautiful sapphire pendant necklace that Graham had given her, and a beautiful crown of flowers sat atop her soft blonde waves. If anyone would have told Poppy last year that her urbanite best friend would be getting married on the farm wearing a flower crown, she would have laughed at you, but things changed when she found Graham.

"Hannah, you look so beautiful. I don't think I've ever seen a more beautiful bride," her mother said as she pulled her into a hug. She pulled her back looking at her, wiping her tears.

"Mom, stop. You are going to make me cry and I just finished my makeup," said Hannah.

After they all finished getting ready, they made their way down to the field that had been set up with chairs and a breath-taking amount of flowers. Though Hannah had left the city behind for small town life, this wedding was a mix of small town charm and big city elegance.

All three of the girls and Hannah's father were waiting to walk down the aisle. Graham stood under an arch over-flowing with flowers. He looked handsome in his kilt. Hannah's brother, Brett, and Poppy's brother, Sam, stood up with him. Graham had made fast friends with Poppy's brother. Probably because they both enjoyed working outside and were a specific brand of laid-back but over-bearing all at the same time.

Sam and Poppy grew up very close. That is what happens when you run a family business like the orchard. As infuri-ating as he was, he looked handsome standing up there next to Graham. After Josie made her way down the aisle, looking hangover free, it was Poppy's turn. She made her way down the aisle looking for familiar faces, most of these faces were city faces and too fancy for their quaint little town, but then Poppy found a familiar face. A smiling face that was just about as comforting as a smile from her own family. Josh Turner's smile always just seemed to feel like a warm hug, some things about Mystic falls had changed in her time away, but not him. Josh was just the same as she remembered him.

When it was Hannah's turn to come down the aisle everyone turned and watched her walk, but not Poppy. One of her absolute favorite moments of a wedding happened when everyone turned to see the bride. She always made a point to be watching the groom standing up front. She had learned it from one of the rom-coms she and Hannah watched growing up, but it was true. There was something powerful about the moment when he set eyes on his bride coming down the aisle, it was often missed, but Poppy never missed it.

And Graham didn't disappoint. At the exact moment Hannah came into view, his breath caught, his eyes teared up and his mouth fell open for a split second. He stood there in his kilt with his red hair tied back, momentarily frozen at the sight of his bride. Poppy had to wipe a tear from her own eye. That is what love looked like, and that is what Poppy wanted more than anything.

Poppy kept her eyes peeled during the ceremony for the woman who gave Hannah her love spell. If she came, Poppy was going to ask for a spell of her own. She was happy for Hannah, but she wanted her own happy ending.

About halfway through the ceremony, Poppy spotted her. There she was, a short round woman with wild, red hair with streaked with gray. Poppy decided she would find a way to talk to her during the reception.

When the ceremony was over, everyone headed to the reception. Poppy sat at the head table between Hannah and Josie and looked out over the people gathered. It was time for Poppy to give her speech, and she had spent so much time preparing what it was exactly she wanted to say. Sam had just finished his speech about finding a new friend in Graham and toasting to the love between them, and now it was Poppy's turn. She took the mic from the DJ and stood.

"I look out tonight over this sea of faces all here to celebrate Hannah and Graham. Some of the faces are familiar. They are here to celebrate with a child they watched grow in the summers who is now a new member of our little town, and we are so excited to have Hannah and Graham here in Mystic Falls. Others of you know city Hannah, the tough-as-nails lawyer who doesn't take any crap. I have had the privilege of knowing both sides of Hannah. In the past year she has spent here in Mystic Falls I have watched something truly magical. I have watched both sides of Hannah become one this year. She is country Hannah, the eight-year-old I used to play with in the creek that separates our houses, and she is city Hannah, the badass lawyer who is going to tell you exactly what she is thinking.

Part of the reason she was able to bring the two facets of

her that exist into one amazing person is due to the love between her and Graham. I have watched their love from day one. I saw the way they argued when they first met, both of them have tempers." A few knowing chuckles came from the crowd. "I've also seen the way they defend each other. I've seen the way they support each other. I've seen the look in each of their eyes when they think no one is looking, that look that says, 'I am the luckiest person in the world.'

I think that is all any of us want. We want a love like theirs. We want a love powerful enough to move mountains, safe enough to truly be yourself, and fun enough that you feel so truly blessed that this person loves you. May we all someday find a love like Hannah and Graham."

She raised her glass. "To Hannah and Graham." taking a sip from her champagne flute, she looked to see tears running down Hannah's cheek and a warm smile on Graham's face.

She sat back down as the servers brought out dinner. "How'd I do?" she asked Hannah.

"Terrible. You made me cry," said Hannah with a smile and hugged her. She looked over at Graham who just held up his glass to her with a warm smile.

After the dinner was over and the dancing started, Poppy tried finding the woman before she left. She spotted her slipping away and making her way to the parking lot.

"Hey!" Poppy called after her. The woman turned and gave Poppy a warm smile, slowing to allow Poppy to catch up with her.

"I was hoping to catch you before you left," Poppy said.

"What can I do ye, deary?" asked the woman. She had a kind voice and a twinkle in her eye, much like she did the day she made the spell for Hannah.

"You're the woman from Ren Faire, right? Do you

remember me? I was with Hannah when she bought the spell," said Poppy.

"I remember ye, dear."

"I know what you did for Hannah." There was no use beating around the bush. Poppy wasn't exactly the 'beat around the bush' type anyway.

"I'm not quite certain what you are referring to, lass," she said with a knowing grin.

"Okay. Okay. I got you," Poppy answered back playing along. "Let's say, I wanted a spell like the one you gave Hannah. One to help me find my own hunky highlander. What should I do?"

"I'm afraid I don't know a spell to bring you a hunky highlander, but I have been known to whip up a successful love spell in my day."

"Okay, that then. I want that."

"Well, if just so happens I have one with me just for this very occasion." said the woman giving her bag a small pat. "The one I have for you will work a bit differently, but I think it will work all the same." She reached into her bag and pulled out a small vial.

"What do I need to do?"

"Ye're a determined one, aren't you lass?" the older woman smirked at her.

"Yes. I'm ready to figure things out and start living my life. I feel like someone hit the pause button on my life years ago, and I just can't seem to get it going again," Poppy said as she took the vial from the woman.

"Now what ye're going to do is brew yourself a nice cuppa tea. Add this little potion to the tea," she said gesturing to the vial in Poppy's hand. "And while you drink it, write down whatever it is ye're searching for on a wee slip of paper. Then I want ye to fold up the paper and tuck it under yer pillow. All that's left then is to finish the tea and drift off to sleep."

"That's it?" Poppy asked warily. "Hannah had a spell she performed under the moon."

"No, that's it for this particular spell," the woman answered back. "Just bear in mind that not all spells work the same. Some people's love is somewhere across space and time, some are much closer. Just keep an open mind and follow your heart. I promise it will not steer ye wrong."

Poppy examined the vial. It was a small glass vial filled with a shimmering iridescent liquid and a cork stopper poking out the top.

She looked up to thank the woman, but she was gone. Not like walked away gone, like gone gone. It was a little unsettling, but Poppy was anxious to try the spell.

"Hey Poppy, what are you doing out here?" she heard a familiar voice call to her.

She turned around to see Josh. They had been in the same class together since first grade. He was a person who was always just around. Although Poppy hadn't thought that much about it before, he was very attractive. He was tall with a muscular build, but he was handsome in this boy next door kind of way. His eyes were a deep blue that sparkled against perfectly tousled brown hair. He was friendly and helpful and always had a warm smile on his face. Even though Poppy didn't know him extremely well, he was naturally comforting. It was just nice to know people like Josh existed.

"I was just on my way back. I came out here to say goodbye to someone," Poppy said as she made her way over to him.

"How about a dance?" he asked with a soft smile.

"Haven't you had enough dancing with me?" she asked.

They were both in the community theater's production of Little Shop of Horrors. Josh was playing the part of Seymore, which always struck Poppy as funny. Seymore was supposed to be this nerdy little guy, and Josh was far from that. But he could sing and that is all that really counted in their little theater. Poppy, of course, was playing the part of Audrey. She loved being in the shows in Mystic Falls, but she had once dreamed of seeing her name in lights somewhere else, but here she was back in this town. A town where everyone knew everyone, but everyone especially knew her because of the orchard.

"Nah, I never get enough dancing with a beautiful woman," he said as he held his arm out for her.

She threaded her arm through his and allowed him to lead her back to the reception and onto the dance floor. Looking around she took in the night. Hannah and Graham were lost in each other, gone and hopelessly in love. Sam and Jackson were dancing, Jackson whispering something in his ear while Sam laughed. The sun was setting on this September night and the fairy lights twinkled above the dance floor. There was something magical about this moment, besides the magic spell sitting safely in Poppy's purse.

Josh took her hand and spun her with ease and caught her in his arms. He was quite debonair. As they danced, Poppy looked up and saw the first star in the sky. She couldn't help but think of that spell in her purse. When she got home, she would put it into motion, and hopefully, soon she would be dancing at her own wedding and starting her own adventure.

CHAPTER 2

Poppy

When Poppy got home that night, she took the vial from her purse. The woman said to add it to her tea and drink before she went to bed. She was exhausted from the day, so she was looking forward to bed for a couple of different reasons. After she showered and washed away the makeup and the hairspray, she put on her comfy pajamas and started to make some tea.

A small creak of the floorboard alerted her to her grandmother's presence. She entered the kitchen in her housecoat and slippers. Gran was a small woman. Poppy had been taller than her since fifth grade. The rest of their family seemed to take their height from her grandfather, but her slightness of stature did nothing to deter from her position as the strong matriarch she was.

"How was the rest of the wedding?"

"It was amazing," Poppy said with a dreamy smile on her face.

"It was a lovely ceremony," said Gran.

"It really was. I'm so happy for Hannah. She and Graham look so happy. I want that," Poppy said wistfully.

"Don't worry, darling," said her gran. She gently patted her hand. "Your time will come."

Poppy had always been a hopeless romantic with big dreams. She felt like there was more to life than what existed here in Mystic Falls. She wasn't quite sure what she was looking for, but she was hoping the answer was in the potion in her purse on the table.

Poppy got a mug down and poured herself some chamomile tea. "Okay, well, I'm off to bed Gran," she said as she stopped by to kiss her on the cheek.

"Goodnight sweetheart."

Poppy left the room and grabbed her purse that contained the little vial. It was time. Tonight, was the start of a fairytale of her own.

Poppy climbed the stairs to her bedroom. It was the same room she had slept in since she was a little girl. She had gotten away for a few years when she went to college. But after her grandfather died, it was all hands on deck to manage the orchard. Of course, she moved home, but she never thought she would be here this long. She had updated the room as much as she could, changing the wall color and adding some framed photos instead of tacked up posters, but there was only so much she could do. Being almost twenty-eight living at home and working the register at her family's orchard was a little soul-crushing. There had to be more to life than this. More adventure. More romance. Just plain more.

The vial in her hand was the answer.

Poppy sat on her bed and placed the cup of tea on her nightstand. Opening the drawer, she pulled out a notebook and a pen. What was it she was looking for? She wished she knew. She closed her eyes and took a deep breath, trying to clear her mind, to hone in on what it was that she wanted. Taking the pen, she wrote the three words that came to her. Contentment. Love. Adventure. These things seem simple, but they had always been just out of her reach.

Holding the vial in her hand, she pulled the little cork out of the glass vial and sniffed it. Nothing. It had no odor. She wasn't sure what it was, but she was ready for what it could bring. Tipping the vial, she dumped the contents into her cup. The liquid swirled and shimmered in her tea.

Now is the time, she thought. Bottoms up.

She drank the tea in little sips at first because it was still quite hot. As she blew on it, she thought of what it would bring. Hannah told Poppy she had asked for love. She had asked for a man she wouldn't have to take care of. Graham was great for her. He took care of her. He noticed her needs in a way no one ever had, even her family. Hannah was absolutely in love with him. It was a magical thing to witness. Everyone could see the magic. Although no one knew how truly magical it felt, except them.

Poppy wanted love, but more than anything she wanted adventure. She wanted a life that was as big as she was. And while, yes, she was a big person, her body was nothing compared to her personality. She was larger than life. All her life, Poppy had been told she's too much. She never really knew if they were talking about her body, her loud mouth, or her straight forward attitude, but she tried to just let it go. Her gran always told her not to let people bother her. "Don't be limited by the small minds of people in this small town." Those words helped Poppy keep her sparkle in those tough times. Poppy was who she was, like it or not. And this was her time. She was going to get out of here and claim the magic for herself.

Poppy took another sip of the tea, now cool enough to

drink, and downed the whole thing in a few gulps. She set the mug down, pulled the blankets up, and went to sleep.

When sleep finally found her, she had the strangest dream. She was walking through the forest filled with a dense fog. And even though she was surrounded by trees and green underbrush, it smelled of beer and peanuts. After walking down the path for a little bit, searching for something she couldn't quite put her finger on, she came to an elevator in the woods.

After inspecting it, she pressed the up-arrow button. A bell sounded and the doors slid open. Poking her head in she checked it out, trying to decide if it was to be trusted. Taking a deep breath, she walked in. Instead of their being floor numbers, there was only one button marked clouds. Giving it a push, the door closed, and the elevator shifted beneath her feet. The elevator dinged and the doors slid open revealing that she was actually up in the clouds. Poppy tested the cloud with a foot to see if she could stand. They easily supported her weight, and she stepped out and they felt solid beneath her feet. She walked to the edge of the cloud and looked down.

It was the main street of Mystic Falls, the sleepy little town she had lived in her entire life. Mystic Falls was a small town that consisted of three stop lights, a handful of bars and restaurants, a library, a little theater, a few other shops, and a gas station.

There was a festival, because there was always a festival. She could see everyone who lived there gathered. Hannah and Graham were there, looking ridiculously happy, and Poppy was once again, not jealous at all. Then she saw Sam and Jackson enjoying themselves. Josh Turner was standing next to them, but he didn't seem to be enjoying the festival, he was searching the skies for something. Further down she saw her gran standing next to her dad. She had to stop for a moment as her heart fluttered and she saw her mother standing right beside her dad. She looked up, right at Poppy and smiled.

"It's coming, Poppy. Trust in yourself and follow your heart. I love you, I have been watching over you. Your time is coming, darling. Just make sure you can find a quiet place in your heart to hear the truth."

The dream dissolved away to the sound of Poppy's alarm clock. She had to get up and get ready for work but would have given anything to go back into that dream. The voice of her mother was still ringing in her ears. When Poppy was a child, her mother had gotten cancer, and when Poppy was twelve, she passed away. It was a long time ago but losing her mother at such a young age shaped Poppy. If she was honest, it was probably a big part of why she could never move away. She clung to all the wonderful memories she had of her mother, and all those memories were here.

She wasn't sure what all of that meant, but she would be forever grateful for the witch. Even if the spell didn't help, she had the comforting sound of her mother's voice in her head all morning, and that was more of her mother than she had had in years.

CHAPTER 3

Josh

osh Turner walked into play rehearsal at the Little Theater on the Square, the community theater of Mystic Falls. This wonderful little theater had been host to many shows and some of his happiest memories. It was a place he could relax and be who he was. And right now, he counted himself as lucky, because he was playing one of his all-time favorite roles opposite one of his favorite people.

He was thrilled to be playing Seymore opposite Poppy's Audrey. Poppy Smith had been a constant in his life. The whole Smith family had been a constant in his life if he was being honest, but there was something special about Poppy. Anyone who ever met Poppy could tell there was something about her. She had this energy around her. She was so full of life. It was contagious and it was something Josh needed in his own life.

He entered their little theater and saw most of the cast hadn't yet arrived, but the long dark hair cascading over the back of one of the seats belonged to his favorite cast member. Poppy was sitting in the front row looking down at her phone. Her dark hair flowed down her back and a signature flower tucked behind her ear. Poppy always had flowers tucked in her hair. Josh loved that about her. If he was being honest with himself there wasn't much about Poppy that he didn't love.

"Hey Poppy," Josh said as he sat behind her and gave her hair a gentle tug.

Poppy startled and turned in her seat. When she registered it was him, she smiled broadly up at him. That smile blossomed inside of him.

"Did you hear the news?" she asked. Her face was even more lit up than normal, and since she had a face that could light up a room on a normal day it almost hurt to look at the light coming off her today.

"No, what's up?"

"I'm not actually sure yet, but Steve said he was going to be about thirty minutes late to rehearsal and we should just run lines until he gets here. He's picking someone up from the train station," she said smiling.

Steve was the director of their show and local high school English teacher. He moved to Mystic Falls a few years back. Before that he was a teacher in Albany.

"Who is he getting?" Josh asked.

"I don't know, it's a mystery. He said it was someone to help with the show." She beamed at him. "Who do you think it is?"

"I don't know. Did he say anything else?" he asked

"That's it. It's intriguing though, right? I love a good mystery."

"Alright Nancy Drew, why don't we run lines then," he said, getting his script out. "Where is everyone else?" he asked. While it was a small cast, there should still have been more people there for their scheduled rehearsal, plus the music director who was not there either.

"I think it was just us here until later tonight."

"Right, well let's start running lines."

"You're no fun." She frowned at him and turned in her chair, getting out a bottle of water.

Even though he knew she was joking, her words stung a bit. He was plenty of fun. She just didn't know the real him, but sadly not too many people did. Poppy and Josh shared something in common, and it wasn't something anyone would ever hope to have in common. Both Poppy and Josh had lost their mothers the same year, Poppy's to cancer and Josh's to a car accident. And while Poppy had an amazing family to fall back on, that wasn't something Josh had. Life had been a struggle, but he kept the smile on his face and did what needed to be done. Maybe that was why he was so drawn to Poppy. She was so full of life, so full of joy. Josh needed those things.

They both moved to sit on the floor with their backs resting on the stage and began running lines.

Poppy shifted and pulled her legs up crossed legged on the floor next to him. Her thigh nudged his, and then she just left it there resting against him. Josh felt a zing at the contact and a warm glow at the fact that she didn't move it away.

They were supposed to work on their big song today when they would kiss. Josh wished he wasn't so excited to kiss her. He had been reminding himself all day it was their characters kissing, not them. Of course, he would be respectful and not make it weird. Poppy had never shown any interest in him, but a guy could dream.

"It was a beautiful wedding don't you think?" Poppy asked, interrupting his thoughts.

"What?" He asked, snapping out of his head trying to figure out what she was talking about.

"The wedding this weekend, Hannah and Graham. It was beautiful," she said with a wistful smile on her face.

"Oh, yeah, it really was."

"They seem really happy, did that bother you? I mean since you used to date Hannah?"

"What?" He wasn't sure where this was coming from. Yes, he dated Hannah, but that was years ago now. It wasn't anything serious, just a summer fling. Later that year he met Abbie, who he had been with for years after that, they had even been engaged. "No, Hannah's great. What we had was nothing serious. I wish nothing but the best for her and Graham."

"Ya know, that summer you and Hannah got together, I was so jealous," Poppy admitted.

Josh felt his heart drop right out of his chest. "Jealous? Jealous of what?"

"Of you and Hannah, but you apparently have a type, you like them serious and blonde."

She was no doubt referring to Abbie who was very serious, at times downright unpleasant.

"I wouldn't say serious and blonde is my type," he protested.

"It totally is. You picked Hannah, and then Abbie. Serious, check. Blonde, check."

"Okay, let's stop there, Hannah is fun to be around, you know that better than anyone. As for Abbie, we all have lapses in judgment sometimes" Giant lapses in judgment that last for years in the case of him and Abbie. "Plus, I once asked out a fun, beautiful, girl with dark hair and brown eyes, and she turned me down," he smiled over at her.

"If you are referring to when you asked me to prom, that was a long time ago."

"I'm just saying, if I ever had a chance with you, things may have been different." The words were out before he could take them back. They danced in the air between them. He wanted to pretend he hadn't just said that. Poppy meant too much to him, the thought that a slip of the tongue would make things weird or make her uncomfortable for even a moment spiked his anxiety and his heart fluttered in his chest. Finding the courage, he looked at her.

Her eyes had a sparkle he had never seen before, and his anxiety evaporated. Her tongue ran across her bottom lip and Josh's heart raced and felt a familiar stir in his pants. Poppy reached out and took his hand. Looking down he saw her painted nails; her thumb was even painted with a daisy. Poppy and her flowers. His thumb grazed over that painted flower.

He looked up and saw her face. The look on her face was not one Josh recognized. There was an earnestness where her effervescence usually was.

"It's funny how you can know someone your whole life, but never really know them. I did like you that summer," said Poppy.

And just like that, Josh's world was thrown off its axis. He had been in love with Poppy Smith since fourth grade when they sat next to each other on the bus on their way to a field trip. She was like a magnet. He was always pulled to her, but she never showed any interest. He had managed the courage to ask her to prom. But after she turned him down, he closed the door on the idea of them as a couple, but never on her. He couldn't imagine a world without Poppy Smith.

Now he knew. He knew that Poppy had liked him at one point. Those words had just come out of her mouth. That was not something he was going to forget. And now she was sitting here on the floor next to him, her leg resting against his and her hand in his. There was something magical in this moment. A spark of anticipation danced between them. It was like nothing he had ever felt.

"Used to like me? As in not anymore?" he said. He watched her. He watched a slow smile spread across her face. She looked down at their hands joined on his lap. The thumb with the daisy painted on it grazed lightly against his own thumb. Something clicked into place.

She looked up at him and took a shaky breath. He hoped she felt it too, whatever this was. The air was electric with the spark dancing between them.

Just then the door thundered open and in walked the director, one of the cast members and someone Josh had never seen before.

The magical moment that existed between him and Poppy evaporated as she pulled back her hand and quickly moved to stand.

"Oh good, you're here. I just saw the girls pull up in the parking lot. I called the rest of the cast early tonight. I have a surprise," said Steve as he strode confidently to the stage.

Poppy stood up. Josh ached at the absence of her and the magic of the moment that had happened between them.

The director and this stranger took the stage as the other cast members started to filter in and took a seat in the first few rows.

"I would like to introduce you all to Damien St. Cloud."

This guy took off his sunglasses and smiled. He stood there in a leather jacket and ripped jeans, looking like a perfectly manicured James Dean. He smiled and waved. Josh fought the urge, but couldn't help himself, he turned to look at Poppy. Her kilowatt smile shining her light up there on the stage, on this obnoxiously handsome stranger.

"Sadly, Ms. Maple had to leave town to take care of her sister who had a fall. We needed a music director, so I reached out to Damien. He's an old student of mine and is currently between shows... on Broadway."

There was a collective gasp and Poppy gave a little squeal

and clapped. Josh felt a rain cloud settle over him. He watched as Damien ran his hand through his hair and winked at Poppy.

"I look forward to working with all of you. I'm here for two weeks. Let's get this show up and running."

"Places for Suddenly Seymore," called the director and rehearsal had begun.

CHAPTER 4

Poppy

*P*oppy had been watching for signs since she did the spell Saturday night. She had been disappointed when she didn't wake up to find her own highlander that first morning, but she kept a watchful eye for anyone new or any possible meet cute on the horizon. The spell had brought Hannah her love and she trusted in the magic to do the same for her. Although that day nothing happened. After her shift at the orchard, she went to the bookstore in town and stopped by the Elbow Room for a drink that night. Nothing out of the ordinary though, just the normal Mystic Falls stuff.

She woke up Monday still on the lookout. Looking for a stranger in town or someone when she was working the register at the orchard, but nothing. Some tourists picking their own apples, a field trip, and a few locals picking up produce, but no sign of her soulmate yet. So, she worked the register and snuck back to the kitchen to bake some pies.

Baking was the only thing that made her job at the orchard tolerable.

It wasn't until rehearsal that night she actually got the magic she had been hoping for. She had been running lines with Josh, and for a moment she had thought maybe something was happening with Josh, but Poppy knew her spell had worked when she saw Damien St. Cloud walk in the door. This was it. He was her soulmate. She smiled up at the ceiling thanking that wonderful little woman for her magic.

She watched as he walked onto the stage, and when she found out he was an actual Broadway star, she squealed with excitement. This was even better than a guy from the past. This was a sexy Broadway star that could help to finally get Poppy's life going somewhere. She could already see herself back in the city, living in the hustle and bustle, and maybe even seeing her name in lights. This was it. It was time to find the piece she'd always felt was missing.

He was going to be there for two weeks. Poppy knew what she had to do. She had just watched her best friend fall in love. Now she would make Damien St. Cloud fall in love with her.

"Alright places everyone for Suddenly Seymore," called the director.

Poppy and Josh took their places. They played through the scene where Seymore finally tells Audrey how he feels about her. Audrey has trouble accepting it because of how bad her life has been, but she finally does. And does so with a truly epic duet. Although Poppy and Josh were not your typical Seymore and Audrey, something about the way they sang together made it magical. Their voices blended well.

When the scene was over Poppy looked out into the theater to see the director and Damien whispering in the back.

"Great job, Damien has some notes," Steve called out from the back of the theater.

Damien stood up and strode to the stage. Poppy watched with desire as he jumped up onto the stage, his muscles rippled underneath the plain white t-shirt he was wearing after losing the leather jacket.

"That was good, but Poppy, I think you could be supporting those notes à little more. I think that will help you hit those high belter notes. Try this."

He placed one hand on Poppy's upper back and one hand on her stomach. "Take it from the key change, and keep this tight and supporting," he said as his hand patted her stomach.

Poppy was trying to figure out how all of this was making her feel. He was touching her, but in a professional capacity. *Don't make this weird*. Also, he had his hand on her stomach, and while Poppy owned her body and all that it was, her belly was still that part of her body she hadn't quite learned to love as much as the rest. But this was professional. He was a professional. He would not judge her squishy belly, even though his was rock hard.

She sang the song again, Josh standing next to her singing his part. Damien's hands heated her skin. As she sang the higher notes, he gently pushed against her belly to make sure she was supporting the note.

"Lift," he said as she hit the high belt at the end and the sound just soared out of her with ease. The sound of it surprised even her. That last high note was tough, and she just sang it like it was nothing.

When the song ended, she looked over at Josh, mouth open in shock. "Oh my god, that was amazing," he said. She beamed at him.

"Great Job, Poppy," Damien said. He removed his hand from her stomach but the hand on her back remained in place. "You're really talented, you could go far with a little more training." His hand started rubbing her back.

Poppy looked over at him and he winked at her. Poppy was undone. She couldn't believe this man was her soulmate. She needed to learn more about him.

AFTER REHEARSAL the cast generally went down the street to the Elbow Room for a couple rounds of drinks and some karaoke. It was one of the few bars in their sleepy little town and one of Poppy's all-time favorite places.

"Hey Poppy, you headed to the Elbow Room?" Josh asked her in his casual welcoming way.

"Of course, I am going to check in with Steve before I head out. I'll meet you down there."

"Sounds good." He finished packing up his bag and got ready to head out.

Poppy walked to the back of the theater where the director and Damien were talking.

"Good rehearsal tonight Poppy, I think we are really coming along," said the director.

"Thanks, I just wanted to come and ask you if you guys wanted to come down to the Elbow Room with us." She looked over to Damien. "It's a local karaoke bar we go to after rehearsal sometimes."

"I don't think I can join you tonight," said the director. Poppy wasn't really too concerned if he would join, he very rarely did. But she was very much hoping that Damien would come.

"I would love to go. I want to live the small town life while I'm here," he said with a wink. That was the third wink he had given Poppy tonight. Poppy couldn't remember the last time anyone winked at her, let alone three times in one night.

"Great, would you like to walk with me? It's just a few blocks down the street."

"Sure, let me just finish up here and I'll meet you outside."

"Okay, that sounds great. I'll meet you outside." Poppy smiled at him. Her heart fluttered with excitement as she went down to the front of the theater to collect her things. She packed up and looked around. She was the last cast member there, most of them were already down at the bar.

She walked out and sat down on a bench and pulled her phone out. She was dying to text Hannah and tell her about everything. Tell her about the spell. Tell her about Damien. She even wanted to tell her about Josh and the weird moment she had with Josh before Damien came. There were definitely some sparks there. But with Hannah in Scotland on her honeymoon, she decided to just take a selfie in front of the theater.

The door to the theater swung open and out came Damien, he had this swagger and confidence that seemed to pull her in. He was just what she had asked for in the spell. He had a life bigger than this little town. He could help her to finally have a big adventure. And he was absolutely gorgeous, so that always helped. And really, Poppy would much rather have a handsome Broadway star than a time traveling high-lander. Things were much simpler that way.

"Hi Poppy, lead the way to your local watering hole," he said with a grin.

"Excuse me?" she asked, a little taken back. *Watering hole? What did he think this was, the wild west?*

"It's just an expression, Lead the way to the bar. I am interested in seeing how you all live."

He put out his arm and Poppy took it, and they walked down to the bar.

How we all live? Poppy thought. That was kind of a weird

thing to say, but he was from New York City though, so this place probably did seem pretty small to him.

Oh well, he was here, and she had work to do to make sure this love spell worked.

CHAPTER 5

Josh

There was a chill in the morning air as Josh walked down main street. He was helping his sister out at the Mystic Falls Inn. It was one of his many jobs. Money had always been tight for him and his sister growing up, so Josh became a jack of all trades. He did a little bit of everything from tending bar, driving Uber and being a handyman. Today that was his job. His sister was the general manager at the local inn, and she often hired Josh to fix things up.

His task for that day was sanding down and staining the gazebo at the inn. He needed to get this done before the weather turned too cold. And with it being late September, he was already pushing it. He needed to finish the sanding today.

Walking to the hardware store for some supplies gave him a moment to think. The events of last night had thrown him. First, there was the electrifying moment with Poppy. He could not get the feel of her hand in his and the look in her eyes as she slowly licked her lip out of his mind, and he didn't know what to make of it all. And then there was the interruption and that guy. Damien St. Cloud. His name was as pretentious as he was.

He set the supplies down on the counter and Theo Williams, the owner of William's Hardware, started to ring him up.

"What are you working on today?" Theo asked.

"I'm sanding and staining the gazebo at the inn," he said, taking out his wallet.

"If you are looking for any help I know my nephew, DeMarcus, learned a lot helping you put the deck on the back of the Elbow Room last summer," Theo said as he rang him up.

"He's a great kid. I'm hoping to get this done today and tomorrow, but next job I get working over the weekend I'll call him up."

"Thanks, Josh. See you soon." Theo handed the bag and bucket of stain to Josh.

"Thanks Theo. Tell Vivian hello for me," Josh said as he headed to the door.

"Will do!" he called back.

He knew some people didn't like small town life, they found it suffocating. Josh, on the other hand, enjoyed it. It comforted him that people here knew him, and that people here looked out for one another. He enjoyed that if he walked into The Corner Cafe, Mae would ask him if he wanted his usual and bring him French toast, scrambled eggs, and bacon, or give him a cinnamon muffin and coffee to go. He liked that when he went into Fipps Market, Mr. Fipps would stop and talk to him and ask about his sister. If he went into Mystic Falls Books, Katie McPhee would ask him to get something off the top shelf and give him a free cup of coffee. This town was predictable and often called on him to help, and he was more than happy to do so.

Turning the block, he saw someone he didn't recognize moving a table into an empty storefront. It was a woman struggling with a table that was about the same size as she was. Josh set down his supplies and rushed to hold the door and take the table from her.

"Let me help you with that, ma'am," he said.

"Why thank ye, Laddie. It is appreciated," she answered back.

Josh entered the empty storefront and saw that it was full of boxes and a couple chairs. He couldn't tell what type of business she was moving in.

"Where do you want this?" he asked as he easily maneuvered the table into the small store.

"Oh, just set it down right there for now, I still need to figure out where things are going."

"What kind of business are you starting?" he asked looking around the room. Setting down the table he noticed a little wobble to it.

"A magic shop," said the woman plain as day.

Josh stopped and finally took note of the woman. She looked vaguely familiar, but he couldn't quite place her. She was short and round with a head full of wild red hair that was starting to gray. She smiled right at him, and Josh could almost sense a magic twinkle in her eye.

"A magic shop? like a magic and joke shop?" he asked.

"No, a real magic store. I tell fortunes and sell herbs and spells to people who need them," she said.

"Huh..." he said, taking it all in with a gentle nod. "I didn't know our little town needed a magic shop, but the best of luck to you. Do you need help with anything else?"

"Well, if ye don't mind, I do have some shelves out there that are mighty heavy for me. Would you mind bringing them in?"

"Of course." Josh found the purple VW bus and got to work unloading shelves.

Once he had them all unloaded, he looked around.

"Your accent, Are you Scottish?"

"Aye, but I left Scotland a long time ago."

"Well, whenever they get back in town I will have Graham stop by. He just moved to the area from Scotland."

"Oh, I am very familiar with Hannah and Graham," the woman said with a smile.

"Yes! That is where I recognize you from. You were at their wedding."

"Aye, I was."

Josh suddenly remembered the gazebo and the time schedule. He needed to get started.

"Well, ma'am, I need to get going, but if you need help with anything else. I'm pretty easy to find. My name is Josh Turner," he said as he flashed his notoriously friendly smile and held out his hand. She took it and gave it a gentle shake.

"Well, Josh Turner," she said knowingly. "I expect I will be seeing ye around. Ye may call me Bridget."

"Nice to meet you, Bridget."

He gave one last look at the table he brought in and gave it a gentle nudge. "Your table seems to have a loose leg." On closer inspection he could see the leg had been fixed, but not well. "I can get this fixed for you if you want. I think it just needs a new leg."

"Oh, don't trouble yerself, lad."

"No trouble at all, consider it a welcome to town. I'll get it in a couple days."

"Well thank ye very much," she said.

"It's my pleasure ma'am. I'll see you later."

Bridget gave him a smile and Josh turned and left. As he walked to car, he couldn't stop thinking about the woman. He couldn't help feeling like there was more to her than meets the eye. He was definitely going to keep an eye on her, she seemed like someone who could shake things up around here.

JOSH'S SHOULDERS and arms felt heavy after spending most of the day sanding. He was ready to call it quits for the day and head home to take a nice hot shower before rehearsal. Cleaning up his tools and heading in to find his sister to say goodbye, he found her behind the front desk.

"Hey Lexi, I'm taking off. I'll be back tomorrow to finish it up."

"That sounds good. I'll be home probably around ten."

"Working both shifts again?" he asked.

"Yeah, with Brandy out on maternity leave we are trying to make it work."

His sister was quite possibly the hardest worker he had ever known. He worried about the toll it would take on her, she had been working full time since she was sixteen. It did pay off last year when she got the promotion to manager of the inn, but she worked hard for it. He tried to lighten her load where he could.

"Okay, I'll bring you some dinner when I head back in town for rehearsal tonight," he said.

"How is the play going? I haven't really had a chance to ask you about it. I know that Damien St. Cloud is here for a few weeks. How's that?" she asked.

Josh sighed and fought the eye roll. Damien St. Cloud. Where to even begin? Josh didn't like the guy, and Josh liked everybody.

"He's... something."

"You don't like him?" she asked. She smiled at him, already knowing the answer.

"I didn't say that."

"You didn't need to. I get it. He keeps asking for turn down service. He actually snapped his fingers at Aggie while she was cleaning his room. Who does that?"

"Damien St. Cloud does that," he said.

Josh was normally a happy-go-lucky sunny kind of guy, but that man was a dark cloud hanging over Josh's head. Maybe it was him, or maybe it was because he had interrupted something that felt like an important moment between him and Poppy. He thought something was finally happening between them after all this time, and now nothing. Josh was ready for him to leave. The show went up next week and he would be gone, and that couldn't happen soon enough.

CHAPTER 6

Josh

Josh pulled the theater door open. He was tired from the day, but he was excited to see Poppy. There was still a small part of him that hoped they could get back to that moment they had before Damien St. Cloud had arrived. Josh had felt the pull to her his entire life, but in that moment, that magnetic pull between them had been so palpable it took all of his self-control to not slide his hand into her long sleek hair and kiss her perfectly kiss-able mouth.

But that glimmer of hope was gone when he walked in and found Poppy. She was sitting down in the front row, leaning close to Damien, her hand rested on his arm and the light she gave off shining directly on Damien St. fucking Cloud. Shoving down his disappointment, he took a breath and put a smile on his face. That familiar jovial Josh smile masked his feelings as he walked down to join the rest of the cast.

His mood continued to sour through the rehearsal. Poppy

was giggling and making eyes at Damien all night. Damien seemed to be bolstered by her. He didn't seem to return the interest rather than revel in it. While jealousy was the main emotion coursing through Josh's veins, he was also angry. Poppy deserved someone who would return the energy, not just absorb it.

It didn't sit well with Josh, none of it did.

When rehearsal ended, Josh found Poppy by herself for once this evening. He decided to make his move.

"Hey Poppy, good rehearsal tonight."

"Thanks, you too. Damien is really helping me to perfect my craft. Isn't he amazing?" Poppy asked.

Josh's mind played through the rehearsal. He just kept replaying Damien's hands on Poppy when he was coaching her. Damien telling Josh on multiple occasions to 'just watch' as Damien sang through Josh's part with Poppy. He pushed the anger deep down. He had lots of practice pushing down his emotions, he was a top notch feelings stuffer.

"Yeah... He's great." He wasn't sure if that sounded sincere or not but at this point he was pretty far from caring. "Are you going down to the Elbow Room tonight? I was thinking about heading down there."

"Yeah, let's go. I just need to finish up a few things here."

"Okay, I'll wait and walk over with you."

Poppy cocked her head to the side and smiled at him. "You're the best. Just give me a sec." She turned and disappeared backstage.

Josh took a deep breath and ran his hand through his hair. He was going to tell her tonight how he felt. The timing for them finally seemed right, with the exception of Damien St. Cloud.

"All set!" Poppy said as she came out and grabbed her purse. "Shall we?"

Josh nodded and held the door open and gathered courage for the talk he was hoping to have.

WALKING into the Elbow Room always felt like walking back in time. It was this dingy little dive bar with an ancient karaoke machine. They didn't even have any digital selections, just an old school book of cd's and sticky selection books with songs that stopped somewhere around 2005. It was a vibe all its own and people around here loved it.

"What do you want to drink?" Josh asked Poppy.

"I'll take a cranberry and vodka with a splash of club soda and a lime."

Josh headed to the bar while Poppy went and snagged them a book and a table. It was a slow night, just a couple tables filled with regulars. Josh came back with the drinks and joined Poppy while she was flipping through the book.

"What are you going to sing tonight?"

"I'm not sure yet." she said not looking up from the book.

Josh's fingers drummed nervously on the table. He had chickened out on the way over, but it was now or never.

"There was actually something I wanted to talk to you about," he said tentatively. Putting his feelings out there was very vulnerable and being vulnerable was hard for him.

Poppy looked up at him with her normal Poppy smile, but after she looked at him her eyebrows drew together slightly.

"What's up?" she asked.

His heart was pounding in his chest. He rubbed his clammy hands on his jeans. His anxiety was starting to spike. Taking a deep cleansing breath, he tried to center himself for this conversation.

"It's about yesterday..." He paused. He needed the words to come out right, but they were getting all jumbled up in his head. Poppy patiently waited for him to continue.

"When we were running lines together. It felt like we --"

He was cut off by the sound of some of the cast members and Damien St. fucking Cloud loudly entering the bar. Poppy turned around and beamed at them. "Over here guys! I'm sorry, can we talk about this later?"

"Yeah, sure thing." Josh's heart fell to the floor, and he glowered over at Damien who was at the bar getting a round of drinks.

Damien walked over to the table holding some shots in his hand. "I got a round for the table." He set the shots down and passed them around.

"Oh, thank you!" Poppy said. "What are these?"

"It's one of my favorite shots from the city. You're gonna love it." he said with a wink at Poppy. Poppy returned his wink with a smoldering gaze. Josh's friendly smile never left his face, but he was feeling far from friendly right now.

"I just love this little bar. It is so old school. So different from anything in the city. You really have to come out into the world and venture out to find that stuff like this still exists. There are people who still live this way," Damien said.

"And what way is that?" asked Josh.

"This! This bar is like a time capsule. This town is like a step back in time. It's great. I can do so much character research here --" Damien continued talking, but Josh was done listening. Damien had everyone hanging on his words. Josh took that moment to check his phone because he could not listen to him drone on about how backwards this town was. This town that basically raised Josh. They were not some zoo exhibit for people like Damien St. fucking Cloud.

He noticed a couple texts and missed calls from his sister.

"Excuse me, I am just going to step outside really quick," he said to Poppy. Poppy turned and nodded, and then quickly turned her gaze back to Damien.

Josh walked outside. It was getting late, and the autumn

air was getting colder. Main street was quiet. The only things open now was this bar and the bistro a few blocks down. He pulled up his sister's number and called her.

"Josh," she answered the phone.

"Yeah, what's up Lex, I just saw that you called."

"Yeah, my car won't start...piece of shit," she grumbled. Josh could hear her slam the hood.

"Do you need a jump?"

"I think so. Do you mind?"

"I'll be right there." He hung up and took a deep breath. He looked in the window, but he didn't see Poppy. He wanted to go tell her he was leaving and see if she wanted him to come back to give her a lift to her car. Walking back in he scanned the room. Poppy and Damien were both gone, and a pit formed in his stomach.

"Hey guys, I need to head out for a minute. Have you seen Poppy? Since we came together, I just want to let her know I'll be right back."

"I think they went out on the back patio," answered one of his cast mates.

That didn't make sense. It was getting cold tonight and neither of them smoked, so why were they on the back patio? Josh made his way through the bar to the back door that let out onto the patio. He pushed open the door and stepped outside. It was a simple wooden deck he had built last summer with lights strung up and a couple of tables.

He didn't see them initially, but then he did. They were in the corner Poppy's back was against the wall and Damien St. Cloud was kissing her. Not just a kiss, no, this was full blown making out. Poppy's hands on his back and fisting his hair. His hand holding Poppy's hip and the other one looked to be feeling something a little higher.

Bile rose in his stomach. He had no claim to Poppy. One moment that had felt monumental to him clearly did not feel the same to her. He may think Damien St. Cloud is a pompous ass, but it would appear Poppy didn't share the sentiment. His heart pounded in his chest. His cell phone slipped from his hand and landed with a loud thud on the wooden floor of the patio.

Poppy and Damien stopped and looked over to see Josh. Poppy's lipstick was smeared around her mouth. The flush in her cheeks and the flush on her chest was evident. She looked well kissed. A wave of overwhelming desire to march over there and punch Damien St. fucking Cloud in the face overtook him, and he wanted to kiss Poppy in a way that she would never even think about kissing anyone else. Ever. But Josh had honed his skills in stuffing his emotions and putting a smile on his face for years, so he would not do that.

"Can I help you with something?" asked Damien.

Yeah, you can take your hands off my girl, douchebag. That is what Josh wanted to say. Instead, he said. "I'm sorry to interrupt, but I have to take off. I just wanted to make sure Poppy had a way safely back to her car."

"I got her, my man," he said with an entitled smirk on his face.

"You sure?" Josh looked at Poppy. *Say no, say you will come with me, say this is nothing and not what I think it is.*

"Yeah, I'm good." That was all she said, still looking aroused and so kissable.

Josh nodded and turned and left. He booked it out of the bar and briskly made his way to his car cursing the day that douchebag came to town.

CHAPTER 7

Poppy

Poppy woke up the next morning grinning from ear to ear. Last night had been one of the best nights of her life. She had asked for a love spell and that love spell did not disappoint. Two days after performing the spell Damien St. Cloud came to town. He was meant for her, and after last night there was no doubt in her mind.

She had felt the chemistry between them since that first rehearsal, but last night after he took her out onto the patio and kissed her stupid there was no doubt in her mind where she belonged. She belonged right here in Damien St. Cloud's bed. He was staying at the inn on the edge of town and last night he took Poppy back to his room. Last night she made love to her soulmate for the first time.

The sounds of the water let Poppy know he was in the shower. She stretched and remembered the night. While the sex had not been as earth shattering as the kiss, it's okay. Lots of women don't climax with new lovers, right? It wasn't the first time she didn't quite get there with someone new. So, they had a few kinks to work out. Hannah and Graham definitely had some kinks when Graham first arrived, so it's totally normal. Last night they had come back after a few drinks at the bar and Damien was just a little drunk, that is why he finished and rolled off her and fell asleep. It happens. They would figure it out.

Poppy's alarm on her phone went off. She looked for it in a panic. Her alarm was set for her to give her enough time to get to the register when she was home and not when she was in an inn clear across town from her car, which she needed to drive home. She shot up and started pulling her clothes on. She gathered her things and looked around the room to see if there was anything else.

Slipping her shoes on she knocked on the bathroom door. "Hey, sorry to run, but I have to be at work in thirty minutes."

"What?" he yelled back over the water.

She opened the door and poked her head in. "I have to get to work." She wanted to ask him for a ride back to her car, but she didn't want to impose.

"Ok, see ya later."

That was it. Poppy waited for more, but that was it.

"Ok... I guess I'll see you tonight."

"Yeah, I'll see you then."

Poppy closed the door and took a breath. That isn't exactly soulmate behavior, but they would get there. She left her room and started down the hallway. If she could find a way to her car, she might be able to get to work on time.

As she pulled the front door of the inn open, she walked right into a big solid chest. She looked up. Josh. Perfect. He was always right where she needed him.

"Poppy, what are you doing here?" he asked in surprise.

She did not want to answer that question. She was feeling a little confused and unsure and those are not emotions that sat well with Poppy.

"Hey, can you do me a favor? I need to get to my car so I can get to work. Can you drive me?"

"Sure," he said flatly.

"Thank you so much, you are a lifesaver."

"Don't mention it," he said. Poppy looked up at him. His normal Joshness was gone. He looked distant and upset. That is no way for Josh Turner to look. Josh Turner was a golden retriever personified. Looking at him like this felt like watching those videos online where the dogs look sad or are waiting for their owners and you just feel a visceral need to make things right.

"What's up? Are you okay?"

He shook his head like he was shaking something off. "Yeah, I'm fine. You just surprised me. Let's get you to your car."

They walked to the lot and Josh beeped his SUV and opened the door for Poppy. She climbed in and he shut the door behind her.

As he opened the door and sat down in the driver's seat she asked, "What are you doing at the inn this morning?" She immediately regretted the question because it was one she did not want to answer herself.

"I'm doing some work around the inn for my sister. I sanded the gazebo yesterday. I was coming back today to stain it."

He didn't ask why she was there again, and she gave a sigh of relief.

"I didn't know you did that kind of work. Don't let Sam know, he will rope you into working his grand ideas for the orchard update. He roped Graham in weeks after he arrived."

She waited for the easy banter that usually happened between them, but he sat there silently driving them back. So, she filled the silence, as she often did when there was any.

"I knew you were a bartender. You bartend over in Glendale, right?"

He just nodded. Poppy would not be dissuaded though.

"I can't believe we open next Friday. Do you think we'll be ready? It always seems like it's never going to come together, but then it always does. At least this time we have Damien's expertise. How lucky are we?"

Josh's knuckles turned white as he gripped the steering wheel. "Pretty lucky, I guess," he muttered.

They pulled up to the theater's parking lot and Poppy hopped out. "Thank you so much, I might make it back in time. Here's hoping my gran doesn't notice I'm in the same clothes as I was last night. I mean I am a grown woman, but she still treats me like I'm a teenager."

Crap. Poppy did not want him to ask about why she was there, but she pretty much said it herself right there didn't she.

Josh didn't respond to that. "Have a good day, Poppy."

And that was it. She closed his door, and he pulled off. *That was weird*, she thought. She had grown so used to Josh Turner's smile and charming warmth being a constant in her life. When it was gone, she didn't like it.

Not one bit.

CHAPTER 8

Poppy

*P*oppy made it through her workday. Her gran either hadn't noticed, but most likely was just ignoring the fact that she magically showed up at the register in the same clothes she left in yesterday. But Poppy just put her head down and made it through her shift, but her mind was everywhere.

She wanted to text Damien and tell him how amazing last night was, but she didn't actually get his phone number. While things were a bit strained this morning, and she was a bit put off by the way he was treating her, everything had been great at rehearsal and even at the bar. But once they got to the inn, it had just felt like a hook-up. It wasn't the soul shaking love she was hoping for, but they could grow. She just needed to trust the process.

Then there was the whole Josh thing. And if she was honest with herself, this was bothering her way more than the Damien thing. His face and demeanor in the car had been playing in her head over and over today. She needed to make him feel better. Something on a cellular level in her felt wrong when he was upset. That was new, and she had no idea what to do about that.

She had been trying to get back to the kitchen all day. On slow days she went back to the kitchen at the orchard and baked. That was her happy place. When she couldn't get her head on straight, she could always go back there and make something and feel better. She knew Josh loved the cinnamon muffins from the diner in town. She decided she would make him some apple cinnamon muffins to take to rehearsal tonight. They had been slammed all day. She did manage to get the apple diced and mix up the batter between customers. Then she finally got them in the oven as she finished up her shift.

She popped her head in her dad's office.

"Hey Dad, I am going to go get ready for rehearsal, but I just put some muffins in the oven to take to rehearsal tonight. Can you take them out when the timer goes off?"

He looked up at her from his desk, which was covered with messy stacks of paper. He handled most of the business side of things at the orchard. He had been an accountant when he and Poppy's mom got married and he put those skills to work here keeping the books and managing accounts and orders.

"Sure thing, Pumpkin. How's the show coming? I heard at the diner this morning something about a Broadway star here in Mystic Falls," he said.

"You heard right. Damien St. Cloud." Poppy beamed at him. "He's here to be the music director until Ms. Maple gets back."

"I bet you're excited about that," he said with a knowing smile.

"He's really talented." She took one of the tootsie rolls from the bowl on his desk and unwrapped it. There was always a bowl of tootsie rolls on his desk. While she didn't particularly like tootsie rolls, she could never pass up the nostalgia they gave her of visiting this office when it was her grandfather's. "He's really going to help our show."

"That's good, Pumpkin. I gotta get back to these numbers. Sam has some orders coming in and I have to do some payroll."

"Okay daddy, just don't forget about the muffins," she said and popped the tootsie roll in her mouth.

"You got it, Pumpkin."

Poppy headed to the house that was just across the yard from the store and nestled back between two big maple trees. After taking a shower and getting cleaned up she headed into the kitchen to get the muffins she made for Josh ready to take to rehearsal. She loaded them up into a basket and headed out the door.

Poppy made her way into rehearsal with minutes to spare. She had been scattered all day. It always seemed like when her day started with running late, she ran late all day.

They hadn't started rehearsal yet, and she was happy about that. She wanted to give Josh the muffins she brought. She walked in and looked up on the stage.

The set was really coming together. When they left last night there were some unfinished platforms, but now the walls were up and with a little paint it would start to look like the rundown florist shop it would be. Then she spotted Josh. He was up on stage screwing in the last panel. The way his muscles flexed and his bicep strained against his black t-shirt kept pulling her gaze. He set down the drill and picked up his phone as Poppy walked up behind him.

"Hey Josh, just the man I was looking for!" she said with a smile.

He was startled and fumbled his phone until it landed

with a thud on the stage. Bending to pick it up he turned to look at her with a look on his face she couldn't quite read.

"I hope you have a good case for that thing, you seem to drop it a lot," she said with a smile. He just looked at her. "The set is looking great! Did you do all this today?"

Wiping the sweat from his brow with the back of his hand, he nodded.

"Right, well I made these for you." She handed him the basket of muffins.

"You made these for me?" he asked.

"Yeah, you seemed upset this morning, and Josh Turner should never be upset. I noticed you like the cinnamon muffins from the diner, so I baked you some apple cinnamon muffins."

"You did?" he said. He looked up at her and smiled. Something inside Poppy's soul clicked into place when he smiled up at her. She would do anything to make him smile. She wasn't sure where that feeling came from, but it sure was there.

That little bubble of a moment popped when Damien came in. She hadn't even noticed him until he was putting his arm around her and taking a muffin from the basket.

"Aww, Poppy brought muffins, guys," he called to the rest of the cast. "Come and get them before we start the run through."

They all made their way over to Josh's muffins to help themselves. Poppy wanted to stop them, but she wasn't quite sure what to say. After the cast had cleared out, she looked down at the basket that now only had three muffins.

"At least we have a small cast," she said with a weak smile.

"It's okay, no one has ever baked me muffins before. Thank you, Poppy." He took the basket from her. Looking into her eyes, he gave her an honest smile. "I would have shared anyway, so no harm done."

Poppy did notice the look he gave Damien though; Josh didn't seem to care too much for him. She wasn't sure why. He was so talented. She watched Damien play the piano and run a song with the do-wop girls. She smiled and thought about what it would be like to live in New York with him and how city life would be. Sure, maybe she was getting ahead of herself, but they were soulmates. Her love potion brought him here.

"Holy crap, Poppy, these are the best muffins I have ever had in my life," Josh said.

"Do you really think so?" she beamed at him.

"Yes, these are delicious," he said, taking another bite. "These are way better than the ones at the diner. Do you sell these?"

"Whenever I have time, we sell baked goods. We almost always have pie, but we have a full kitchen at the store for all the apple butter and jams. So, I bake to sell when I get the time." Something inside her warmed at his compliment.

"Well, text me next time you make these, and I will come and buy them all."

Poppy felt something growing inside of her. If she had to guess it was pride. Pride in her baking. Pride in the orchard. Pride that she had made Josh happy. Those weren't things she usually took pride in, but it felt really good.

"I'm gonna go put on some clean clothes before the run through, but really, thank you, Poppy. I mean it."

Oh, for Christ's sake, Poppy was blushing. She never blushed, but she most definitely was. She nodded and smiled dumbly as Josh made his way to the dressing rooms to change his clothes.

"Places for act one," the director called out.

"Thank you, places," they all answered back.

Why on earth was Poppy's heart fluttering? She shook it off and got ready to start.

Damien motioned her over. "Hey Poppy, come here for a second." She walked over to him as he was sitting down at the piano. "I just wanted to remind you to really support the high note at the end of the opening number. You were a bit flat last night."

"Right, got it." Taking notes from music directors should not make you want to spit fire, but she did right now. *She wasn't the only one who fell flat last night,* she thought. A lot more happened last night and he was acting like she was no one. She walked backstage fuming.

When rehearsal had finished Poppy was getting her stuff to head home. She was tired after not getting much sleep last night and her emotions were a mess because the person she believed to be her soulmate was acting so differently than he had last night. She just wanted to go to bed and hit reset.

"Hey, do you have a second?" She turned to see Damien standing behind her. He had the same look he had last night.

"Sure, what's up?"

"I just wanted to ask if you wanted to go over your solo a few times?" He asked.

"Sure," she said. She was unsure, but she did like the look Damien was giving her.

"Hey Steve, we are going to stay and practice a little bit. I can lock up when we are done," he called to the director without taking his eyes off Poppy.

Poppy licked her lips and felt a heat building inside her.

"Sounds good, see you tomorrow," he said.

When he left it was just Poppy and Damien. Damien made a quick sweep of the room making sure they were alone. Then he pushed her against the wall and pressed into her.

"I have been dying to do this all night," he whispered in her ear. Poppy could sense the heat in those words and tilted her head exposing her neck to him.

"You have?" she asked. He started kissing little kisses down her neck.

"I have," he said between kisses.

Poppy breathed him in. He smelled so good. He smelled fresh and clean, and like expensive cologne. Poppy ran her hand through his hair, and he gave her neck a bite. She gasped and he pushed his leg between her thighs and Poppy moaned at the friction and pressure.

"I wasn't sure, because you were acting like nothing happened last night, and we both know something amazing happened last night."

"Poppy, I'm just being professional. I want you." he said against her neck, kissing her one last time. "But that's obvious," he said. He pushed her against the wall with his hips, grinding his erection into her. She gasped again and he took her mouth and kissed her. He kissed her deep with the same passion their kiss last night had. His hands explored her body and his tongue danced with hers.

"Come back to my room with me," he said.

She wanted to, she really wanted to, but she also really needed to get some sleep. And her gran was gracious enough not to say something last night, but she knew that courtesy would not be extended to the second day.

"I can't. I really want to, but I have to get home and get some sleep tonight."

"You don't have to stay over. Just come over for a little bit."

Poppy thought about it, she tried to push away how good his lips felt on her neck and how good his hands felt on her body. Poppy was not now, nor had she ever been a booty call, and she didn't plan on being one for him. As much as it pained her, she would say no, and their relationship would be stronger for it. This was just the beginning for them.

"Damien, I would love to, but I really have to get home

tonight. I want to get up early and get some baking done for the store."

"If you must," he said, kissing up her neck. He gave her one last kiss. "We should go then. Bring me some more of those muffins again. They were delicious."

"Right," she said. He had assumed those muffins were for him. Baking for him hadn't even crossed her mind. He didn't seem like the kind of guy who would appreciate a good muffin. He seemed more like the kind of guy who would be concerned by the carbs in a muffin, at least that was a pleasant surprise, because she couldn't care less about carbs.

He pulled away from her and went to turn off the house lights. All that was left was the glow of the ghost light on the stage.

"Alright, let's get out of here. I'll see you tomorrow."

They walked out of the theater. "I'm this way," she said, nodding her head to the right.

"I'm this way, so I guess this is where we part."

"Looks like..." She waited. She wasn't sure what for. For one last kiss? For him to walk her? Anything?

"Welp, good night." He turned and headed down the sidewalk.

Poppy slowly started down towards her car. Something felt off, she was putting up with stuff from this guy she never would have normally. She was trying to trust the process. If they could make this work this could be the start of something new and different for her. She couldn't help but wonder how the spell felt for Hannah. Had she been this uncertain? Hannah would be home next week, and she couldn't wait to talk to her. She needed to hear how the love spell felt for Hannah. She knew Graham and Hannah did not like each other at first, so maybe these mixed emotions were normal?

As she turned the corner, she saw Josh standing by her

car holding her basket. Her heart swelled. While she wasn't sure what was happening with her and Damien, it was a comfort to know some things never changed. Josh Turner being one of the things, and she was realizing more and more lately how much he was this pleasant constant in her life.

"Hey, you waited for me?"

"I just wanted to give you this back." He handed her basket back. "I put the last muffin in a Ziplock bag. It'll be a great breakfast tomorrow. Thank you so much, I was having a bad day, but that helped."

Poppy couldn't help the dopey grin that was plastered across her face right now. "You're welcome."

"Really, it was very thoughtful of you."

"No problem." Her car was right next to his, she took the basket from him, and walked over to her car. "I'll see you tomorrow," she said as she got into her car.

"Good night, Poppy," he said as he watched her get into her car.

Poppy took a moment and smiled to herself. He just called her thoughtful, that felt really nice. Poppy was often called things like, bubbly, funny, fun-loving, but she was also called things like scattered, emotional and a time or two self-absorbed. Thoughtful was a new one, and she liked the way that one felt.

CHAPTER 9

Josh

It was Friday night when Josh sat down on his couch. It had been a busy week and he was happy it was over. He had worked a few bar shifts after rehearsal a couple nights and had been doing work at the inn, plus finishing up the sets. He was beat. However, there was no rest for the weary, he picked up the phone and turned on his Uber app. He had had a job since he was fifteen. Life was hard and it was all about the hustle. Which is why he had all the side hustles.

Theater was the only thing he really did for himself. Theo Williams had built the sets for years and asked Josh to help. Once the people there knew Josh could sing, he was asked to be in the chorus of shows. He found that he really enjoyed being on stage. Getting to be someone else for a while was a nice break from his own life sometimes.

He plated himself up some leftovers and sat down to watch Netflix. He turned on a comfort show that always made him laugh.

As he finished his bowl of warmed up fettuccine, he heard his phone ding. He had an Uber call. He claimed the ride and headed out the door to the inn where the pick-up was.

As he pulled up, he saw Poppy sitting on the front steps of the inn all by herself. She was looking at her phone. Her shoulders were hunched and some of her hair hung in front of her face. She didn't look like herself, she looked upset. If he had to guess, he wagered the cause for her current state was a current resident at the inn. Anger surged in him, but he bit it back. He checked his phone to see who he was here to pick up. It was under the name Sam Smith. It only just then dawned on him that Poppy was using her brother's account.

He stopped and instead of just rolling down the window like he would for any other passenger, he put the car in park and got out to talk to Poppy.

"Hey Poppy, did you by chance call an Uber?"

She looked up at him and gave a half smile.

"I did, I should've known you'd be my driver," she said, sounding a little defeated.

"I mean, I can let Ol' Henry come and pick you up, but I have it on good authority his car smells like feet." He gave her a small smile. "There are only so many of us in Mystic Falls."

"No, it's fine. I'm kind of glad it's you" she said with a weak smile.

Those words pulled him to her more. He walked over the stairs and offered her a hand. She took it and the same magnetic pull was there. It felt like he was being pulled into her orbit. He just wanted to pull her close and hold her. It took all of his willpower not to do just that.

"You are probably wondering why I'm here?" She asked.

That was actually the last thing he wanted to discuss with her. He knew why she was here, and he did not want to discuss Damien St. fucking Cloud with her.

"I came to work on my character with Damien," she continued.

Josh nodded and kept his eyes on the road. Why was this dickhead hiding her? If he was dating Poppy Smith, he would be shouting it from the rooftops, not treating her like a secret. And he would never make anyone he was dating call a fucking Uber. He kept his eyes looking straight ahead so Poppy wouldn't see his contempt for that man.

"Where to, Poppy?" He asked.

"My car is in town by the theater. Can you just take me there?"

"Sure thing."

Josh tried to calm his racing mind. In his head all he wanted to do was hold her and tell her that she deserved much better than him. She deserved so much more than the way he was treating her. She deserved someone who would dote on her and help her to shine her light brighter, not someone who would use her and hide her light, but that wasn't his place. He had no say in how Poppy lived her life. He had no claim to her, no matter how much he wanted to. And he really wanted to claim her, protect her, worship her, cherish her, but none of that really mattered if Poppy didn't want that too.

Josh glanced over and Poppy was scrolling on her phone, frown still firmly planted on her face. He gripped the steering wheel as they turned onto Main Street, driving until he saw her car. Putting his car in park he turned to look at Poppy. Her dark hair was down and there was a stray lock falling across her face. His hand twitched with the need to tuck the strand behind her ear. But then what next, because if he was that close, he would want to touch her face, and if he touched her face, he would want to kiss her full delicious lips, but that is not where they were. So, he just smiled at her and waited for her to finish what she was doing.

She reached for the handle, but hesitated. "Hey Josh, can I ask you a question?" The look on her face was tentative. Josh was not used to seeing the look on her face. She usually knew exactly what she wanted and exactly how to get it.

"Of course," he answered.

"What do you think about Damien?"

Fuck. This was not what they needed to be talking about.

"I think he's talented..." was all Josh could think to say.

"I know that, but I mean like as a person. Do you think he's a good person?"

"I don't know him, so I can't really say," he answered, hoping it would be enough to change the subject.

"I know, but what is your impression of him? What are your thoughts?"

"I don't see how my opinion of the man makes any difference."

"It makes a difference to me." Poppy paused and looked Josh in the eyes, the look on her face pulled at something inside of him. It pulled at his need to protect her, but also to bear his soul to her and that was new. "You are such a great guy and I trust you. I've known you most of my life, and I'm feeling confused right now. Hannah is gone and Sam is staying over at the Glenn's and is so busy and I just haven't had anyone to talk to. Please, just tell me what you think."

Josh tried his best to navigate this minefield. He didn't want to say the wrong thing. Situations like this spiked his anxiety. He didn't want to say things to upset Poppy. Telling the truth in this situation could upset her, but if she needed someone to talk to, he would of course be there for her.

He mulled his words over carefully before he said, "I think he is talented and I'm glad he is here to help the show, but I also don't trust him very much. I feel like he is trying to work an angle, I just don't know what it is. He is only here for a couple weeks, and I just don't want to see you get hurt."

She paused. "Hurt? Why would I get hurt?"

"Poppy... if we are being completely honest here. I know there is something going on with you two. I just worry that he is using you."

"Using me?" Her eyebrows drew together, and she gave Josh a defensive look.

Fuck. This is exactly why he didn't want to talk about this.

"Maybe it's not my place, but I just don't want to see you hurt when he goes back to New York."

She looked at him and let that sink in. She took a deep breath and sighed.

"Can I ask you something?" he asked tentatively. "And please don't answer if I'm out of line, but what is going on between you two? This is the second time you've been at the inn, and I saw that kiss on the patio. I'm just concerned about you, Poppy." His hand did finally go up and sweep that strand of hair behind her ear. She looked up at him, he saw the exact moment her wall went up and she shone her light like a security light.

"I appreciate it, Josh, I really do, but no need. We are just two adults having adult fun."

"Just as long as he's treating you well." He was kicking himself for even bringing it up, but it needed to be said.

"We're good, no worries. I'll see you tomorrow night... Well, not tomorrow it's the weekend, no rehearsal, but Monday night. See you then." She flashed her kilowatt smile and got out of his car.

He stayed there and watched to make sure she got in and her car started up, then he drove off, making his way home. Once home he saw his sister's car in the drive. He collected his thoughts because he was not prepared for twenty questions with his sister. He looked at the time, it was already almost eleven. Hopefully she would be asleep because she was not prepared to talk about anything right now, especially anything involving Damien St. Cloud. So, he turned up his music and took some time to collect himself.

After a couple deep cleansing breaths, his chest was less tight, and the panicky feeling was not gone but at least it was manageable and some days that was the best he could do. Turning off the car, he headed inside.

When he got in, he found his sister in the kitchen heating up a frozen dinner. "Why are you eating that garbage? I could have cooked you something," Josh said.

"This is fine," she said as she cut a slit into the plastic film and put it in the microwave. She turned around and looked at him. It was the discerning look like he was a puzzle she needed to piece together. He knew that look all too well.

"What's wrong?" she asked, her brow furrowed.

"Nothing's wrong, I just got home from an Uber call," he said quickly, turning to go back into the living room.

"'Nothing's wrong', says the man who was just blaring Radiohead Creep from his car. Like I don't know that is your wallowing song."

"I don't have a wallowing song," he called back from the living room, not looking back at her.

"Everyone has a wallowing song, and yours is Creep by Radiohead. It has been since you were fifteen."

She was right and he knew it, but he didn't want to talk about it. That moment with Poppy before Damien had arrived had stirred up old feelings. Yes, he had pined after her all through high school, but he had moved past it. Yet here he was again in her magnetic field being pulled in by that killer smile she had. He didn't want to get into all that with his sister.

"Can we please just drop it?"

She stood there in the archway that separated the kitchen and the living room looking at him. Their relationship had been forged a long time ago, she took care of him. The roles were set. He was a grown man, but to her he was still her baby brother.

"Okay, as long as you're okay," she finally said.

"I'm fine," he said, flopping down on the couch snagging the remote, ready for the night to be over. He had the weekend to try and recover from this terrible night. Monday would come soon enough then he would have to face Poppy and Damien again. He should have just kept his mouth shut, but he just wanted her to be happy. If only Ms. Maple hadn't left, he had a feeling everything would have played out differently. But here they were, he would just have to try his hardest to enjoy the show.

CHAPTER 10

Poppy

The last week of rehearsal flew by, and they were getting closer to opening night. It was the final dress rehearsal and Poppy was feeling nerves. It was beyond the normal nerves she felt with every other dress rehearsal. Things being up in the air with Damien was unsettling. She was still trying to find her footing with him. She knew he just thought this was a fling, but she needed to talk to him. She knew this was more. She just didn't understand how their story would weave together yet. It was going to. It had to. The spell had worked for Hannah. Poppy was just going to trust the process and do her part.

She was packing up the cookies she had made to take to the cast and crew. During this show, she had started to really rekindle her love of baking. She brought something new almost every night, but tonight she was bringing her famous chocolate chip cookies. Chocolate chip cookies were one of the things Poppy remembered making with her mom, so they were the epitome of comfort food to her.

The kitchen door swung open, and Sam walked in. Sam and Poppy were really close. Poppy had felt his absence since he moved out, given moved out was kind of a stretch, since he moved to another house on the property. He and Jackson had moved in after they got married and fixed it up, but for the past two weeks they had been staying at the Glenn's farm. They were caring for the animals there while Hannah and Graham were gone. Graham had started raising some goats and sheep for a petting zoo for the farm and they needed around the clock care.

"Hey sis, long time no see," he said as he walked over to her and ruffled her hair.

She glared at him because he knew she hated that. But then she smiled, because she really had missed him being around.

"I know, we haven't really talked in weeks, how ya doing over there?"

"Good, I'm ready for Graham and Hannah to get back. I am falling behind on the picking schedule. Do you have any time --"

"No!" She cut him off. "I'm not here for the manual labor of it all. I run the store, you do that stuff. That's the deal. The deal we were born into."

Sam paused. "What's that supposed to mean?"

"It just means I don't want to get even more involved. I don't want to be stuck in this orchard for the rest of my life."

Sam rolled his eyes and walked over to the sink to get a drink.

"What?" Poppy asked.

"I'm just tired of this whole thing, Poppy. I love you more than life, you know that, but I am so tired of hearing you bitch and moan about the town and the orchard. I'm sorry we don't live up to your standards."

"Well, I have been talking to Damien, and he thinks I should move to the city."

"Who?" Sam looked at her skeptically.

"Damien. Damien St. Cloud."

Sam looked at her and gave his head a little shake.

"Damien St. Cloud! He is this Broadway star who came to help with the show after Ms. Maple had to leave town. He thinks I should move to the city. I know he would help me get on my feet there and give me a place to stay."

"He said he would?" Sam asked skeptically.

"Well no... not in so many words, but we are together --"

"Woah," He held up his hands. "You guys are together?"

"I mean, yeah... I think."

"You think?" He looked at her incredulously.

"Yeah, I mean we haven't really talked about it, but I know we are meant to be."

"Poppy --" The look on his face right now was one that drove Poppy absolutely insane. It was half protective big brother, half exasperation, and wholly condescending as fuck. It was the last part that just made her so mad. She wanted to be taken seriously.

She wished she didn't feel like such a child sometimes. Poppy was a grown woman, but the family dynamic was fixed, and she didn't know how to get out of it. She would always be the overprotected little girl as long as she lived here. She knew losing her mother at such a young age made her family put her and her brother in a bubble and protect them at all costs, but she needed to get out of it. Sam did it somehow. He was seen as an adult, and he would eventually take over the running of the orchard entirely. He loved the orchard. Poppy just didn't. She didn't like the physical labor and the outdoors and the bugs of orchard life, the only thing that made it tolerable was baking.

"Don't! Don't talk to me like I'm some flighty girl with my

head in the clouds. I know what I'm doing, and I know what I'm risking if I move to the city, but it is my decision. And I know that Damien and I are meant to be because I did a love spell and he showed up the next day."

Poppy hadn't really meant to tell her brother that last part. But there it was, and there was no taking it back, and she wasn't ashamed. Performing a love spell and basing life decisions because of it wasn't exactly something out of character for her, but she knew other people wouldn't understand.

Sam's face fell. "Poppy, where is all this coming from?"

"I see what you and Jackson have, and I see what Hannah and Graham have, and I want that. I want something big to happen. I want my life to start. I am almost twenty-eight years old and still living at home, in the same room I grew up in. My life feels eternally on pause and I don't know why. Ever since moving home I feel like I am in some weird limbo, and I can't stand it anymore. I felt something shift the day he came."

The picture of her and Josh sitting together in front of the stage running lines shot to her head like a movie, clear as day. She could see what he was wearing, she could smell his fresh scent mixed with an earthy scent, she could actually feel his hand in hers. She could feel that pull.

"Poppy... where'd ya go?" She snapped her head over to her brother who was waving her hand at him. "Ya kind of zoned out there. Look, all I'm saying is don't base important decisions on some guy you have known less than two weeks."

"You're right. I'll think about it," she said, still trying to get her head back on straight after that intense flashback of sorts.

"Well, I gotta get back to work. I'll see you later. Jackson and I have tickets for tomorrow."

"Good! See you later."

Sam walked out of the door and Poppy was left trying to figure out why she had the intense flashback of Josh of all people. She thought back to last night, it was one of many she spent with Damien. There was something there, right? She would make her intentions known with him tonight. It was time.

Poppy walked into the final dress rehearsal with her basket of cookies and the decision to talk to Damien after the show and finally figure all this out.

Final dress went great, her scenes with Josh were flawless. Their voices sounded good together, but she couldn't fight the butterflies about the talk she needed to have with Damien tonight.

After the run-through, she changed and washed off all the stage makeup. She was one of the last people there. No Damien, so she decided to head over the inn and talk to him.

Her heart pounded in her chest as she walked the hall to his door. She gave a small knock, and moments later Damien was at the door. He looked at her with those blue eyes, his hair slightly ruffled and looking effortlessly handsome.

"Poppy, what a nice surprise. What are you doing here?"

"I wanted to talk to you about something."

He held open the door and she walked in. Once the door closed behind them, he flashed her a smile, and slowly stepped into her space. He pushed her back against the door and he was there pressing into her and kissing her neck.

"Damien... I wanted to talk to you."

"Talk after." He glided her into his room and pulled her shirt off and then pulled off his own. Talking later sounded okay to Poppy.

But after another unsatisfying tryst with Damien, Poppy laid there thinking. It shouldn't be like this. If he was her true love, it shouldn't feel this way. This is just not how she saw her love spell working out. He came back to bed and Poppy headed into the bathroom to clean up and pull herself together. They needed to talk.

She went to wash up and took a good look at herself in the mirror. There she was in her underwear covered in little cherries and her crop top with her Sagittarius constellation. Her long sleek hair was messed up a bit and her lipstick was long gone. Sure, her unsupported breasts hung low, and she could see the faint stretch marks on her belly peeking out, but she still thought she looked good. She looked like Poppy, even if she wasn't acting like Poppy.

She was going to give this one last attempt. If this didn't work out, she would just have to find a way to jump start her own life. She would be better off making her way on her own than she would be with him if things didn't change soon. Her faith in the process was on shaky ground. Maybe the love potion didn't work for her. She hated this feeling.

She walked out to find him in bed.

"Hey, Damien, can we talk now?"

"Uhhh... yeah, sure. What's up Poppy?"

"I just wanted to talk about where this is going and what we are doing?" she said very matter of factly.

"What do you mean?" His eyes darted quickly away from her.

"I mean, once you go back to the city, what is next for us?" She sat on the bed next to him.

"Poppy..." he sat up and looked at her. "I think that what we have now is so special that we don't need to think about what is next. The world may keep us apart, so let's just live here, in this moment." He brought his hand up and cradled her face.

"What does that mean? Is this just a hookup?"

"Poppy, this is so much more than a hookup, you know

that, but let's not worry about tomorrow. Not tonight. Tonight, we both need our beauty sleep to be ready for opening night tomorrow."

"Ok, so we will talk tomorrow?" she asked timidly.

"Of course, tomorrow we will figure out what our place in the universe is," he said as he moved his other hand to her face. "And we will accept what may come. That is the life of an actor, Poppy."

"Okay," she said, trying to parse the meaning of his words.

He stood up and started to help her gather the rest of her clothes. She got dressed and got her purse together. She left his room and headed down the hallway herself. She felt so foolish. The facade that was Damien St. Cloud was cracking and she couldn't believe she let herself fall into this. She was better than this. While she had let herself feel trapped here, the obligations of a family business were intense, she was never someone to allow herself to be defined by a man. What she was capable of did not depend on someone like Damien St. Cloud.

She got in the car and wasn't quite ready to go home. She felt so stifled at home, but whatever this was with Damien didn't feel right either. If the fulfillment she was looking for wasn't there and it didn't seem to be in her love spell and Damien either, where was it? Where was her place in all of this? She was just so lost.

She decided to drive by the theater. When they were leaving rehearsal, they were putting the show on the marquee and the show posters up. She always loved when those went up and decided to drive by and take a look.

As she drove through the quiet town, she noticed the little space by the bookstore was full. She didn't usually come into town this way, and she hadn't seen this before. She pulled over and got out of her car and walked right up to the window to look in. It was a magic store. There were shelves with dried herbs and oils. Bookshelves filled with books and tarot card decks, little baskets of crystals and larger crystals on display. In the middle of the store was a little purple table and chairs she recognized. The sign that hung above the table read *Bridget's Love Spells and Fortune Telling*. Was it the woman from the Ren Faire? Had she opened a shop in town? Unfortunately, the sign on the door read closed.

She knew what she had to do. She would be back here tomorrow, and she would talk to this woman and find out once and for all about her spell.

Right now, though, it was time to get home and get some sleep. Tomorrow was opening night, and she needed a full night's sleep to be at her best.

CHAPTER 11

Poppy

Opening night was here. Poppy was ready, but she had something important to do first. She had performed a love spell to bring her true love and then a dreamy Broadway star down into her lap. She loved the idea of leaving town with him and falling madly in love and living a glamorous life in the city. But she was starting to think she loved the idea of the life and not the actual man attached to it.

She was hoping a certain witch would give her some answers. The spell Hannah had been given was pretty clear, but Poppy couldn't figure hers out. The timing for Damien made sense, but it couldn't be him. Hopefully there would be some answers here.

She opened the door to the tinkling of a bell above her head. "Hello?" she called out.

A head popped up from behind the counter. "Oh, hello dearie, how can I help ye today?"

"Hi, do you remember me? I asked for a spell at Hannah's wedding."

"Of course, I remember ye, lass. How is yer quest for love?" she asked. Her bright eyes twinkled.

"Well... not good," Poppy said.

"Oh no, my dear, tell me all about it." Bridget made her way over to the table and chairs in the store and sat down. She pulled out the other chair and indicated for Poppy to join her. Poppy sat down and looked at her hands tightly clasped on the table.

"Well, I thought I knew how it was going to play out. After I took the potion someone new showed up in town, and I just kind of assumed it was him, but it hasn't gone at all like I thought it would."

"These things never do, my dear." She gave her hand a reassuring pat.

"Are you sure it worked? I wanted to find love. I mean I did what you said, I made the tea, wrote down what I wanted, and I just don't think it worked."

"Do ye love him?" She waited patiently for the answer. Poppy thought about it, she wanted to say yes, but she knew she didn't. Not even a little.

"No," she said eventually. "I thought I could, but I don't."

"Love is a tricky thing," Bridget continued. "It takes two people. Two people willing to sacrifice for each other. Two people willing to do the work. Two people whose biggest desire lies in the happiness of their partner."

Poppy looked at her and nodded. She wasn't sure what to say. She wanted to feel like that, but that wasn't how she felt about Damien.

"I have a certain gift with love spells and potions," Bridget continued. "I loved my Fergus so fiercely. We gave up so much to be together that even now, though he is gone, I still feel him with me just as clearly as I did when he was next to me. That is the love we are all looking for."

"But how do I know? I know Hannah and Graham didn't like each other at first, but now their love story is fairy tale stuff."

"I cannot answer that for ye, my dear. Only you and yer love can know the answers to those questions." She patted her hand on the table and gave her a sincere smile, "But I can tell ye to trust yerself and the path. Yer love story is coming. Some of us have to move heaven and earth to find our true love, but that is not the case for everyone. Just be open and follow yer heart."

"That's it? Follow my heart?" Poppy scoffed. She had been hoping for some real guidance and not some crappy follow your heart Hallmark card stuff. She was really struggling here.

"I wish there were an easier way, but that's the secret."

"You bring Hannah a Highlander from the 1700's and I just have to follow my heart. That doesn't seem fair."

"My dear, none of us have the same love story, but I promise ye a happy ending."

Poppy sat there waiting. For what she wasn't sure, but that was not it. There had to be more to it than that.

"Well, my dear, I think ye need to make yer way over to the theater. Ye have a show to put on," she said through her thick Scottish brogue with a glint in her eye.

"But what am I supposed to do about Damien?" she asked, impatience seeping through.

"Follow yer heart, my dear."

"What kind of nonsense is that? Follow my heart," Poppy muttered.

The old woman chuckled and put her hand on Poppy's. "I see ye are frustrated, but ye should have seen Hannah and Graham when they came to see me the morning he arrived. I didn't have any answers for them and I'm afraid I don't have any for ye. Just --"

"Follow my heart. I know." Poppy's shoulders slumped as she looked at the woman. The woman smiled back a kind smile and gave her hand another little pat.

"Well, ye better be getting down to the theater."

"Right, well, I'll see you later," Poppy said as she turned to leave. She walked out of the store, the bell tinkling over her head. *Well, that was pointless*, she thought to herself. She had hoped for an answer and got none.

Follow your heart, what kind of advice is that?

Poppy made her way to the theater. She was one of the first cast members to arrive. It gave her some quiet time to get ready for the show. Life had been chaotic recently, and she needed to center herself. Sitting on the stage she walked through the show in her head. Then she went down to the make-up room to start getting ready.

There was always a magic energy to opening night. There was buzz in the air that just radiated through everyone. As the cast started trickling in the magic buzz grew. After she had her make-up on, Poppy went to get into her costume. When she entered her dressing room there was a big bouquet of flowers sitting on her table. It was big and color-ful, some people brought roses, but this bouquet had so many different kinds, even some poppies. She hoped they might be from Damien, but she kind of thought in the back of her head they were probably from her father. She looked at the card and felt a shiver.

> To my leading lady,
> Break a leg tonight, I know you are going to steal the show. It has been an absolute pleasure being the Seymore to your Audrey.

Josh

She couldn't believe he had gotten her flowers. She loved flowers. Maybe it was because of her name, but flowers were definitely her thing. Thinking about Josh made her smile. He was someone who had been around, just this reliable dependable great guy. She wasn't sure why nothing between them had ever happened, maybe it was because he dated Hannah a few years ago, but it wasn't that. He was always there, and she liked that.

Everyone was gathering for the cast meeting. Poppy's eyes scanned the crowd of people for Damien but didn't see him. Her eyes did stop on Josh though. He looked different. He looked distracted. She wondered what was going on, maybe it was just opening night jitters?

As she walked over to the crowd, she did see a familiar face. One she had not seen in a couple weeks. There at the piano bench sat Ms. Maple.

"Alright everyone, I have an announcement. It seems as though Damien has been called back to the city. So, as sad as we are to see him go, we are happy to have Ms. Maple back with us." The director clapped her on the back and she smiled at everyone and she gave a little wave.

"So Damien just left?" The words were out of Poppy's mouth before she even had time to think about what she was saying.

"I'm afraid so. He was offered a job back in the city and he needed to leave."

He continued to go on and get everyone hyped up for the show, but Poppy was lost in her thoughts. She had been so sure Damien was brought to her by the love spell, but it never really felt right. He never really showed that he cared for her more than a convenience fuck, and in that depart-ment he wasn't great. The fact that he had never gotten

Poppy off during sex should have been a red flag. But the fact that he seemed to hide what they were doing should have been a red fucking banner in the sky. Poppy was not something to be hidden away. Poppy lived her life out loud, she always had. Why on earth had she stopped for some mediocre Broadway star?

It was all because of that love spell. Well, that was done now. Poppy wasn't going to think about the spell anymore. Getting out of this town didn't begin and end with Damien St. Cloud and shame on her for acting like it did.

It was time for her to do some major self-reflecting. She needed to figure out what it was that she wanted, and start taking steps to get it. Maybe she would stay in Mystic Falls, maybe she would leave, but sitting around and waiting for life to happen needed to be over. It was time she took charge and started steering her life and not just waiting to see which way the wind blows. 'Follow your heart' was crap advice when she didn't even know what her heart wanted. It was time to figure it out.

"Alright, let's warm up those voices," Ms. Maple called from the piano. She started playing scales and everyone started singing. Poppy looked over at Josh, and he was watching her with an expression she couldn't quite read. He had been around Poppy her entire life, why is it that now Poppy felt acutely aware of him? She looked for him in rooms. She brought him muffins when he was sad. And right now, she wanted to go over and give him a big hug and thank him for the flowers. Where was all this coming from?

It was just about time for the curtain to go up. That feeling that buzz in the air was palpable. If there was ever a way to bottle and sell that energy that would be amazing. Everyone was at places in the dark, quiet wings backstage waiting for the overture to start.The magic and energy of an opening night is a high all actors and theater folk know well.

Poppy was jostled a little bit and a large hand settled on the small of her back. She turned, and there was Josh Turner, strong and steady. Poppy was just about ready to vibrate clear off the ground with nerves and pent up energy.

"Break a leg," he whispered in her ear.

"Right back atcha," she answered with a smile back as the opening chords of the overture began to play.

THE SHOW WENT WELL, and the cast's hard work paid off. Curtain call was over, and they had just smashed opening night. The cast was bustling with energy. When the curtain closed Poppy nearly leapt into Josh's arms. His strong arms wrapped around her and picked her up off the ground.

"Great show, Poppy. You absolutely killed it!" he beamed at her.

"You too. I think that was the best we have ever performed." She smiled up at him, his arms still around her waist. The pull between them was intense. He ran his tongue over his lips and Poppy fought the urge to kiss him. She wanted to press herself into him until no space existed between them.

"Great show everyone! Go see your fans and then we have the Elbow Room tonight for a private cast party," said the director.

The entire group cheered and made their way off the stage, but Poppy and Josh were still there, looking at each other, stuck in this moment.

"I think I better go find my family," Poppy said as she pulled herself out of Josh's embrace.

"Of course, I'll see you at the cast party," he said. He flashed her a smile that she felt deep in her soul.

Poppy went out and found her family. Sam swept her into a big hug. How is it that Poppy missed him while he had been right next door? Then she hugged her dad and her gran. They all told her how great the show was and how good she did. She tried to be in the moment and listen to them, but she could not stop thinking about that moment she and Josh had just shared. Maybe it was just residual energy from the show. They were in love on the stage, so maybe that had just bled over into real life.

As she talked to her family, she felt people push past her. It was always packed after shows, people visiting with their family who came to the show, and it was loud and chaotic, the type of energy Poppy thrived in. But even with this type of attention on her, she found herself searching for Josh in the crowd.

CHAPTER 12

Josh

After the show Josh went out into the house to find his sister. On his way, he was stopped by Mr. Fipps, owner of Fipps Market.

"Josh," he said, reaching out to grab his hand. "Great job up there tonight. Is there anything you can't do?"

"Thank you, I'm so glad you enjoyed the show. Performing with a cast like that makes it easy. Have you seen Lexi?"

"Yeah, she's towards the back."

He clapped Josh on the back one more time and Josh went looking for her.

"Josh." He heard his name called again and turned to see Vivian Williams, whose husband had helped Josh with the sets. She pulled him into a hug. "You were great! How you remember all those lines I'll never know. You and Theo did a great job on the sets."

"Well, he taught me everything I know about tools, so I'm

sure if the sets look good it's all because of the skills of your husband."

"You're too modest, Josh," she said with a warm smile.

"Have you seen Lexi? I'm trying to find her." His eyes scanned the crowd again. "Oh, I see her. If you'll excuse me."

"Tell Lexi hello for me."

"Of course, have a nice night," he said as she pulled him into one last hug.

He managed to make his way over to Lexi without being stopped, again.

"I wondered how many people would stop you on the way over," she said to him with a smirk.

"Well, what did you think?"

"That you are amazing. That's what I always think." She reached up on her toes to hug him. He hugged her back tightly. The two of them were a pair. Josh was 6'3 and muscular and Lexi was 5'2 and round. The only thing that even hinted at the familial relationship was their piercing blue eyes.

"Do you want to come to the cast party?" he asked.

"I'm not in the cast," she said dryly.

"I know, but you're always invited," he said in hopes of reassuring her.

"I appreciate that, but I have an early morning at the inn."

"Okay, but as long as you know you are invited."

"I do, thank you. You and Poppy sounded great up there tonight."

"Yeah, it felt really good tonight," he said as he ran his hand through his hair.

"Well, baby brother, I'm going to get going, but as always I'm so proud of you." She pulled him in for one last hug. "I'll see you at home."

As she turned to leave Josh scanned the theater. It had mostly cleared out. There were still some cast members visiting with family, and there was Poppy with her family. He couldn't help but smile as he watched her talk to her brother. Her father beamed with pride. Her gran, tiny in stature, stood well with the other tall members of the Smith family. Jackson was talking to her gran with a kind hand on her back. There was something about the Smith family that always pulled at his heart. Anyone could see the love they all had for each other. He never grew up with family around him and it was something he always wanted. He yearned for that sense of unconditional love and support. It had always seemed like a dream and something unattainable for him.

He caught Poppy's glance. She gave him a big smile and it warmed his heart. He nodded at her and gave a small smile then headed backstage to the dressing rooms to get changed.

Josh had finished changing and was getting ready to head over to the Elbow Room when he saw Poppy come into the greenroom. She was still in costume and make-up.

"Hey!" she said in greeting. "I'm surprised you aren't at the bar yet."

"I'm getting ready to head over." Josh replied. "Do you want me to wait and walk with you?"

"Oh, you don't have to do that."

"It's not a problem. You were spectacular tonight, Poppy. I mean it."

She smiled, and if Josh wasn't mistaken, she even blushed a bit.

"Right back atcha, Turner. What a great opening night! I'm gonna change as fast as I can. I'll be right back."

"Take your time. I'll be here."

She disappeared into the dressing room and Josh took out his phone and started to scroll. It had been a crazy day. One of those days where emotions had been high and all over the place. At least it ended on a high note. He pulled up social media, which he very rarely checked, but right now it was full of congratulations from the townspeople who had seen the show. Someone had even posted a picture they snapped during the show of him and Poppy. She was stunning. He could look at that picture all night.

"Okay, I'm ready," Poppy said as she came out of the dressing room. "And really thank you again for the flowers. They are so beautiful."

He just nodded bashfully, not sure what to say. "Should we head out?"

"Yep!"

They left the theater and started walking the couple blocks to the bar. The air was crisp, and Poppy pulled her light jacket around her. Josh ached to put his arm around her and warm her up, but he just pushed his hands deep into his pockets and listened to her talk about the show.

"I think this was one of the best opening nights I've ever had!" she exclaimed. "I mean nothing went wrong. NOTH-ING! Something always goes wrong, but not tonight. You were incredible. I mean that, Josh."

He glanced her way, and she was smiling that kilowatt smile of hers on him and he basked in its warmth. Josh could listen to Poppy ramble on forever.

"You had the audience eating out of your hand with Grow for Me, Josh, you really did. I peeked out and they were all just so engaged."

"I heard the applause after Somewhere That's Green, Poppy. You were the real star tonight, let's be honest."

"Humble as always... I'll take it though. I was a star tonight." she said with a joking smile on her face.

"In all seriousness though, you were incredible tonight," he said.

She stopped and looked at him, waiting for his full attention.

"In all seriousness, Josh, you were incredible tonight."

He always felt uncomfortable receiving compliments, but he decided to just take it. It did feel pretty good.

"Thank you, Poppy."

They had made their way to the elbow room and the cast and crew and many family and friends were already singing and drinking. Josh put his hand on the small of her back.

"What can I get you to drink?" She opened her mouth to talk, but Josh continued, "Cranberry and Vodka, right? With a splash of club soda and a lime?"

"You remembered my drink?" She beamed at him. "Yes please! I'll go grab us a table and a book."

Josh ordered the drinks and joined Poppy at the table. As he set the drinks down, Poppy noticed his hand.

"What happened to your hand?" she asked as she lightly traced his knuckles that were bruised and swollen.

He quickly pulled it back. "Nothing, just banged it at work today."

His knuckles were swollen and bruised because of a certain visitor, but he did not want to talk about it. He had never hit anyone before in his life, fighting wasn't something that was in his nature, but sometimes it was necessary and punching Damien St. Cloud in the face was worth it.

He had been working at the inn earlier that day when he heard him talking on the phone in the dining room. Telling whoever he was talking to that he had 'a stage five clinger' and he planned on staying for opening night, hitting it one more time, and going back to the city. Josh saw red after that. They got into a confrontation and after he said some unspeakable things about Poppy, Josh lost it. His sister broke up the fight, kicked Damien out of the inn and he found a way back to the city.

"Do you guys want to play Karaoke Roulette?" asked one of their cast mates.

"Fun! I love when we do that!" answered Poppy. Josh

smiled and nodded, glad to see Poppy happy and for the subject change from his hand.

"Number 876" calls out the DJ, "Mariah Carey Always Be My Baby. Who knows it?"

One of the do-wop girls, Keisha, took the stage and started to sing. The night went on like that, drawing random numbers and seeing who knew it. It was always a good time, sometimes people knew it and they rocked it, other times no one knew it, and someone had to fumble their way through. Either way it was fun.

As the night went on people talked about the show and congratulated each other. Josh heard lots of people wondering why Damien left early. Poppy was not among them though, which surprised him. He was happy about that because he had been worried she would be upset.

"Number 223, Leather and Lace by Stevie Nicks and Don Henley. A Duet! Who's gonna sing this one?"

"I can get the Stevie part!" calls out Poppy. "You know I love Stevie Nicks." She took the stage waiting for someone to join her.

Josh knew the song, but he waited to see if anyone else wanted to sing. When no one joined her, he stood up.

"Looks like Josh and Poppy are performing again." called Alan, the DJ.

He looked up at Poppy who was smiling right at him. Climbing up on the stage he stopped and grabbed the second microphone. "Thanks, Alan," he said as he took the mic from him. The music started and Poppy started singing her verse. When it was his turn, he thought this song might have been a mistake. It hit a little too close to home to his actual feelings for her and they weren't acting. When it came to the part of the song they sang together, he was surprised when her hand slipped into his.

He looked over at her and all time seemed to stop. She

was looking at him and singing right to him. The world around them fell away as they sang to each other. There was something different about this moment. It felt like the moment they shared in front of the stage before everything had gotten screwed up. When for the briefest moment of time he thought he might have a chance with Poppy before Damien and before everything that had happened.

When the song ended, they stood there for a moment, hands clasped. The pull of her magnetism was so strong it was taking all his strength to not pull her to him and kiss her perfect red lips. Her gaze held his, and he would swear she could feel it too.

The rest of the bar erupted into cheers as Poppy slowly turned to them, bring both of them back to reality. Poppy smiled at them and bowed. Josh watched her and they headed back to their seats.

"You two are so incredible together," said Emma, one of their cast mates.

"She's a great leading lady," Josh agreed. "Let me get you another drink," he said to Poppy as she sat down.

"Thank you," she said with a look in her eyes he wasn't quite sure how to read. He needed a moment after that, he felt overwhelmed with emotion.

The rest of the night went by fast. The cast was fun, Josh loved the family of The Little Theater on the Corner. This was one of the few places where he truly felt like he could be himself, but it was getting late, and he had to work tomorrow and another show in the evening.

"Hey, I think I'm gonna head home," he said to Poppy.

"Wait for me, I'll walk back to the theater with you," she said. "I just want to say goodbye."

She got up and Josh watched her as she made her way around the room, stopping to hug everyone and share a laugh. He was mesmerized, the way she would toss her head back and laugh out loud, seemingly without a care in the world. It lit a fire somewhere deep inside of him that maybe one day he could feel effortless joy like that.

"Ready?" she said as she made her way back to him stopping to grab her bag.

"Ready," he said with a nod as he opened the door for her.

The temperature had dropped even further since they left the theater. He watched as she shivered in the cool night air. She was only wearing a lightweight jean jacket that she pulled tightly around her. He shrugged off his jacket and slipped it over her shoulders. Her breath caught with surprise when she realized what he was doing. She looked over at him with a small smile and pulled his jacket around her.

"Thank you. You are such a gentleman."

"I try," he said with a smile, trying not to feel uncomfortable in the moment.

"Ya know, I'm glad Damien wasn't there tonight. It was much more fun this way."

"I agree," he said with a small chuckle hoping to hide just how much truth he felt in that statement.

"I'm not sure what I even saw in him," she said.

Damien was the last thing he wanted to talk about tonight, but he was glad she seemed to be coming to her senses after the interaction he had with him today at the inn. He shook out his hand at the memory.

"Me either, you can do so much better than him."

"I can, but I think I need to focus on me. I think I got swept up in all of that because I'm always looking for a way out of Mystic Falls, and really I'm not sure why. Why I want to leave, why I don't seem able to, why I just feel so antsy all the time."

"I hope you figure it out. You deserve to be happy, Poppy. You deserve everything you have ever wanted." He meant that, sure he had a dream of being with Poppy, but he would never want her to settle, and he could never leave Mystic Falls. It was his home.

"You have always seemed so content here. How do you do it?" she asked.

"What do you mean?"

"You seem to really like living here," she said.

"I do really like living here. I guess I just look around and see so many people in this town as my family. Mr. Fipps, Theo Williams, Mena at the diner. These people know me, and I know them. You don't get that everywhere. I feel lucky to live here."

They walked the last couple blocks in silence. Poppy seemed to be lost in thought.

"Are you okay?" he asked.

"What?" she looked over at him as if being pulled out of her own thoughts. "Oh yeah, I'm fine. Just thinking about some stuff."

Poppy's car was only about half a block away now.

"Well, here's your jacket, thanks for letting me wear it," she said to him. Her face looked earnest. That wasn't a look that naturally seemed to find her face often.

"You sure you're okay?" he asked, taking his jacket from her.

"Yeah, I'm just trying to figure some stuff out."

"I'm a pretty good listener if trying to figure out loud would help?"

"Thank you, Josh, I appreciate it, I really do." She reached out and hugged him. He pulled her close to him. She laid her head on his shoulder as he held her close. He could hold her like this forever, holding all of her softness against him. Taking a deep breath, she pushed away.

"Are you good to drive?" He asked.

She nodded. "Yeah, I'm good." She stopped and looked up

at him and for the second time that night, time seemed to stand still. "Good night, Josh, thank you for everything. I'll see you tomorrow."

"Good night, Poppy."

She unlocked her car and got in. He watched as she started it up, she smiled and waved at him as she put it into drive. Waving back, he walked over to his own car. He slipped his jacket back on. It smelled like her. Taking in a deep breath he smiled at the scent of roses and Poppy.

CHAPTER 13

Poppy

Kids raced around the orchard's store trying to get in line first for cider.

"No need to push, there is plenty of cider and donuts to go around. Please line up in an orderly fashion so we don't spill anymore," Poppy said through a forced smile.

Field trip day was Poppy's least favorite day at the orchard. On these days she never had enough time to get back into the kitchen to bake. Not only that but the kids were loud and messy.

She was happy Sam had made such a success of the orchard. When they were growing up, it was just an orchard. They had the trees. Sometimes people would come and pick their own, sometimes they would just buy them at the store front. They always had cider, apple butter and some jellies and apple pies, but it was nothing like it is now that Sam took over. Which was good, this had meant good things for her family. She just couldn't quite find her place in it, nd it seemed like since her talk with Bridget, all she had been able to think about was her place in things.

A sharp scream came from the kid third in line. Poppy looked up and saw her pointing to the boy in front of her who had blood streaming out of his nose.

"Oh Joel, your nose!" The teacher grabbed a handful of napkins and shoved them to his face. "He always gets nosebleeds," she said, turning to Poppy with an uncomfortable smile. "Class, Ms. Jacobs will help you get your cider and donut. Then go sit at the picnic tables," she called out to her class.

The other teacher stepped up to the line.

"Come on, Joel. Let's go get you cleaned up," she said, leading him out of the store.

Poppy finished helping all the kids get their cider and donuts and was wiping down the counter as the teacher came back in.

"I set you back a donut and some cider," Poppy said to the teacher, turning her back to get them.

"Thank you, I appreciate that."

Poppy handed the teacher the donuts and set the cups down.

"You all have really made some changes in the past couple years, huh?" asked the woman.

"We have, my brother has been working hard to try and attract some tourist attention."

"Well, I say keep it up, these kids loved it this year."

Poppy smiled nicely at her, "Well thank you, I will let him know."

The kids finished their snacks and Poppy let out a slow sigh of relief as the last teacher stepped onto the big yellow bus. She smiled as it pulled away. If she went back to the kitchen now she would have just enough time to get in some pumpkin squares to take to the show tonight.

The past week had been the run of the show. It had been going really well. Performing with Josh was like a dream. He was talented and she loved to listen to him sing every night. They had really gotten close during this show, and it made her happy. There were some feelings for him blossoming, but she was trying to ignore them. 'Follow your heart' was what she was told to do, she was still trying to figure out what it was that her heart wanted. She had been looking online for jobs and apartments in the city, but she couldn't find anything she liked. Nothing felt right.

Rummaging under the counter she pulled out the big sheet pan and poured the batter in and put the bars in the oven. Baking was something that she had been doing a lot lately. It gave her time to clear her head and kept her in one place long enough to think about it. She didn't feel any closer to knowing what it was that she actually wanted, but the more she baked and focused on listening to herself, the less that antsy feeling of being ready to run took over. So that was a start, right?

After getting the bars into the oven, she set a time and then walked back out to the front. The store needed to be tidied up a bit. Field trip days were hard on the store, so she went about straightening the gourds and pumpkins. It would have been close to closing time a few years ago, but Sam kept things open longer so people could stop by on their way home from work. Luckily during the run of the show someone always came about this time so she could go get ready. She was going to talk to Sam about getting full time help up here soon with the way their little orchard was growing.

Poppy tried to picture herself here, working here. She tried to picture herself moving away. Nothing felt right. The timer dinging and she went to get the bars out of the oven. They smelled delicious. She set them out to cool so she could frost them before she left tonight. *I wonder if Josh will like the pumpkin bars.* She found herself wondering. He crossed her mind a lot since the run of the show.

Something else that crossed her mind a lot was that duet they sang at the opening night cast party. She kept replaying that in her head. There was a moment between them, and a look in his eye, she thought he was going to kiss her. And if she was being honest, she was disappointed that he hadn't. She was trying not to focus on that right now. She needed to figure out what she wanted before she would let herself be swayed by someone else again. But something about the thought of him slipping his jacket over her shoulders made her smile.

"What are you smiling about?" she heard a familiar voice ask.

Turning she saw Jackson coming in.

"Hey! Long time no see stranger!" Poppy gave him a hug.

"Poppy, I saw you last week."

She pouted. "I know, but it feels like forever. I have been so busy with the play and with you and Sam staying over at the Glenn's farm, I haven't seen you."

"I know, but it was nice to pretend to be bougie for a couple weeks over there. Their place is nice, like NICE nice."

"I know, I think that is what happens when your family is so wealthy, they pass down country estates like they're beat up Chevy's," Poppy joked.

"Sadly, we're back in our house. Hannah and Graham got back a couple hours ago, so Sam and I are back at home."

"Well, I am glad to have you guys back, even if it's just a little closer."

Jackson's eyebrows drew together, and he tilted his head and looked at her. "What's going on with you? Something's up?"

"What do you mean?"

"I don't know, you were all smiles when I came in with this million miles away look, and now you seem off."

Of course, Jackson could tell, he could always tell. It was a sixth sense that both she and Jackson had, the ability to sense when someone was holding out on the good gossip. Poppy looked away because she didn't know what to say.

"Spill."

That was really all the encouragement she needed. "Okay, so did you hear about the guy from Broadway who came for a couple weeks to help with the show?"

He nodded and gestured for her to go on.

"Okay, well. We kind of hooked up."

"What? I heard he was hot," he gave her an approving nod.

"Oh yeah, he was. Sadly, he was also lousy in bed."

"Ain't that how it goes…" he said with a slow shake of his head.

"Anyway, it's a whole thing, but I kinda had it in my head that we were meant to be, and he was my ticket out of here."

He made a knowing face and nodded.

"Anyway, he's gone." she continued. "He just left before opening night without even a goodbye, and I'm not even that upset about it. I'm just trying to figure out what it is that I truly want, ya know."

"Oh, I know, the age old Poppy dilemma."

"I think it is just time for me to make up my mind and choose once and for all. And in a crazy turn of events, I'm starting to think maybe I should just let the universe win on this one and find a way to be happy here." Jackson's eyes got big. "Don't you dare tell my brother! I'm still figuring it all out. I just need to decide once and for all."

"I won't, but for what it's worth, I hope you stay. I love your brother, but you make life interesting around here."

"Right back atcha!"

"Anyway, I'm here to tell you to go get ready. Apparently,

Nicole couldn't make it tonight, so I'm covering until Sam finishes up for the day."

"Thanks, I'm gonna go hop in the shower. Two more shows and then we are done. I'm gonna miss this one. Performing with Josh has been really fun." She could feel the dopey grin that crept across her face when she talked about him. She tried to push it away, but it looked like Jackson already saw it.

"Mmm-Hmmm, you two look like you're having a little more than fun on stage."

"We are just good actors."

"I've seen your acting, Poppy," he said with a straight face.

She fake gasped. "Rude! Anyway, I gotta go get ready. Byeee!"

"Bye Poppy," he said with a smile.

She headed off to the house. She should have known she couldn't fool Jackson. Whatever these feelings were with Josh, she needed to put them the back burner. It was probably just from being in the show together. At least that's what she was trying to convince herself.

CHAPTER 14

Poppy

It was closing night, and Poppy had mixed feelings about it. Those feelings came at the close of most shows. There is something special about cast bonding and the magic of theater that always came with the disappointment of the close of a show. She didn't know if it was saying goodbye to Audrey or not getting to see Josh as much as she had grown accustomed to, but she was really sad to see this show end. She knew what the answer was, but she just wasn't quite ready to admit it to herself yet.

The show went off without a hitch and after curtain call she felt that same hand on her back she felt after opening night. She knew the feel of that hand well by now and she turned blindly into his arms and buried her face in his shoulder. He held her and gently rubbed her back.

"It has been one of my biggest pleasures playing opposite you, Poppy Smith. This show will always have a special place in my heart."

Poppy pulled away from him and quickly wiped a tear

from her eye. If she were to cry right now the mascara would become a problem of epic proportions and those fake lashes would look a hot mess, so she needed to pull herself together.

Looking up into Josh's eyes she thought she saw the same emotion, but it was dark backstage.

"Let's go see who's out there tonight."

"After you," he said, placing his hard on the small of her back guiding her through the darkened stage. She loved that he did that. There was something so centering in that kind of a touch, she would miss that.

As they walked out to greet the audience, Josh was of course stopped and talked to almost immediately. It looked like Aggie who had worked at the inn almost all of Poppy's life was here with her grandson and stopped him to talk.

Poppy was wistfully taking it all in when she felt a hand on her shoulder, she turned to find Hannah smiling at her.

"You were amazing, Poppy! How have I never seen you on stage before?"

"HANNAH!" Poppy pulled her into a bone crushing hug. "I'm so glad you're back!" She let go and stopped and looked at her best friend then pulled her in for another hug. Hannah was a good six inches shorter than Poppy, but they shared a very similar round build. While Hannah's hair was soft blonde waves, Poppy's was sleek and dark. Then her eyes were pulled up by the towering Scotsman standing behind Hannah smiling at her.

"Well done," said Graham.

"Thank you." A small chuckle bubbled up in Poppy. She was so glad Hannah was home, she needed to talk to someone who would understand the whole crazy situation she was in.

"The whole show was wonderful, but you and Josh did such a great job," said Hannah.

"Thank you," Poppy said again, pulling her into another

hug. "I'm so glad you guys are back. Hey, what are you guys up to after this?" asked Poppy.

"Nothing that I know of," Hannah said. She turned to look at Graham who gave a little shrug.

"You guys have to come to the cast party! It is that last one. We are meeting down at the Elbow Room. It will be fun," Poppy pleaded.

"Sounds good to me," Hannah said looking up at Graham.

"Aye, sounds good to me too," Graham agreed.

"Yay! I'm so glad. I'll meet you guys over there, just let me go change."

Poppy left to go backstage. By the time she made it back she was the only one still in the dressing room. Everyone had already cleared out and made their way to the cast party. Poppy quickly washed off her makeup and got her things together. She looked through her bag for her cell phone but remembered that she left it backstage.

She made her way to the prop room where she had been sitting during the show. When she went to grab it, she saw Josh around the corner at the prop table checking his props.

"Hi," she said softly. "Are you going to the cast party?"

Josh looked at her and just nodded. His eyes were filled with something, something deep, she didn't know how to read.

"Are you okay?" she asked as she walked over to him.

"Yeah," he said in a low gruff voice. "I'm okay."

Poppy walked over to him as if being pulled by some force she couldn't see or identify but she could feel. The prop room was a giant 'L' and the prop table they were at was sat towards the back and hid them from view of the door.

Prop rooms in theaters were interesting places. They are this hodgepodge of things you would never find in real life. There was a leg lamp from when they did A Christmas Story and piles of vintage suitcases stacked on the floor, flowers hanging over their heads, wig heads stored in the back corner, piles of dishes and an old victrola. It was like a real life page from an eye spy book.

"I saw Hannah and Graham out there tonight, you must be glad to have them back," Josh said with a soft smile that didn't quite reach his eyes. He seemed far away. There was something almost haunting about the way he looked right now. This was not how she was used to seeing him. Josh was like a touchstone to her. He was a constant. She never quite realized it before now. He was always there. He was supportive and happy and made everyone feel so warm and welcomed, but who did that for him?

She walked over to him unsure what her plan was but knew she needed to close the distance between them. Poppy looked up into his eyes, trying to figure him out. Who was Josh Turner and why did he feel like a stranger but also felt like home all at the same time?

"Poppy, can I ask you something? What on earth was it that you saw in Damien?"

That brought her right out of whatever moment she was experiencing.

"What?"

"Damien. Why him? What did you see in him?"

Poppy's brain struggled to keep up. She wasn't sure where all this was coming from. He had been gone for a week, and if she was being honest with herself she hadn't actually thought that much about him since he left. She had been too busy trying to figure out her own stuff.

"I mean I get it, he was this hotshot Broadway star, but he was kind of a dick," he said.

Poppy couldn't help but laugh. Why was she laughing right now? He was right, he was kind of a dick, kind of a major dick.

"I don't know," she shrugged. "I guess I just got wrapped up in the idea of him. But trust me, that spell is broken."

Josh looked at her and took a step towards her. His eyes burned with something Poppy had never seen before and it almost took her breath away.

"You're done with him?"

"I was done with him even before he disappeared."

Time stopped and stood still between them, neither of them talking or moving. They just looked at each other as if they were both trying to figure out the next move. A loud bang pulled them out of the moment.

"What was that?" he asked.

"I don't know," Poppy said. He stepped around her and walked to the door. The giant metal door to the prop closet had been closed. Josh jiggled the handle, but the door didn't budge. Poppy walked over to the handle and tried to open it, still stuck tight. She wasn't sure why she tried it if he couldn't open it, then she sure wouldn't be able to.

"Looks like we are stuck," he said, his gaze falling to Poppy's lips.

Her hand still resting on the lever to open the door, she licked her lips and watched as Josh's expression tightened. "So, it would seem."

Josh banged on the door and Poppy called out, "Hey, anyone out there?"

Nothing.

"It's okay, I'm sure someone will come by in a minute," Poppy hadn't taken her eyes off of Josh. She was drawn to him like a magnet.

"I'm sure when you don't show up to the cast party they will send a search party," he said with a soft smile.

Time ticked on and they didn't hear anything out there. Poppy moved to sit on the stairs that led up to more prop storage upstairs and Josh leaned up against the door. A loud growl from Poppy's stomach interrupted the silence. She put her hand over her stomach and laughed.

"I didn't have anything to eat before I came. It was a busy day and I'm starving!" she said.

"Just a minute," Joshed moved to the back of the room and pulled out a small Tupperware container. "I snagged these from the green room. I know the rules about no food in costume or in the prop areas, but sometimes I get hungry during the show." He opened the container to show her two pieces of the banana bread she had brought.

"You are a lifesaver." She took the Tupperware from him and broke off a corner of the bread and started eating. Josh settled down on the stairs next to her. Their legs touched and she relished in the feel of his leg against her. Whatever was happening between them felt right, and it felt different than anything Poppy had experienced before.

"Josh, we have known each other our entire lives. We have been in school together since the first grade and both of us have mostly stayed here in this town. Why has nothing ever happened between us?"

Josh choked on the banana bread and sputtered. "What?"

"I mean it, this isn't a big place, why didn't anything ever happen between us?"

"I don't know, I mean maybe timing? In high school, I had such a crush on you, and worked up the courage to ask you to prom, but after you turned me down, I never thought you felt the same way."

"Yeah, I wanted out of this town in high school," she sighed.

"You left for college, then I was with Abbie, and we were together for a long time. Timing was just never right."

"You guys were engaged right?"

"Yeah, but I don't want to talk about her right now." He

turned to look at her. His eyes flashed with hunger. "I just want to clarify. You have no feelings for Damien St. Cloud."

"None." Poppy said. His hand was on her knee, and it felt like life.

"Are you interested in anyone else, Poppy?" His hand started to slowly move up her leg. She nodded because her brain could not form words, all it could focus on was the sensation of his hand on her leg and the need to kiss him.

"Poppy, can I kiss you?" he asked, meeting her gaze. She nodded again as his hand found its way up her hip. He raised his other hand to cradle the back of her head and lowered his head closer to hers. Poppy was on fire. She felt so drawn to him. He licked his lips and Poppy could not resist the pull of him and closed the distance. Their lips touched in this perfect kiss.

Poppy had never experienced a kiss like this before. Energy zinged right through her, she felt pulled to him. She wanted to be closer to him. She felt like she would never be close enough. Poppy parted her lips and Josh was right there. His tongue slipped into her mouth, and it stirred up a desire in Poppy she had never felt before. She ran her hands through his hair pulling him closer, he responded by wrapping his hand around her waist and pulling her close to him. This moment was utterly magical. The pull to him was so magnetic she would never be able to separate from him.

There was a buzzing sound neither of them were aware of. They were both entranced in this kiss, not wanting to break the magic of this moment. But when her phone buzzed clear off the table, she broke away.

"My phone, I totally forgot. That's why I came in here." She stood up from the staircase but was suddenly dizzy from the absence of his mouth and his hands on her. He reached out his hand to steady her.

She walked over to the spot where her phone had clattered down to the floor and picked it up. Hannah was calling her, and she quickly answered.

"Hey," she sounded like she was yelling over loud music. "Where are you?"

"Josh and I got locked in the prop room, can you send someone to get us out?" She looked over at Josh who was giving her the classic Josh Turner smile. The smile that just radiated his goodness, she had to smile back.

"Oh my gosh, yeah, I'll send someone over."

"Thanks, see you guys soon."

She hung up the phone and sat it on the table.

"So, it looks like someone is coming to let us out."

"So, it would seem," said Josh. He got up from the stairs and walked over to her. "Then it looks like I'm almost out of time to do this." He reached up his hand and cradled the back of her head and claimed her mouth. While their first kiss was all spark and exploration, this kiss felt like he was claiming her. That he was afraid this would be their last kiss. Like if they walked out of that door it would all be over and they would go back to just being Josh and Poppy, but Poppy knew in her heart there was no turning back after that kiss, or this one for that matter.

He brought his other hand up and cradled her face. She gave a little moan and put her hands on his hips and pulled her to him.

The door clicked open and the two pulled apart.

"Hey, sorry, I didn't know you guys were in here. Luckily, I was still here cleaning up," the box office manager said.

"No harm done, Ken," Josh said with a smile.

"Just lock it back up when you guys are finished. I'm just about done here for the night."

"You got it. Do you need any help?" Asked Josh.

"I'm just about done, finished vacuuming the foyer now

and that's about it. Thanks for the offer but I will see you guys over at the Elbow Room."

"See ya there," Poppy said as she flashed him a smile.

"I'll walk you over, are you ready?" Josh asked.

"Yep, I just need to grab my bag." Josh put his hand on the small of her back as she made her way back to the dressing rooms to get her stuff.

Well, this night didn't turn out as Poppy had intended, but she thought she knew what the witch meant now. Follow your heart. She still wasn't sure what her heart wanted. Whether she wanted to stay here in Mystic Falls or head out on her own, but Josh Turner was a definite twist in the script she hadn't planned on. While he may not have been the object of her desire, things could change. And if Josh Turner kissed like that, things could definitely change.

They made their way over to the bar where neither of them really knew how to act around each other. Everything was so new, and Poppy was just trying to play it cool, Josh seemed to be following her lead.

Poppy could only hope that things changed soon, because she wasn't sure how long she could play it cool.

CHAPTER 15

Josh

Country music blared as Josh wiped down the bar. He was picking up a daytime shift at the Lucky Saloon, the bar he worked at in the next town. It was always quiet during the day which gave Josh plenty of time to think. Last night had been incredible, that kiss with Poppy was amazing, but the earlier events in the week not so much.

"Hey, Josh, if you wanna ride the bull at two I'll do it at one," said Jess, the waitress on today. She looked the part when she came in with long blonde hair in low pigtails, tight jeans, and a flannel buttoned down, but tied right above her belly button.

"That works."

Part of this place's appeal was the mechanical bull right in the middle. The staff took turns riding it on the hour. When Josh first started, he wasn't very good, but after some practice he was probably the best bull rider in the place. Now he loved getting up there, his hips took over and he rode. He had even gotten good enough that he could do some tricks.

Josh used his day shifts to practice and then on the night shift he could rake in the tips. On a good night he could make over six hundred dollars. All the money was going straight to the bank. He had his eye on a very special house in the heart of town, not too far from his sister, but far enough they could both get a little bit of space. And if riding this bull for people would help, it was something he would gladly do.

The bell rang and Jess entered the ring and hopped on the bull. The small lunch crowd cheered, and she rode and smiled. Josh continued making drinks and working the bar.

When the next bell sounded an hour later, it was time for Josh to get out there. He hopped in the ring and climbed onto the bull. It started out slow and he easily kept pace, but they soon turned it up a bit. Josh smiled. He liked it when things got a little hard to hold onto. Raising his hands in the air he rode it out, his hips rolling in time with it.

As the music changed, he decided to practice some of the more complicated moves. He used the handle that hung above the bull to lift himself up, turn around, and drop himself on the small area on the bull ahead of the handle. When the next big buck came, he propelled himself off and caught himself with the mere strength of his thighs on the back of the bull. He heard Jess call his name and cheer. He then turned himself back around and stood on the bull like a surfboard and got the small crowd to cheer. He let one of the big bucks take him back into sitting as he finished the song out.

When the song was over, he dismounted and headed back to the bar, but someone standing there pulled him up short. There he was, looking right into the face of Poppy. She was looking at him with her perfect red lips slightly parted and a flush that was crawling up her chest to the tips of her ears. Something about the sight of her here and the look on her face did something to his heart, it just swelled, and that wasn't the only thing swelling at the look of those perfect pouty red lips.

"Hey Poppy, what are you doing here?" he asked as he closed the distance between them. Her mouth was still open, and she appeared to be having trouble finding words. "Don't tell me you're speechless. I think this is the first time I've ever seen you speechless"

"I didn't know you could do that," she said in a breathy voice.

"Oh that? I do that a few times a week," he said with a slow smile.

"And twice on Saturdays," the waitress from behind the bar chimed in.

"Hey Jess, I'm gonna take my break now, you got this?"

"Yep, I got it covered."

"Come out back with me," he said to Poppy. He put his hand on the small of her back and guided her out onto the back deck.

"I'm happy to see you, but what brought you out all this way Poppy?"

She seemed to have gained some equilibrium. "I brought you these," she said as she shoved a Tupperware container of muffins into his hands. "I made some for the store today and I had some leftovers. I went to the inn to take them to you, but your sister told me you were working out here today. And since I have the rest of the day off, I thought I would bring them here to you," she said all in one breath.

"Thank you, that was very thoughtful of you." Josh smiled and took the container from her arms. His stomach gave an appreciative rumble at the sight of his favorite muffins.

"Where did you learn to ride a mechanical bull like that?"

"I've been working here for a couple years. We have to take turns riding every shift. It's a good time."

"You are really good at that.... like *really* good."

"Thank you," he answered back with a chuckle. He wanted to scoop her up and kiss her, but they hadn't talked about anything since their mind blowing kiss. Josh wanted more, but he didn't want to scare her if she wasn't sure how she was feeling. But the way her eyes were perusing his body, he thought she might just feel the same way.

He got a muffin out of the basket and peeled off the paper and took a bite. These really were the best muffins he had ever had.

"I really appreciate this, Poppy." And he wasn't lying. Growing up it had really kind of been him and his sister against the world. When someone went out of their way to do something nice for him, it meant so much.

"What time are you off?"

"I'm working a double shift today, so here till close tonight."

Poppy sat down on the picnic table next to him. She sat close enough that her thigh pressed into his. Hers was soft and giving, if felt good against his hard thigh. He let his hand rest on her mid-thigh, careful not to go too high, but oh how he wanted to. After last night he couldn't stop thinking about her. He had made it through the cast party on his best behavior, but barely.

"Are you busy tomorrow?" she asked.

"Nope, I was planning on taking the day to just relax and recover. Do you have plans?"

"Nope," she said as she turned to look at him. She licked her bottom lip, and Josh would almost swear she did that on purpose. Then those beautiful soft lips turned into a small smile.

"Let me take you out," he said, as he tucked a strand of hair behind her ear. The smile on her face turned into a bigger smile and shone so bright it warmed his heart.

"Okay."

"Tomorrow, I will pick you up at one and take you on a picnic. How does that sound?"

"That sounds amazing, I'll bring dessert."

'I'm sure you will,' thought Josh, hoping maybe Poppy could be dessert.

CHAPTER 16

Poppy

*P*oppy's heart had been all a flutter since she went to see Josh at work. She had no idea he could ride a bull like that. It was impossible to watch him ride that thing and not think about what it would be like to sleep with him. She was a wreck. The vision she had of what his hips would do on top of her had her constantly wet. In fact, last night she got out her vibrator and gave herself multiple orgasms at the thought of those hips of his. She even envisioned turning the tables and riding him.

Poppy tried to shake those thoughts. She'd woken up early that morning and decided to start baking. It was her day off in the store, so she busied herself in the kitchen. It used to be her dream to open a bakery somewhere, but she never thought of doing one here. If she was honest, she had many dreams of that sort, but none of them had much staying power. This one could be different. This could be a good start for her, and Sam loved it when she baked for the store. But she wasn't quite sure yet. Thinking about what she actually wanted had made her realize this opportunity was right under her nose. So, this morning she was baking. She had made some apple cider doughnuts, a dozen apple pies, and some cinnamon apple swirl bread.

As she was packaging some of it up the kitchen door opened, and her gran walked in.

"Something certainly smells good this morning," she said, giving Poppy a warm smile. Her eyes scanned the kitchen taking in the doughnuts, pies, and loaves of bread. "My you have been a busy girl this morning."

"I was just in the mood to bake," said Poppy with a shrug.

"Usually, you don't set foot in the store on your days off."

"I know, I just couldn't really sleep, so I decided to bake instead." She offered her gran a doughnut.

"Are these my mother's recipe?" she asked.

"Of course. These are the best doughnuts, and the only ones I know how to make, but I'm hoping to branch out," she said as she surveyed all she had made this morning. "Do you want to help me package all of this up and get them out to the store?"

The two of them worked, getting everything ready for sale. "Leave out a couple turnovers. I am going on a picnic with Josh today and I told him I would bring dessert."

"Going on a picnic with Josh Turner?" her gran asked with a raised eyebrow. "Is there something going on between you two?"

"I don't know yet. Maybe? I think I like him."

"He's a very sweet boy, Poppy. Be careful with him."

"I think you have the advice backwards gran, aren't you supposed to warn him not to hurt your little girl?"

"I know sweetheart, but he has had a rough life. I love you with every beat of my heart, you know that, but you're a little flighty sometimes."

Poppy was a little taken back by this conversation. This is not what she was expecting.

"What do you mean he's had a rough life? I've known him my whole life," Poppy said.

"I know you both lost your mother's that same year and that is hard. But you had a loving place to land. You had me and your grandfather, you had your own father, who's an amazing dad. Not everyone has that."

Poppy nodded, trying to take in what she was saying. The more she got to know Josh the more she realized she didn't *really* know him at all. She had this idea in her head of who she thought he was; this happy, nice guy who would give anyone the shirt off his back. She was still certain he was that, but he had more layers than she had thought. Poppy found herself wanting to know all of them. She wanted to know about his life and make sure he was never sad ever again. That was a thought she could not bear. She was also very interested in learning more about the Josh she watched on the bull.

After they got all the items for the store packaged up, Poppy went upstairs to get ready for her date. A picnic. She wasn't sure what that meant when it came to getting ready. Like a cute picnic dress for an easy park picnic? Or did she need something a little more outdoorsy, was there hiking involved? Hopefully not too much hiking, Poppy wasn't averse to hiking, but she wasn't what you would call outdoorsy. She decided she would text Josh to find out.

> Poppy: Hey, So I'm trying to figure out what to wear, will there be walking involved? Woods? I need more information than picnic.

> Josh: Just a little walking, nothing too crazy. I'm sure whatever you wear will be perfect. Perfectly Poppy.

Perfectly Poppy, that made her smile. She couldn't help but feel the giddiness bubbling inside her.

Poppy: OK, I'll be ready

JOSH SHOWED up at one on the nose. He was very punctual, because of course he was. She was sitting out on the porch swing enjoying the fall day when he came. Most people here loved the fall but living at an apple orchard the fall was busy. Poppy was glad to have some time off.

Josh got out of his SUV and walked up to the porch. "Hey, are you ready?"

"Yep, let's go."

He took the container with the turnovers from her hands and led the way to the car. He popped the back gate and set them in. Poppy spied a picnic basket and a blanket. She didn't remember the last time she'd been on a picnic. This was nice.

Josh opened the door for her, and Poppy climbed in. She had decided to go with jeans, a big sweater, and some of her favorite boots. She felt cute and comfy. Josh's car was spotless, she knew he drove Uber, but it was pristine. Poppy chuckled thinking about the state of her car. Half of her wardrobe resided in the back seat, scrunchies on anything a scrunchie could go, because she always decided she wanted her hair up halfway through the day, water bottles and charging cords everywhere, and of course a big poppy hanging from the rear-view mirror. It was quite the comparison to his. His car even smelled like a new car.

As Josh started down the driveway Poppy couldn't help but to feel excited, but she found herself to be a little nervous as well. She fiddled with the hem on her sweater. Josh looked over at her and smiled and took her hand. There was that zing. *What was that?*

"So, where are we headed?" She asked.

"There is a spot by the waterfall that I have loved going to ever since I was a kid. I thought I would show you."

"That sounds amazing."

They pulled up to one of the parks outside of town. There were camping grounds and walking trails. This is where the town got its name from, Mystic Falls. If you walk one of these trails a way back you come upon some beautiful waterfalls.

Josh grabbed the picnic basket and blanket. They set off down the trail. A little way down Josh turned off of the trail, but Poppy followed his lead. After a few minutes a narrow trail picked back up.

"We are almost there," he said. Looking back, he smiled that care-free smile he always had, but Poppy was beginning to wonder just how care-free that smile actually was. There was way more to this man than she ever thought.

The sound of rushing water was growing louder. Poppy knew they were getting close to the falls, but she had never been this way before. They came up to what appeared to be a large stone wall about shoulder height to Poppy. Josh put the picnic basket and blanket up on it and turned to Poppy with a smile on his face.

"Up this way," he said motioning his head that she was to climb up the giant rock.

"Umm Josh," she looked down at her body. "I'm not actually built for rock climbing."

"You can do it. My sister can climb up this and I know you can too," he said with an encouraging hand on her arm.

Okay, she was going to try.

"Here let me help you. Put your foot here and grab onto this branch."

She did that and pulled herself up.

"Okay, now next foot here and grab here. Then you should be able to get right up there."

She followed his instructions and was able to step onto the platform. Before she knew it, Josh was right behind her picking up their things. They were so close to the falls she could feel the mist. She turned back to see him watching her and smiling.

"This way." He pointed to a space between two large rocks. Poppy followed him just a little way further. It looked like they were going into a cave of some kind. But as they turned the corner Poppy could see it. There was this perfect little stone ledge with light shimmering in and water cascading down in front of it. They were behind the waterfalls.

"Oh my god. This is beautiful. How did you even know this place existed?"

"I spent a lot of time here as a kid. This has always been one of my secret places." He looked around and took it all in, then got to work setting up the picnic. Laying the blanket out, he motioned for Poppy to join him as he pulled out a bottle of wine and poured her a glass.

She took it, her eyes were still scanning this place. It was filled with this magical glow as the light streamed through the waterfall. He got a cutting board and set out beautiful fresh fruit and cheeses. Then he reached in and pulled out two sandwiches wrapped in brown paper. He handed her one and she took it with a small smile. Poppy had dated for fun in the past, she did lots of things for fun, but something felt more serious about this date with Josh. And it was over-whelming her a little bit.

"This is amazing, I don't think anyone has ever done anything like this for me before," she said quietly.

He gave a bashful smile and set a plate down in front of

her. She unwrapped her sandwich and it was something out of a magazine. It was a fresh baguette with arugula, tomatoes, fresh mozzarella, and a balsamic drizzle.

"Where did you get these?" she asked. "They look delicious."

"I made them," Josh said.

"You made these?" she asked. Then she took a bite. It was so good, the bread was toasted and a little crispy, the fresh mozzarella was creamy, and the Balsamic vinegar brought it all together. "These are amazing."

"Thanks, I'm glad you like them." Josh reached into the basket and pulled out a bottle of water and opened it and took a drink.

It was then that something struck Poppy, she had never seen Josh drink. He was at the Elbow Room all the time, bartended at the saloon, was it possible that he didn't drink?

"No wine for you?" she asked.

"Nope, I don't drink," he said as he took another bite of his sandwich. And there it was, yet another layer to this enigma of a man.

"Like ever?"

"Nope. I've never had a drink."

"Like ever?" she asked again, astounded.

"Nope, I just never saw the appeal, I guess."

She thought about that. They both sat there silently eating their sandwiches.

"The more I get to know you the more I realize how little I actually know. You're a mystery, Josh Turner."

"What can I say, I'm just full of surprises." He cocked his eyebrow and gave her a look that shot straight between her legs. The picture of him on the mechanical bull, and the way his hips rode with it, invaded her thoughts. She couldn't help but think of those talented hips burying himself into her over and over. He moved so nimbly.

"Penny for your thoughts, Poppy," he said, pulling her out of her dirty thoughts.

"Oh, you don't want to know my thoughts," she responded without really thinking. She set her half-eaten sandwich on her plate.

"Oh, now I really do," he said, shifting his weight closer to her.

Poppy grinned and shook her head.

"Tell me."

"Not a chance, Turner," she grinned at him.

At that, he pounced. He dove next to her and grabbed her sides, tickling her. He pulled her on top of him and she laughed. "Tell me and I'll stop."

Poppy laughed and tried to catch her breath. "Okay, okay, I'll tell you."

CHAPTER 17

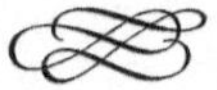

Josh

"Victory!" Josh cried. They were now both laying on the blanket with Poppy's body strewn over his. She looked at him and he became acutely aware of how close they were. He could feel his cock twitching to life with her soft body in his arms and her breast pressing into his chest.

She bit her lower lip, and he watched as she dragged it through her teeth. Breaking his gaze, she looked away. Was Poppy feeling shy? There was a first time for everything.

"I was thinking about watching you ride the bull." Her gaze turned back to his. There was a fire in her eyes he had never seen before.

"Were you? What exactly were you thinking about?" he asked in a low raspy voice.

The fire stayed right there in her eyes, and he could see the exact moment she chose to be brave. "I was thinking about how good you looked riding that bull, how your hips rode the bull..." Her tongue traced out along her bottom lip.

"And I was thinking about what your hips would feel like riding me the same way."

At that moment Josh lost what little control he was holding on to. He slid both of his hands into her dark hair and claimed her mouth. The feeling when he kissed her was like nothing he had ever experienced before. It was like the palpable force pulling them towards each other like magnets, like he would never be able to get close enough to her. His tongue dove into her mouth and claimed his space. Her hands clung to his arms and his skin heated under her touch.

He flipped them so Poppy's back rested on the blanket, and he caged himself over her. He looked into her dark eyes. She smiled up at him with a gaze that fueled the fire burning deep inside of him. He had wanted Poppy his entire life and could not believe this was actually happening. A smile crept across his face as he brushed her hair away.

"What are you smiling about?" she asked.

"I just can't believe this is real. That I'm here with you, in this place that has been my safe space for so long, and I'm here with you. Kissing you." He lowered his head and placed a sweet tender kiss on her mouth. She smiled up at him and his heart swelled in his chest.

"I'm glad to be here too. Thank you for showing me this spot."

He kissed her mouth again. This time he slowly sipped at her lips, taking his time, drinking her in. Her fingers sought out the bare skin of his back at the hem on his shirt. He deepened the kiss, and she returned it with just as much passion. He let his hand trace along the curves of her body. His hand rested on her hips and hitched her closer to him. She gave a little moan, encouraging him further. Her blunt fingernails dug into his back as his hands explored over her soft belly and up to her full breasts. He let his fingers trace a light circle around the nipple pebbling under her sweater, their mouths connected the entire time.

Josh pulled back and looked at her. He needed to show her pleasure, needed to hear her come apart. He let his hand find the hem of her shirt and he kissed gently up the side of her neck until he was at her ear. His teeth sunk into her earlobe, and she gasped. His fingers found the bare skin of her belly.

"Can I touch you, Poppy?" he rasped in her ear.

She gave a breathy reply, "Yes."

He let his hand slip under her sweater. He relished the smooth softness of her belly as his hands traced upward and gently squeezed her breast. He lifted up her shirt and his cock was screaming at the sight of her soft skin and her purple lace bra, her dark nipple pebbled under the fabric, and he licked it over the fabric and sucked it into his mouth. She gave a sharp cry of pleasure, and he knew he had to make her come right now. If she would allow him, he would pleasure her right here in this cave, the sound of rushing water blocking her cries from the world and echoing in here just for him.

His hand left her breast and traced over her belly, coming to rest on the button of her jeans.

"I wanna make you come right here, princess. Will you let me give you pleasure until you scream, and you remember exactly who made you scream?"

"Oh my god, yes!" she cried. She started to undo her pants. Josh's hand stilled hers, "No, I'll do all the work. Your only job is to enjoy yourself."

His hand undid the button of her jeans and slowly pulled down the zipper as his teeth lightly scraped over her nipple. He slid his hand under her underwear until he was holding her sex in his hand. It was warm and already slick. He carefully slid his finger between the folds, and she gasped. He sank his finger in and she dug her nails further into his shoulder. At the slight sting he pumped in another finger. Poppy spread her legs further and moved to slide her pants off her hips to give him more room to work. His fingers slipped up to that delicious bundle of nerves and made a slow intentional circle. Her breath caught in her throat, and he increased the pressure. The feel of her slippery clit between his fingers had him itching to explore her with his mouth, but he would wait until he had all the space and time to pleasure her how she deserved to be pleasured.

She started to grind against his hand, he could tell her release was building inside of her. He pulled his hand back and watched with amusement as she scowled at him. That pouty mouth egged him on, he kissed it and started working slow circles around her clit again. He watched the pleasure dance across her face. She closed her eyes and bit her lip. He pulled his hand back one more time. Her eyes shot open looking at him, begging him for the release building inside of her.

"Are you ready to come now, Princess?" She looked at him, her mouth opened and panting, and she nodded her head. He claimed her mouth and pushed two fingers inside of her. Then his thumb found her clit and began to circle it as his fingers pumped in and out. Her hips started grinding against his hand. He increased his pressure until she was panting into his mouth, and he devoured the pleasure. He could tell she was getting close, and he needed to see her face.

He needed to see what she looked like falling apart on his hand.

She moaned and her breath caught. Her eyes flew open and locked onto his. He didn't speed up or change the pressure. He was there, steady, giving her exactly what she needed. Then her head fell back, and she cried out. He could feel her body pulse around his hand, and he helped ride the waves wringing out every ounce of pleasure he could. He had never seen her look more beautiful than she did right now. Her breathing slowed and he slid his hand out and licked his fingers clean while she watched. He adjusted her pants and sat back to look at her.

She reached for his pants, and he stopped her hand and then brought it up and pressed a gentle kiss into her palm.

"Not this time, princess."

"But--" she started to protest.

"No," he gave her a sweet kiss. "This time was all about you. You don't know how much pleasure I got from watching you, that is enough for me right now."

He watched her expression change, and he would swear he saw her eyes glass over for a short moment. He brushed the hair sticking to her damp temples away and kissed her again.

"And if I have my way, Poppy. I will do that again and again. You are so pretty when you come, princess."

She sat up and he handed her some water.

"Wow... That was amazing," she said, still panting a little.

The glow in his heart expanded. Her eyes locked on him, and she gave a small smile. He cradled her face and his thumb grazed slightly over her cheek. That pull he felt towards her was still strong, but now it was coupled with this desire to claim her, to please her, to give her everything she has ever wanted and fulfill all her fantasies.

That thought scared him. Was he capable of giving a woman like Poppy everything she deserved? He wasn't sure what he had to offer. His life was kind of a mess. It always had been kind of a mess. He wore his happy-go-lucky mask well, but she deserved more than someone's mask. Josh knew how to make people comfortable. He knew how to make people happy, but he was always afraid if they saw the true him, they would realize that he didn't really have anything to offer. And while he did know that wasn't true, here looking at her, he didn't know how he would ever be enough for her.

Her hand closed over his and she nuzzled into his hand. The simple gesture made him smile. Even though he was afraid of letting her in, of someone knowing all of him and not just the happy-go-lucky mask that he showed the world, he had to try. She deserved a whole person, and he did trust her, even though he was terrified.

"What's wrong?" she asked as she sat up and brushed her fingers over the furrow on his brow.

"Nothing," he said. He held her hand and kissed it again. "Absolutely nothing is wrong. What do you say we get into those turnovers you brought?"

After they ate dessert, Josh packed up the picnic and they headed back to the car. He dropped Poppy off and walked her up to the door. It was almost like they were in high school again, only in high school he never made girls come in the forest, so this was much better than that. They kissed goodbye and he headed back to his car. He didn't know what was next for them. He knew what he wanted, but he didn't want to rush her. It felt like he was on the edge of something really big, he didn't know if he was more terrified or excited, but he was going to try. He was going to be brave because it is not every day you get this close to your dreams.

CHAPTER 18

Poppy

The Glenn farm was as picturesque as a New England painting. As Poppy pulled up to visit with her best friend, she stopped to take it all in. It was mid-October and the leaves were turning colors in the trees that lined the farm. Down the hill was their charming barn, horses out to graze in the field, and there was Graham, out in his kilt chopping wood. He smiled up at her and waved. She waved back, glad they were home. There had never been a moment she needed to talk to her best friend more.

She climbed the steps to the kitchen and walked in. "Hannah, where are you?" Poppy needed to find her and talk fast since she was on her lunch break.

"I'm in my office, just one sec." Hannah came around the corner and Poppy attacked her with a big bear hug.

"Woah... I miss you too, Poppy," she said with a chuckle.

"How was your honeymoon?" Poppy asked. She was trying to be polite, but she needed to talk to Hannah about this love spell situation and Josh and Damien. She was just about to pop.

"It was great! I loved Scotland, I think it might have been a mixed bag for Graham, he was happy to see Scotland again, but it was also kind of hard because he didn't recog --"

"I got a love spell," Poppy blurted out.

"What?" Hannah looked at her, her mouth gaping.

"I stopped Bridget, the witch, at your wedding and asked for a love spell. I performed it that night and two days later this Broadway star showed up in town."

"Woah woah woah, slow down. You got a love spell?" Hannah asked.

"Yes," Poppy said and gave a silent plea for Hannah to keep up and let her get this out. "She gave me a potion to put in my tea before I went to bed. I did it. I had a super crazy dream, and then two days later Damien St. Cloud came into town because Ms. Maple needed to go take care of her sister and we needed a music director to help us finish the show."

"Ok," Hannah said, waiting for her to go on.

"I thought he was my soulmate. We hooked up the whole time he was here, but he was a low-key dick and things never felt right. Had you been here a week ago I would have been talking to you about how things were with you and Graham when he first arrived. I knew you guys had some growing pains." She paused and took a breath while pacing around the kitchen. Then she continued, "So I thought that's what this was, but then I went to Bridget's store--"

"Her store?" Hannah interrupted.

"Yes! There's that too. She is here in town. She set up a shop. But anyway, Friday before opening night there is an announcement, Ms. Maple is here Damien got called back to the city and is poof gone. I tried to text him but haven't heard anything back." She took a deep breath. "Anyway, long story short, I think my soulmate might be Josh Turner."

Hannah's mouth fell open and she cocked her head to the side and just stared at Poppy.

"My sentiments, exactly," Poppy said as she flopped down onto one of the chairs at the kitchen table.

"Woah," said Hannah "That's a lot."

"Tell me about it," Poppy said as she picked up one of the candies in the bowl on the table.

"Ok, so you're sure it wasn't the guy from Broadway?"

"I mean, pretty sure. He was full of himself, and we were always sneaking around, and I never had an orgasm with him."

"You never had an orgasm with him?" Hannah clarified.

"No, but I thought maybe it was just a growing pains thing. How did the spell feel with you and Graham?"

Poppy watched as her best friend's face glazed over with a sappy smile. "Well, I mean, we did fight with each other at first, but there was no way either of us could have fought the spark that danced between us every time we touched. And once we kissed it was all over. I tried for a minute to fight it, but I knew I was powerless. Okay, back to you, why do you think it is Josh?"

"Okay, so after things were a flop with Damien, I went to see Bridget and she was all like 'follow your heart" which is bullshit advice if I've ever heard any."

"Stop, you went to see her? I'm just trying to keep it all straight," Hannah said, trying to follow Poppy's animated storytelling.

"You were gone too long Hannah."

"Well excuse me for getting married."

"You're excused, now keep up."

"I'm trying!" Hannah said, chuckling under her breath with amusement.

"Yes, Bridget is here. I went to see her when I was feeling like things with Damien were not what I wanted. She told me to just follow my heart. I tried to think about it, I mean I have always wanted to get out of Mystic Falls, but it seems the more I think about it the more I question if that is what I truly want. I mean if I really wanted to leave that badly, why am I still here?"

Hannah just nodded, knowing Poppy clearly wasn't finished.

"See this is the thing, because of that I wouldn't think it was Josh because all I have ever wanted to do was get out of this town, and Josh Turner is the walking embodiment of this town. Being in love with Josh Turner is like being in love with the town itself."

Hannah nodded, no one would deny that. Josh was a staple in this town. He knew everyone, had worked every-where, and was basically the heart of the town.

"But there was this moment right between us before Damien showed up. And then on closing night we kissed in the prop closet, and it was the best kiss of my entire life. I just want to be close to him, physically close, it feels like this magnetic pull, like I can't fight it. And then yesterday he took me on a picnic and made me come so hard I couldn't see straight."

Hannah sat there across the table grinning at her.

"What are you smiling at?" Poppy asked.

"You," she said with a little shake of her head.

"Stop. What do you think?"

"I think it is pretty obvious." Hannah said with a smirk.

"But, like, why?" Poppy groaned. "I wanted this grand epic love story full of magic like yours. While I didn't get a time traveling highlander, I thought a Broadway star might work, but no, it's Josh. Josh Turner. The kid I have known since first grade. Where's the magic in that?" Poppy asked incred-ulously.

"I don't know, it sounds pretty magical to me. Looking for

the love that had been right under your nose the whole time, learning a little 'there's no place like home' magical lesson."

Poppy groaned, but the more she thought about it the more it did make sense.

"How do you feel about Josh?"

A big grin fell across her mouth, and she tried to bite it back, but she knew Hannah had seen it. "I mean he's pretty incredible. Have you ever seen him ride a mechanical bull? It may be the singularly hottest thing I have ever seen in my entire life." Poppy could feel the flush climbing up her chest.

"What? Josh Turner on a mechanical bull?"

"Yeah, we should go see him bartend one night and you can see what I'm talking about."

"I think you know your answer, Poppy," Hannah said.

"What do you know about Josh?" Poppy asked.

"What do you mean?"

"I mean, you dated him. You have to know about him. Like, how did you not tell me he kisses like that? Also why is everyone telling me to be careful with him? He cooks. He can trick ride a mechanical bull. He has never had a drop of alcohol in his life. I just feel like for someone who feels as comfortable as he feels to me, I still feel like I know nothing about him."

"Yeah," Hannah said with a pensive look on her face. "Now that I think about it, I don't really know him that well either. I mean we dated for a couple months, but we never really talked much. I could have told you the kissing part though he's a pretty amazing kisser."

The door to the kitchen opened as Hannah was finishing the last statement and in walked Graham. He really was something out of this world. He was tall and huge and wearing a kilt.

"You better be talking about me, mo ghràdh," he said as he lowered his head for a kiss.

"Of course, I am, my love." Hannah said, smiling at him. "Poppy got a love spell from Bridget at our wedding."

"Oh, ye did, did ye? How is that goin'?" he asked.

"Good, I think."

"She thinks it's Josh Turner," Hannah said.

"Maybe! I just need to figure out what I want," said Poppy.

"That would be nice if he was taken. I wouldn't have to hate him any longer, he seems like a nice enough fellow, but I don't trust any man who kisses this lass and lets her get away," he said, kissing Hannah on top of her head.

"Oh, stop it," she said, pushing him away.

After they finished their visit Poppy headed back to the orchard. She would love to have more time than a lunch break to spend with Hannah, but that would have to be enough for now.

POPPY CLOSED the shop and decided to cook dinner for everyone. She gathered the ingredients and threw together a pot of chili so it would still be warm when everyone else was finished for the day. When finished, she texted everyone to let them know there was chili and cornbread whenever they wrapped up for the day.

Then she started to think about Josh. Because, let's face it, she was always thinking about Josh now. It was just him and his sister in that house, maybe he would like to come over for dinner.

> Poppy: Hey, if you're hungry I made a big pot of chili, come on over.

> Josh: Are you serious?

> Poppy: Yeah, I am getting corn bread out of the oven in 10 minutes. Come over whenever you are ready.

Poppy smiled at her phone. What on earth was her problem? What kind of spell had Josh put on her? Ok, well... maybe she was the one who put a spell on them, but whatever it was it sure felt right.

The family started making their way back for dinner. Jackson was the first one and he started setting the table. Poppy was glad Jackson was here. Since he and Sam got married last year, they weren't around every night, and Poppy missed them. They were still close, but they hadn't gotten together for a family dinner in a couple weeks.

"Hey, add one more place to the table," Poppy said.

"Okay, who's coming?" Jackson asked.

She didn't really want to tell him, because when Jackson got his mind on this, he would be relentless. There would be so many questions. Are you dating? Is it serious? Is he good in bed? Where is this going? And she didn't really have the answers to any of those questions. Why did she think it was a good idea to invite him over for dinner? Oh, right because she missed him. She hadn't seen him today and wanted to see him. This is not something she was used to. She cringed at the thought, but maybe she and Josh needed to have a conversation and figure out just what was going on. She was nervous because she was still unsure where her place was. Josh deserved certainty, but she didn't have that for herself right now.

"Josh," she said as she got the cornbread out of the oven. She hoped if she was holding something hot, he wouldn't be a pest about it. He was oddly silent as she set the pan on the stove next to the giant soup pot of chili. She turned to see Jackson appraising her with his hands crossed over his chest and his eyebrow cocked.

"What?" she asked.

"I'm not saying anything."

"Good."

Over the next couple minutes her dad and gran came in. The room was filled with chatter and laughter and all the warm fuzzies. Sam came in and headed into the bathroom to clean up. There was a soft knock and Poppy went to open the door. She had not expected everyone to be here. Usually, it was tricky this time of year to get them all together, but somehow, they managed it tonight, and Josh was about to be thrown into the middle.

Poppy went to open the door, but instead of opening it and inviting him in, she opened it and then slid out, shutting the door behind her.

"Hi," she said barely above a whisper with an out of character bashful smile.

"Hey, what's going on Poppy?" he asked. Amusement creased his forehead and he chuckled.

"So, when I invited you over, I was not planning on the whole family being here for dinner, and I just wanted to let you know they are all in there."

"I have met your family before," he said with a reassuring smile.

"I know, but that was before we were doing what we have been doing and I just wanted to tell you before you got in there."

"I think it'll be okay, unless you told them I made you scream with pleasure in the woods --"

Her hand flew to his mouth covering the words. "Oh my god! Will you stop?" She slowly removed her hand from his mouth.

"Let's go eat dinner, Poppy," he said. The warm smile on his face settled the nerves that had been bubbling up.

When she opened the door, they were already sitting

down at the table with steaming bowls in front of them chatting about the day.

"Josh, hello dear, I'm so glad you're here. Grab a drink from the fridge and come join us," said Gran.

They got their drinks and sat down to eat. Sam and her dad talked about the orchard, Jackson talked about work, and Gran asked Josh how his sister was doing. It was nice, something about this seemed easy.

"I wanted to tell you what an amazing job you did in the play," Gran told Josh. "I enjoyed watching you and Poppy up there."

"That is very kind of you," he said with a simple charm. "It's pretty easy when you've got such a spectacular leading lady." Under the table he put his hand on Poppy's knee. Her thin legging did nothing to block out the heat of the touch. His fingers gently rubbed her leg, and it made her think about yesterday.

"Are you blushing?" Sam asked. "I don't think I've ever seen you blush before."

"Shut up, I'm not blushing," Poppy said, wishing she could disappear inside her bowl of chili.

Sam gave her an expression only a sister could read. It was an expression that said, *'You are full of shit. What is going on with him?'* And her expression answered back, *'Not now. Please be cool, for the love of god.'*

When they finished eating, Sam left to finish up some work before he was done for the day, and Jackson left with him. Her dad and Gran got up to start cleaning up dinner.

"Please let me help," Josh said, as he got up and took his bowl to the sink.

"Aren't you sweet, dear. No, why don't you and Poppy go relax."

"Are you sure? I don't mind," said Josh.

"I insist," Gran said, taking the bowl from his hands.

"Do you want to go for a walk?" Poppy asked, trying to extract him from the situation.

"Yeah, that sounds good," he said. He looked over to her with the quintessential Josh smile, friendly and reassuring. Only now it made her feel things she hadn't before. This smile made her feel protective, like she would do anything to keep that smile on his face, and she totally wanted to jump his bones... but that was neither here nor there... just new.

They walked over to the door and Josh opened it for Poppy. As they descended the porch stairs, Josh reached out and took hold of her hand. There was a giddiness there, she felt like she was in high school holding hands with the boy she had a crush on. All of this made her feel so alive.

They walked a while, past the closed store and down to where there were rows upon rows of apple trees. The sun was setting and there was an autumn nip in the air, but she didn't feel it walking hand in hand with Josh.

"Hopefully, that wasn't too much for you," Poppy said, breaking the peaceful silence between them.

"No, that was really nice. I didn't grow up with much family. It's nice to be around such a close one."

"I guess. We're close and in each other's business all the time..." Poppy said, trying to make a joke.

"It's love and it's nice," he said with a seriousness in his voice. "It's just me and my sister normally, so I enjoyed that."

Poppy remembered her Gran talking about how things had been different for him because he didn't have much family to fall back on after his mom died. She wanted to know about that. She wanted to know about him.

"So, it's just you and your sister?" she asked, hoping he would share more.

"Yeah, it's been just the two of us for a long time."

"No extended family or anything?" He was quiet as they walked, thoughts churning behind those piercing blue eyes.

She didn't want to upset him, but she did want to know him better. She squeezed his hand. "It's okay, you don't have to tell me."

"No, it's okay. I want to tell you. It's just not something I talk about very often." Taking a deep breath, he squeezed her hand. "But yeah, it's just me and my sister. I never knew my grandparents, and as you know, my mom died when I was twelve, and my dad left soon after that."

This was new information. Left soon after that? That didn't make any sense, who raised them?

"Your dad left?"

Josh slowly nodded his head. "Yeah, he didn't handle things well when my mom died. He tried to be there for the first year, but he was broken. Then he started drinking, he was never violent or anything, just sad. Then he started disappearing for days at a time, then weeks at a time, then one day he was just gone."

"He was gone? What do you mean?" Poppy asked. How could he have just left?

"Just that. He was gone. When I was fourteen, he left. It has just been me and my sister ever since," he said chewing on his bottom lip.

"But she was a kid too. She was in the same class as Sam. So, she would have been, what, seventeen?"

Josh nodded his head, his mouth pulled tight.

"Who took care of you?" Poppy asked, her heart starting to ache for him.

"We took care of ourselves. Lexi turned eighteen a few months after he left, and Grace Peterson helped her get custody of me and gave her a good job at the inn. I got a job at Fipps Market and finished school."

Poppy stopped and looked up at him. She saw him in a way she had never seen him before. Josh Turner was this happy-go-lucky guy with a kind word to say about everyone, always willing to go the extra mile guy. That idea of who he was did not go along with what he had just shared. He had no business being as kind and wonderful as he was with a story like that.

"I'm so sorry. I had no idea."

"No one did, besides Grace of course. I mean, I think some people suspected, which is why Mr. Fipps at the grocery store hired me and gave us a discount on food. Mena at the diner always fed us on the house. The town really looked out for us, but we never told anyone. I think most people just thought he was a drunk and not that he had totally left. So, we had to look out for each other, but really Lexi took care of me."

Poppy couldn't help herself. She wrapped her arms around his waist and hugged him. He slid his arms around her and rested his head against hers. He took a deep breath and snuggled into her.

"Thank you for sharing that, you have no business being as well adjusted as you are."

"Well, I'm not sure I would say well adjusted, we all have our trauma. I've only ever told that to one other person."

She pulled back so she could look into his eyes. "Thank you for sharing that with me, Josh. I mean it. I consider myself so lucky to have someone like you in my life." She reached her lips up to his and gave him a gentle kiss.

He rested his forehead on hers. It was a simple gesture and the intimacy of it settled in her heart. She traced his strong jaw line with the tip of her fingers. "You are an amazing person, Josh Turner. I hope you know that. If you ever need anyone to remind you, I will tell you over and over how amazing you are," she whispered to him.

Lifting his head, he looked right at her. It was a piercing gaze that threatened to overwhelm her. The intimacy of this moment was not something Poppy had ever felt before. She was overcome with emotion when he looked at her like that, but then his mouth slanted across hers. He kissed her, that kiss saying all the words that were left hanging between them. Then he fisted his hand into her hair and deepened that kiss. After that Poppy was only feeling one emotion.

Desire.

CHAPTER 19

Josh

Kissing Poppy Smith was like nothing Josh had ever experienced, and he had kissed his fair share of people. He had even been in love before, but nothing could have prepared him for what it was like to kiss her. This kiss in particular. The first kiss in the prop room had been an awakening to him. He knew he had always had feelings for her, but that kiss made those feelings impossible to push away. This kiss felt like it was shifting his whole world. He would never get enough of her.

He pulled himself out of the kiss and looked down into her deep brown eyes. Her lips looked thoroughly kissed and her eyes swimming with lust, he knew this was it for him.

"Poppy, I don't know if I'll ever get enough of you."

"Good," she purred as she leaned into him and snuggled.

The wind whipped through the trees and the chill ran through them. He held her close and rubbed her arms to warm her up. The apple trees surrounding them rustled in the wind. They had been walking for a while and the sun had set. He had no clue where they were. As another gust blew around them, she shivered against him.

"Poppy, come home with me," he rasped out at her. He wished he didn't sound quite so desperate, but when she immediately replied yes, he was on top of the world.

"Lead the way back to your house," he said.

She took his hand, and they made their way back to the house. He stopped by his car, "If you still want to come over, do you want to ride with me or would you prefer to have your own car there?"

"Would you bring me back in the morning before my shift?" she asked.

"Of course, I'll bring you back whenever you want. Just say the word." The fact that she even had to ask this made him feel like punching Damien St. Cloud all over again.

She reached up and pulled his face to hers in a deep kiss. Leaning over her, his arms caged her against his Jeep. Her fingers traced under his shirt and along his back. His leg pressed against hers. They opened and he settled one leg between hers. He could feel the warmth from her core, and he was sure she could feel him poking her in the belly with his erection, but right now he was so far from caring. She bit his lip and ground against his thigh.

"Are you going to take me home or not?" She asked with a smoldering gaze.

He kissed her one last time as he reached behind her and opened the door. "Get in."

As she turned to get in, he gave that delicious ass a little spank. Poppy looked up at him with a playful smile and he walked around the car and got in. The engine purred to life. He tried not to peel out of there too fast, but the thought of Poppy in his bed was making it hard to go slow.

They pulled up to Josh's run-down little house he shared with his sister. Her car wasn't in the driveway, meaning she was still at the inn. He was happy about that. He loved his sister more than anything, but she was extremely protective of him. And after what happened with Abbie, he wasn't sure how she would handle him seriously dating anyone again.

He pulled in and put the car in park. Leaning over, he kissed Poppy again.

"Well, this is it." He walked around and opened her door.

"How have I never been to your house before?"

"Not many people have. It's not much, your house is much nicer --" Her hand reached up to his face to stop him.

"I'm sure it is lovely," she said with a smile. "But right now, I am not here to see your decor." The look of her face as she said that last part shot straight to his cock which was already straining against his pants.

He opened the door and tried not to be self-conscious. It looked just like it did when his mom lived there all those years ago, but now it was a little sad and run down. Josh worked very hard to curate his image. He was happy and helpful, and people loved that about him. He loved that about him. And on some level that was truly who he was. But there was this side of him, the sad run down side, he never let people see. He had opened up to Poppy in a huge way tonight and he was still feeling a little exposed from that, but this had him wanting to hide.

His eyes darted around the room. It was tidy at least. The dishes were done, and the floor had been vacuumed, but that didn't hide anything. His heart thudded in his chest.

"This is really nice," she said.

He watched her look around and take it all in, everything from the sagging couch that looked like it belonged on the set of Full House, the carpet that was worn thin in the walking path, the wallpaper that had been yellowed by his father's nicotine. Why had he brought her here? The shame spiral started setting in. He looked down and saw that he was gripping her shoulder so tightly his knuckles were turning white. He let go of her and shook out his hand.

"Hey, what's the matter?" She looked up at him and gave him a warm smile.

He shook his head, "It's nothing, sometimes it's just weird bringing people back here. You are only the second person I have ever brought here."

"Well, as lovely as your home is, I did come here to see one room in particular." She stepped closer to him and pinned him in place with her smoldering gaze.

"Right," he said, finding his confidence again. "Come with me." Taking her by the hand, he led her down the hallway.

He opened the door to his room and watched as Poppy walked in taking in his space. He took in her body, *really* took it in. He had tried for the most part not to sexualize her despite the bone level attraction he had for her, but with permission given he was sexualizing the hell out of her.

Her back was to him right now, her long dark hair was down to her mid-back, and his gaze moved further down to her ass. That ass was perfection. He wanted to spank it and watch the ripple that he knew that ass would give. At that thought his cock strained almost painfully against his jeans.

She walked over to his bed and turned around. His gaze rested first on her face, her dark brown eyes burning with lust. He watched as she licked her bottom lip. Her full pouty mouth was so damn kissable. His eyes traveled further down. He relished in watching her, allowing all the dirty thoughts he had ever had about her to run through his head. Giving himself permission to fantasize about Poppy was opening the floodgates of sexual fantasies.

Deliciously slow, one by one, she unbuttoned her shirt, her eyes fixed on his. He saw the peak of red lace as she unbuttoned lower. When she got the last button undone, she slipped the shirt off her shoulders and let it drop to the ground. The sight of her lacey red bra barely containing her perfect breasts had him breathing heavily. He continued his perusal, noticing that her hands were stilled over the buttons of her jeans.

One day he would enjoy undressing her, but right now he was enjoying watching her, allowing himself to take her fully from the Poppy he knew his whole life, who he respected too much to sexualize without her consent, to this moment, when he would take Poppy and greedily eat up any morsel she was willing to give to him.

He looked at her face, her eyebrows were cocked as if asking permission to undress further. He nodded at her, and she slowly undid the button of her jeans and slowly slipped them over the swells of her hips. Her jeans dropped to the floor, and she stepped out of them. He took her in, all of her. The fullness of her breasts, the soft roundness of her belly, and he was hungry to see what was hidden under those panties.

He grabbed the hem of his shirt and slowly lifted it over his head. He watched as she bit her bottom lip. The idea that she might want him as badly as he wanted her was new to him. He had been in love with her his entire life and had always fought those feelings because he didn't think she would ever return them. But that was changing now, and the look on her face was all he needed. He toed out of his shoes and undid the button of his jeans. His cock sprung out as he pushed them down his hips. Spurred on by the look on her face he gave his cock one hard stroke through his boxers. Poppy licked her lips watching him. That small action awakened something in him. The side that needed to possess her and drive her over the edge. He wanted to make her come again and again, knowing that would give him almost as much pleasure as his own release.

"I'm going to worship your body and make you come all night. Is that okay with you, Princess?" he rasped.

Poppy's eyes widened and mouth fell open. She nodded her head.

"Good, now lie on the bed."

Poppy sat on his bed and slowly laid herself back and ran her hands over her body. Josh prowled over to the bed and sat on the end. He picked up her foot and kissed her ankle, then he started kissing his way up her body. He kissed her calves and thighs, not veering inward yet, there would be time for that, and he intended to take his time. As he kissed a little higher, he was almost to her belly, he wanted to make sure she was comfortable. He knew she might be self-conscious about this part of her body because society sucked. But he loved it because it was a part of this amazing sexy woman, and he loved all of her.

"Is this okay, princess?" he asked.

"Yes," she said with a breathy sigh.

He continued his way up kissing her belly and breasts, which were still covered by her bra, then he kept going. He kissed up her chest and kissed her neck and shoulder. Then he started kissing down her arm. When he got to her hand, he kissed the backside of it, then he pressed a kiss to her palm. Her mouth was open, and her breathing had turned into little pants and her eyes were hooded with desire. As he held the heat of her gaze, he took her finger and traced his tongue to the tip. He drew the tip of her finger into his mouth and sucked on it.

She moaned, "Oh my god, Josh, you are so fucking hot."

"And you, Poppy, are sinful perfection."

She bit her lip and her breath shuttered. "Fuck me now," she panted.

"Oh no, princess, we are just getting started."

He laid down beside her and pulled her closer. He kissed

her as he felt her lush soft body pressed against his own. He stopped and pulled back and looked at her, "You are so beautiful," he said between kisses. "I've waited a long time for this." He felt like he could never get enough. He could never be close enough.

He pulled her close to him and delighted in the press of her breasts into his chest. He kissed down her neck as his hands found the clasp of her bra. He undid it with ease and slid it off her shoulder. He adjusted her onto her back and slipped it off completely. Pausing for just a moment to take in the sight of her breasts, he took one in his hand and watched as it was too big for his hand and spilled over. He thumbed her nipple to a peak and then he kissed it and sucked it into his mouth.

His hand slid down her belly and rested at the waistband of her lace panties. Though he wanted to rip them off and devour her, he would do that later. This time he wanted to savor every new part of her. He started to pull them down, kissing along her leg as he went until he slipped them all the way off.

Now he sat between the legs of a naked Poppy Smith, and it was like all of his fantasies come true, although the fantasies could never have held a candle to the real woman spread out naked before him. Pushing her legs wide, he looked at her perfect pussy for the first time. He licked his lips. This was going to be fun. She would be screaming his name by the end.

He ran his finger along the seam between her legs, already glistening with wetness. He pushed a finger in between her folds.

"Mmmm, you are so wet already, princess. Are you ready to come?"

"Yes, please touch me."

"Since you asked so nicely," he slid one finger in and

swirled the wetness around her sex. Her breath caught as he began to swirl that wetness around her clit. He took his other hand and slid a finger inside of her, while he still worked her clit. She was so slick, tight, and warm. He could not wait to sink his cock into this pussy, but he needed to hear her cry out first. He slid in another finger and began working her inside looking for that spot. When her body convulsed, and she cried out he knew he had found it. Then he kept working it and added more pressure to her clit with the other hand.

"Oh my god, Josh, don't stop."

He watched as her breathing increased and her eyes locked onto his.

"Come for me, princess." And then her head fell back, and she cried out. She spasmed around his fingers as she came on his hand. He pulled his hand out and licked his fingers clean. "Good girl. Now I'm going to make you come again."

This time he lowered his face between her legs, her scent was intoxicating. He could live here between her legs. He slowly dragged his tongue up from her entrance all the way up to the clit and swirled his tongue around the little bud. She shifted and moaned in pleasure. That sound was like music to his ears. He would never tire of her sounds when she was lost in passion. He licked down and shoved his tongue inside of her and fucked her with his tongue. Her moans grew louder as his tongue grew bolder. He moved his tongue back up to her clit and slid two fingers inside of her to work her as he circled her clit. Her hand grabbed at his head as he sucked her clit into his mouth. She grabbed a handful of hair and pushed him into her. His tongue circled it and then he gave one last suck, and she broke. She was moaning his name as she rode waves of pleasure. He kept up. He wanted to wring every ounce of pleasure out of her that he could.

She finally pushed his head away and he looked up at her.

Her eyes were hazy with pleasure as she caught her breath. He gave her a moment to come down as his hand traced her lush thighs.

"That was incredible," she said.

"Are you ready for more?" he asked.

"Only if it means you inside of me."

"If that is what you want. I am here for anything and everything you want."

"I want you inside of me."

He reached over to his bedside table and pulled out a condom. He slid down his boxers and kicked them away. He rolled the condom over his cock and laid between her legs. He kissed her lips as he lined himself up with her center. He stopped kissing her and pulled back, he wanted to see her face when he pressed into her. As he slid in, her eyes widened as she gasped. He kissed her as he pushed himself in all the way.

Once he was positioned deep inside of her, he pulled back and thrust back into her. Her hips met his thrust and he knew he didn't have long. He started moving his hips in and out, riding her and grinding into her clit each time. Her fingernails clawed at his back as he worked his hips. Her hips moved with his and she felt so fucking good.

"I'm gonna need you to come for me, princess." And at the words, she clung to his back. She dug her nails in and cried out. He could feel her pulse around him. She did listen well. The thought drove him over the edge. He gave one last hard thrust and came harder than he had ever before in his entire life. Holy fuck. That was the best sex he had ever had, and he prayed she felt the same.

But when he looked down into her eyes, he could tell by her expression it was just as good for her. He quickly got rid of the condom then collapsed down next to her and pulled her to him. She cuddled into him and put her head on his chest. Was it possible that this, cradling her naked body while she absent mindedly stroked his chest, was even better than what they just did? He didn't know the answer, but it sure felt like it might be.

"That was amazing." she said.

He kissed her temple and held her a little tighter. "It was."

She lifted her head and looked at him. "No, I mean like, that was really amazing. I have never come like that in my life. I should've started having sex with you years ago."

He chuckled and kissed her. "I definitely would not have been opposed."

"And you're bossy," she said.

"And you like it," he answered back with a cocked eyebrow.

She bit her lip. "I do."

They both snuck off to the bathroom to clean up. He went into the kitchen to get her a glass of water. He brought it back to her and asked, "Do you still want to stay? What time should I set an alarm for?"

"The store opens at ten so I should be home by nine to get ready."

He set an alarm on his phone, then he climbed back in bed with her and snuggled her until she fell asleep.

CHAPTER 20

Poppy

*P*oppy awoke the next morning to a beeping sound. She batted at the nightstand to turn it off. She turned over to snuggle into Josh only to find the bed empty. Where had he gone? She couldn't quite process what had happened last night. Josh Turner, happy-go-lucky, easy going, Josh Turner had rocked her fucking world last night. She had no idea how dominant he would be in bed or how much of a turn on it would be. Never had she experienced anything like that before and she was dying to do it again, very soon. She had a feeling she had just scratched the surface of what sex with him would be like, and oh man, did she want more.

She was just about to get out of bed to go find him when his bedroom door opened. He walked in smiling his smile that could light up the entire world, carrying a plate and a cup of coffee.

"I know you have to get going soon, but I wanted to make you some breakfast."

He handed her the plate. There was a piece of toast and what looked like a piece of bacon and veggie frittata.

"Oh my god, this looks amazing." She took a bite. "This IS amazing! Did you make this?" she asked.

He nodded and watched her with a content smile on his face.

"First the fancy sandwich, now this. Where did you learn to cook like this?"

"I do the cooking for me and my sister. I have since I was a kid. I like cooking and trying new things," he said.

"There is more to you than meets the eye, Josh Turner."

He rested his hand on her thigh that was still under the blanket. "I had a really good time with you last night," he said.

"Oh my god, me too. It was incredible."

He gave her thigh a squeeze and licked his lips. It sent tingles all through her body.

"And just think, I did a love spell for a guy that was right under my nose the whole time."

"Love spell?" he asked, giving her a quizzical look.

"Oh yeah, Hannah did a love spell and the next day she met Graham," she said casually between bites of the frittata. "So, at the wedding I asked the same woman who gave them their love spell to give me one and the next day Damien St. Cloud showed up."

She noticed the way he seemed to wince at his name. She put her hand on his and continued. "I couldn't figure out why my supposed soulmate was such a douchebag, but I thought I'd better give it a go."

"Ahhh, I see. I was wondering what on earth you saw in that guy. He treated you like shit, and the Poppy I know would never put up with that," he said.

"I would not, but I did, which is dumb. But I think I'm starting to figure some stuff out. I hope that doesn't freak you out."

He flipped her hand, so their hands rested on her leg palm to palm. "Not even a little," he said as he laced their fingers together.

"I am going to have to stop by her shop to thank her," she said.

"Her shop?"

"Yeah, she's the woman who opened the magic shop in town last week," she said.

"Really? Well, I guess I will have to thank her too." He brought her hand up and kissed it. Poppy looked over at the clock and groaned.

"What's the matter, princess?"

She groaned again as he called her that thinking about last night.

"I was just looking at the time wishing we had a little more of it for a little morning fun, realized we didn't, then you called me princess and it gave me flashbacks to last night, and I don't think I can wait, but Sam will kill me if I do not make it there to open the store."

Josh took the plate from her hand and set it on his dresser. He moved closer to her and traced his finger down her cheek. He slid it down around her neck and leaned in for a kiss.

"Don't worry princess, we'll do that again, very soon. But for now, why don't you get dressed so I can run you home?"

His car pulled up to her house. It was surreal. Here she was, returning to the same house she had lived in since she was a kid after having life altering sex with Josh Turner. If you would have told her this would be her life a few weeks ago she would have laughed at you, but here she was. And as he leaned over to give her a kiss goodbye, she was grateful for whatever it was that brought them together, whether it was the spell or not.

Throughout the day Poppy was so distracted, her mind

kept flashing back to the previous night. She kept seeing his face when she undressed for him, feeling whispers of his touch on her skin, and hearing his low rumbly voice calling her princess and telling her to come. Her body seemed to obey him on a core level, and she loved that feeling. She spent so much time in her head and his ability to cut through all the bullshit and turn her brain off was so appealing.

And then of course there were those orgasms. Holy shit. No one had ever made her come like that. She had heard people talk about seeing stars before, but she always thought it was a metaphor. But yesterday she shut her eyes and came so hard she saw lights flashing behind her eyes with each wave of pleasure. All this time who would have thought he was like that. She thought she knew who he was, but she had no clue, and she was starting to believe no one else really knew him either.

Once she got the store open, Poppy made her way back to the kitchen and spent the morning in her happy place before business picked up. The kitchen table was full of muffins she'd made by the afternoon. She finally had enough time to step away long enough to start packing them up.

"Hey Pumpkin, what are you baking up today?" asked her dad as he entered the kitchen.

"I just made some more of the apple cinnamon muffins. They seem to be doing pretty well."

He picked one up and took a bite. His face contorted and he spit it out into the garbage can.

"There's something wrong with these muffins, Poppy," he said as he took a long drink of water.

"What?" Poppy asked. "This is the same recipe I have been using. People love these muffins." She took a bite of one. It was terrible. She spit it out into the trash like her dad. "Those are awful."

She opened the cupboard and pulled out the containers.

The salt container was right there in front. It struck her that she must have used salt instead of sugar in that batch.

"You can't sell those, sweetheart," he said, still drinking water.

"I know," she said as she swept them into the trash. "I can't believe I did that. I'm not thinking straight today."

"We all have off days. At least these turned out good," he said as he snatched a donut and headed back into his office.

She picked up her phone and made her way back out to the register.

> Poppy: I can't even focus today, I keep thinking about last night.

Immediately the three dancing dots appeared.

> Josh: You and me both. I'm trying to do some work at the inn, but I've been distracted.

Poppy couldn't help but smile down at her phone. What was even happening?

"What's got you grinning so big?" Poppy turned around to see Sam bringing in a bushel of gourds to set out. She walked over and started helping him get them put out.

"It's nothing, just texting someone."

"This wouldn't have anything to do with the fact that I saw a certain someone dropping you off at home this morning?"

Poppy didn't say anything. She didn't need to, while her and Sam were not twins, they definitely had that connection.

"What's going on with you two?" he asked.

"I'm not sure, I mean it's new, but I like him, Sam. Like, *really* like him."

"Yeah?" He looked at her with a gentle look in his eyes. "I think he's good for you."

"Me too," Poppy said, thinking about him and talking about him gave her such warm fuzzy feelings, she couldn't help but smile.

"Maybe he'll be the one to finally get you to stay here," he said jokingly to her. And while she still hadn't quite made up her mind, when she thought about Josh it was different than anything she had ever experienced before.

"Maybe, we'll have to see. It is still so new."

"But also, he better not hurt you and all the big brother nonsense, you know the drill."

"Right gotcha, brotherly love and support, with just a sprinkle of toxic masculinity," she said with a smirk.

He laughed. "But in all honesty, he's a great guy. I hope it works." They had finished setting out the gourds and Sam bent down to pick up the box. "Don't fuck it up," he joked with a warm smile on his face.

"I don't plan on it," said Poppy.

He turned to leave, but not before an idea struck Poppy.

"Hey, he bartends over at the Lucky Saloon, it's pretty fun. We should all go out, take a ride on the mechanical bull. You know Jackson would love it," she said.

He chuckled to himself. "He would indeed, yeah, let's do it."

"Perfect!" she said and clapped her hands. "I'll call Hannah later and see if she and Graham want to come. We can make a whole night out of it."

"Sounds fun, but right now let's get back to work."

She rolled her eyes. "You're predictable."

He smiled at her as he headed out of the store. "One of us has to be."

CHAPTER 21

Poppy

The gravel crunched under the tires as Sam's truck pulled in the parking lot of the Lucky Saloon. Poppy had planned a fun night out for everyone to come here and get some people to ride the bull. And if she was being honest with herself, she was dying to see Josh ride that bull again. She just could not get him out of her head.

They all climbed out of the truck, Poppy in jeans, a flannel tied at the bottom near her waist, and some boots she found in the back of her closet. She was always ready to dress for an event. Jackson had dressed up too, clearly in some of Sam's clothes: jeans, flannel, and some cowboy boots.

"Are you sure this place is ready for a gay, black cowboy?" Jackson asked.

"They better be, or else they'll have me to deal with," Sam answered him with a smile and quick kiss. Poppy loved the relationship between Sam and Jackson. Her brother had always been more serious than Poppy and she liked that

Jackson helped him be a little more fun. Poppy and Jackson could be kind of a handful when they got together, but Sam always just rolled with it.

"Hannah and Graham should be here soon. Let's go in and get a table." She fixed the flower she had tucked behind her ear, and they headed inside. Excitement flittered inside of her at the thought of seeing Josh.

They walked in and peanut shells crunched beneath their feet and the smell of beer swam in the air. Poppy looked around and spotted the perfect table where they could see the bull and the bar, perfect for keeping an eye on her beautiful bartender. She looked behind the bar and there, drying a glass, wearing a delicious tight black t-shirt, was Josh. He had a smirk and winked at her, and she felt it zing through her.

"Hey, go claim that table. I'll go get us some beers." She made her way over to the bar and settled herself on a stool.

"What can I get for you, pretty lady?" Josh said with a smile.

"I'll take three beers and a kiss from the sexy bartender."

"Coming right up," he said as he leaned over the bar and kissed her. He turned and bent down to the refrigerator case behind the bar and Poppy appreciated the view. He turned back holding three beer bottles. He saw her face and smiled at her. "Excuse me miss, were you checking me out?" he said with a smirk.

"You know I was," Poppy said as she bit her bottom lip.

"Good," he said with a panty melting smile. How on earth had Poppy been friends with him her entire life and not noticed how incredibly sexy he was?

"Excuse me," a voice from down the bar called. He shot her one last smile and turned to go help the other customer.

As Poppy walked to their table with the beers the bell sounded and one of the waitresses entered the ring in the middle of the bar. "Let's all watch as Jessi tries to tame the beast tonight," a voice boomed over the loudspeaker. The crowd cheered as she climbed onto the bull, and it started to buck beneath her. She was good, but she had nothing on Josh. The anticipation for watching him on the bull again was killing her.

"I'm getting on that thing before tonight is over," Jackson said.

"I would expect nothing less," Sam said.

They enjoyed their beers and the atmosphere. Sure, it wasn't the Elbow Room, but it was a good change of pace. The door opened and Hannah and Graham walked in. Poppy waved them over. Graham seemed to be taking it all in, this wild west theme was probably new to him. Hannah was whispering in his ear as they made their way over to the table.

"This place is something. How have we never been here before?" Asked Hannah.

"I know, it's great. I have only been here a handful of times before, it's pretty fun," Poppy said.

The night went on and they all drank beer and watched people ride the bull. It was a good time. A few more waitresses rode and some of the patrons rode. Some were as good as the wait staff, others were thrown off after their first couple bucks, but the crowd always cheered them on.

Jackson finally worked up the courage to get on. They all cheered, Poppy the loudest, but there was no surprise there. He held on until they had it cranked up pretty high and he got bucked. He got up and bowed in true Jackson fashion and everyone cheered. Sam whistled loudly behind her. Things felt good.

Then the bell sounded again as Jackson left the ring. "Alright, you guys are in for a show, let's welcome everyone's favorite bartender to the ring. Get your tips ready because he never disappoints. Give it up for Josh."

Poppy watched with bated breath. She had been thinking about him on this bull over and over. It was the stuff fantasies were made of. He hopped on and started riding, working his hips. Before long it was bucking away and Josh rode it. Poppy was getting so turned on. On the end of the bigger movements, he seemed to use the momentum to launch himself into a standing position on the bull like he was surfing. He got the crowd going and used the strap that was above the bull to lower himself back onto the bull and moved aptly to the end working it with his hips the whole time. Then he did the trick she had seen him do the first time she saw him ride where he let one of the big bucks propel him from the front of the bull to the back and catch it with his thighs alone and the crowd went wild. Poppy cheered him on. When his time was up, he hopped off and gave the crowd a wave and everyone went crazy.

Poppy turned to look at the table. All of them were sitting there with their mouths slack in a look of surprise. Poppy remembered that feeling the first time she saw him do that.

"I did not know he could do that," Hannah was the first one to say.

"How did he do that?" Sam added on.

"Damn Poppy, he's got to be amazing in bed," Jackson said.

All Poppy could do was grin. They had no idea, but after that show she needed to be reminded of that and soon... like really soon.

The night went on and they had fun. Hannah and Graham decided they were going to get going. Sam was looking tired, Poppy was hoping she had another ride home, so she made her way to the bar when there was a lull in service.

"Hey, I think my brother is getting ready to go, but I was

wondering if maybe the hot bartender would take me home tonight?"

"I think that can be arranged. We close at one and I have to finish some stuff up. But if you want to hang around, it would be my pleasure to take you home," he said as he cocked an eyebrow. Poppy blushed at the look on his face. Oh man, she had it bad, but she wouldn't have it any other way.

Poppy made her way back to the table. "If you guys want to head home, I think I'm going to wait until Josh gets off and leave with him."

"Yeah, you are." Jackson said with a grin.

"Are you sure?" Sam asked, gently elbowing Jackson in the ribs.

"Yeah, I'm sure. You guys head home when you are ready."

Poppy claimed a chair at the end of the bar and watched Josh as he tended bar. He was a natural at this job. He talked to people and made them feel comfortable. He rode the bull again and Poppy could barely contain herself. She was going to jump him as soon as he was off. Oh man, she wanted those talented hips pushing into her again.

The DJ called last call and the crowd started to thin out. Soon it was quiet, and the staff was going about their closing duties. Josh was running some stuff to the storeroom and Poppy was scrolling her phone posting pics from the evening to social media when one of the waitresses stopped by to chat with her.

"So, you're here with Josh?" she asked with a smile.

"Yeah."

"How long have you guys been together?" she asked.

"Not long, but we have known each other for a long time."

"Well, you must be something special, he never really gives any of the girls who are constantly hitting on him the time of day." she said with a kind smile.

"Oh yeah?" Poppy didn't like to think of other girls hitting on him, but she trusted him. That she was certain of, love spell or not, Josh Turner wasn't that kind of guy.

"Yeah, you should see what happens when a bachelorette party comes in," she said with a laugh.

"What do you mean?"

"Here watch this." She pulled her phone from a pocket in her apron and pulled up a video and handed her phone to Poppy. Poppy watched as a woman wearing a bridal veil with penises on it sat on the bull. It started to buck underneath her and before she knew it Josh jumped up onto the bull and settled behind the woman. This girl wearing a veil headband fit firmly between his legs, her back pressed into his chest. She watched as the bull bucked and Josh rode the bull in the same sensual way with this girl between his thighs. When the bull started a gyrating motion, he pushed her chest down till she was flat on the bull and spanked her. He then pulled her back up by her hair and they finished out the ride.

Poppy's mouth hung open. She had no clue two people could even ride that thing, let alone ride it in such a sexual way. Then there was the sight of another girl with Josh like that and it did make her feel jealous, but not angry. It was his job. Right? But why hadn't he told her.

"Wow, I didn't know he did that," Poppy said, handing her back her phone

"Yeah, he makes good money on those nights," she said, returning it to her pocket.

Out of the corner of her eye she spotted Josh watching her from the storeroom door. He stopped and looked at her. Concerned pinched his brows.

"I'm outta here, Josh. You're the last one here. Lock up as you leave," the waitress called to Josh.

"You got it, Jess. Drive home safely."

She turned to leave but he didn't take his eyes off Poppy.

"I just got a few things to finish up then we can get out of here."

Poppy smiled and nodded. She didn't know what to say. Watching that video had thrown her. Could he ride the bull like that with her? She really wanted to try.

They sat in silence as Josh finished up his closing duties. Josh seemed off, but Poppy was in her own head.

"What did she show you?" Josh said finally. He sounded nervous and Poppy felt the need to make it right.

"What? Nothing."

He stopped and looked at her, his eyes flooded with panic and concern. "Poppy, let me explain. It's not what you think it is."

She realized he thought she was mad at him because of what she saw. "No, it's fine, I mean yeah she did show me a video of you riding very... uhh… suggestively with a girl. I'm not sure why I said nothing. I think I'm just processing, but it's totally fine. I'm not upset at all."

"You're not?"

"No, It's part of your job. I get it."

"You do?" he asked. He finished up behind the bar and walked around and stood close to Poppy between her legs. He put his hands on her knees. "I promise it is nothing. It's just a way to make good tips. They have fun and tip well. Usually, they behave themselves when it's all over. I have had a time where some have tried to cross the line, but nothing has ever happened. You have to believe me." Anxiety and panic danced across his face. Poppy couldn't stand to see him like this. She cupped his handsome face, his stubble gently scratched against her hand, and she yearned to feel that gentle scratch in other places.

"Hey," she said softly and waited until he looked into her eyes. "It's fine, I understand the difference between something you do for a job and what we have. I trust you completely. I just..." she stopped.

"What is it?" he asked.

"I guess, I just didn't know that two people could ride those things, and while I did feel jealous watching you ride with another girl and I'm not sure I ever want to watch you do that, --"

"I won't do it anymore," he answered immediately.

"I didn't say that I just don't really want to watch it, but if you still do it, it's fine with me.... I was just wondering..."

He looked at her his eyebrow raised and waited for her to say it.

"I know I'm bigger than the girl you were on that thing with, but do you think you could ride it with me?"

A slow grin crept over his face. "You want to ride with me?"

Poppy grinned at him and bit her lip. She nodded her head.

"Well, let's get you up there, princess. I'll show you how it's done."

"You can ride that with me?" she asked.

"Without a doubt. I got you," he said as he took her hand and pulled her to standing.

She loved to hear those words out of his mouth because she believed them so effortlessly. He really did have her and there was no doubt there.

"Have you ever ridden one before?" He walked her around to the entrance of the ring. She shook her head.

"Okay, you hop on, I'll set the time and keep it going pretty slow. Then I'll hop on. Does that sound okay?"

She nodded as he helped her on. She felt a little nervous as the thing slowly started to rock beneath her. Then she looked behind her as Josh made his way over to the bull and jumped right on. In one swift motion she felt him settle in behind her. His thighs bracketed hers and his hands found her hips. The bull started bucking a little harder beneath them, but Josh was there to anchor her. She felt the slide and caress of his thighs against hers and she had never been this turned on in her entire life.

The bull continued to rock beneath them, one of his hands stayed planted firmly on her hip anchoring her hips to his own as he rode masterfully. His other hand began to explore her body as he kissed down her neck. With each rock of the bull, it started to hit her in all the right places. The sinful feel of his hips rocking into her, his mouth on her neck and his other now squeezing her breast had her so worked up. A moan escaped her lips.

"You like this?" he rasped in her ear.

"Yes," she sputtered out trying to catch her breath, her mind unable to focus. She was filled with so much desire.

"Are you as turned on as I am, princess?"

"Yes," she said.

He brought her arms up so they could reach behind her and hold onto him. "Hold on," he whispered. Then his hands traced down the side of her body as his thighs held her firmly in place. His hand found the button of her jeans and he started to undo them. "Is this okay?" he asked.

"Yes," she cried out as his hand slid beneath her panties cupping her sex as she clung to him.

"Mmmm, you are turned on," he whispered in her ear. "You are so wet. Should I make you come right here?"

Poppy nodded as the bull bucked beneath them. He held her close, one arm wrapped around her right under her breasts holding her to him, the other hand in her pants working small circles around her clit. Those hips still working their magic and his thighs holding her in place. It wasn't going to take long. This was the single hottest moment of her entire life. She could feel the tightness in her belly as his fingers worked their magic little circles and his mouth kissed down her neck. Her hands started to grasp him harder as the pleasure started to overtake her. He kept his pace as she was pushed over the edge.

She cried out and his hand stayed working her through her pleasure. He still held her tight and safe as she came down. He adjusted her pants and steadied her. "Hold on," he said as he took her hands from around his neck and put them on the saddle. He hopped off the back and went and turned it off.

Poppy leaned her head forward and tried to catch her breath. "Holy shit, that was incredible. You better not be doing that with other girls."

"Not a chance, that's just for you," he said with a wicked wink.

"Alright Turner, get over here and help me down. I seem to have spaghetti legs from yet another world rocking orgasm." He smiled at her and made his way over to the bull to help her down. Once she dismounted, she turned into him wrapping her arms around his shoulders, and he snaked his around her waist. She looked up and kissed him. She sipped at his mouth until he opened and then her tongue plundered into his in a deep kiss. They just stood there for a long moment kissing and enjoying each other.

"Take me home, so we can finish what we started, Turner." She looked up at him, her eyes smoldering.

"Lead the way." They left the pit and Josh stopped at the bar to turn off the neon signs that were still lit, locking the door behind them as they left.

Josh

The next morning Josh woke up cradling Poppy in his arms as she slept. The sight of her here in his bed in the morning light, her hair strewn over his pillow, the feel of all her softness pressed into his body, this was something he could get used to. He wasn't sure if he bought the love spell thing she had talked about, but there was something truly magical taking place between them. Given he wasn't the most experienced person in the world, but he had been around enough times to know that what existed between them was not something he had ever experienced before and was definitely something he hoped would last. He knew he was falling for her, he just hoped she felt the same way.

Josh had never been quite so open about some of the dominance he felt during sex. He knew he loved to be in charge during sex and found almost the same amount of pleasure from his partner's release as he did his own, but something about her submission spurred him on more than anyone else. Images replayed in his mind from last night. First them at the bar and her coming on his hand as they rode the bull. That was one of the hottest moments of his life.

But then the sex they had last night when they came home was almost primal. He had feasted on her until she screamed his name. Then he had fucked her from behind. He got to watch her glorious ass ripple with every thrust. He even got a few good spanks in, which to his utter delight she seemed to enjoy just as much as he did. His cock twitched to life as it was nestled between the globes of her ass. He tried to point himself away. Not exactly what he wanted her to wake up to this morning.

Thinking of morning, he turned to check the time on his phone. It was eight and he wasn't sure what time she needed to be at work. It was the time she had asked him to wake her up last time, but this time he wasn't sure if she even had to work or not. He wouldn't want her to be late if she had just forgotten to mention it in the passion of their night together. He brushed the hair away from her face and pressed a gentle kiss to her temple. She stirred awake in his arms. He loved getting to see her like this. There was something so intimate about those first wakeful moments.

She shifted in bed and turned to face him. "Good morning," she said. The sleepiness still clouded her eyes. Josh leaned down and kissed her forehead.

"Good morning. I'm sorry to wake you, I just wasn't sure if you needed to get to work today," he said in a gentle whisper.

She stretched in his arms and smiled at him. "Nope, I'm off today. How about you?"

"I have some errands to run, but I'm off."

Now he saw some life in her eyes, she turned all the way to face him in bed. "Do you want to spend the day together?" She asked.

"I would love nothing more."

She grinned and squealed and hugged him close. *This was it*, he thought. He felt like the luckiest man in the world here at this moment. It healed something in his heart to see the joy on her face at the mere thought of a day with him. And it felt so damn good. Yes, they had only been officially together for a couple weeks, but it didn't matter. He knew he was already falling in love with her. All he needed was the slightest push because he had been living his whole life dangerously close to loving this woman who he never thought he had a chance with. Now that he had the chance, he was going to do his best to keep her.

He held her close as she did a little happy wiggle in his arms. "So, what are we doing today?" She grinned up at him.

"Why don't we start with breakfast?"

They made their way to the kitchen and Josh started making some French toast while Poppy made coffee. They sat down at the kitchen table and ate together.

"So, plans for the day?" Poppy said with a smile. "Can they start with me going home to get a change of clothes?"

"Of course, I'm going to hop in the shower and get cleaned up. Then we can run by your house. I have a table I fixed that I need to bring to the magic shop."

"You fixed Bridget's table?" She looked over at him with puppy dog eyes.

"It was the least I could do if she had anything to do with this," he said. He took her hand and smiled warmly into her eyes.

"I also have to return some of the props from the show to their owners."

"Ok, well let's get started, Turner." She reached over with her fork and stole the last bite of his French toast.

"Did you just eat my last bite?" he asked, with an eyebrow raised. She looked at him and grinned. "It's a good thing you're cute, but you're gonna get it later."

"Promise?"

"Oh princess, you have no idea." He leaned over close to her and whispered in her ear. "You misbehave like that, and I might just have to spank you again." Her squirm in the chair let him know she liked it just as much as he did. "Or maybe I will find another way to make you pay." He bit her earlobe and she moaned.

"I'm gonna go take a shower, and then we can start our day." He gave her a quick kiss and then disappeared into the bathroom. By the time he was done and dressed Poppy was putting away the last of the breakfast dishes.

"You didn't have to do the dishes. I would've taken care of those."

"It's okay, I don't mind. Are you ready to get out of here? I hear my own shower calling my name."

"Let's go," he said as he took his keys off the hook by the door.

They pulled up to Poppy's house as orchard traffic was in full swing. They'd opened about fifteen minutes ago and it looked like there was a field trip today as they drove by one of the big yellow buses.

"I'm so glad I am missing field trip day, I worked on Sunday so I would have today off," Poppy said, with an amused smile as they made their way further down the drive to the house.

"Yeah? Not a kid fan?" Josh asked. He had always seen kids in his future.

"No, it's not that. It is just when there are sixty of them all screaming about apples and pushing each other to get to the cider, it's a lot."

"Yeah, I remember trips to the orchard as a kid."

"Something about taking a field trip to your own house took all the fun out of it," she said.

They pulled up to the old farmhouse that was nestled back from the orchard and walked up to the porch and into the empty house.

"Everyone is working today, so it should be pretty quiet here. Make yourself at home while I hop into the shower." She disappeared up the stairs, leaving Josh downstairs.

He began looking around, taking the place in. This looked like a home. A real home. There was a certain level of coziness that soothed him. Everywhere were signs of a life well lived and loved. There were school pictures of Poppy and Sam on the dining room walls and a piano in the corner covered in framed photos.

He walked over to take a closer look. There was a picture of Poppy and Sam at the Grand Canyon, Poppy looked to be about seven and had the toothless grin to prove it, a picture of Sam and Jackson on their wedding day, a picture of Poppy's parents on their wedding day, next to a picture of her grandparents on their wedding day. This is what a family home should look like. This is what he had been missing. He always felt the absence of the kind of connection family could offer.

Then he picked up the picture of Poppy's mom. It was a frame with two pictures. One picture was of a tired young mother smiling while she helped a young Sam hold a baby Poppy. The other picture was one of her mother starting to look sick with cancer, though a bright smile on her face shone through, with her arms around Poppy and Sam.

That picture was hard for him to look at. It dug at old

wounds that had never really healed properly. These photos were full of the joyful moments, the sad moments, all of it. These pictures showed a life, a life surrounded by a loving family to help you celebrate the good times and hold you through the bad times. He wiped a tear from his eye. He heard the back door open, and he set the picture back down.

He looked up to find Poppy's Gran coming in from the kitchen.

"I thought I saw your car out front. What are you kids up to today?" she asked with the warmth a grandmother's voice possessed. The fact that she called two people in their late twenties 'kids' made him smile.

"We are just going to run some errands," he said. He stopped and gave her a big smile, trying to push through the feelings clouding that smile.

As any gran can, she could tell something was off. She walked over to him and joined him by the piano and looked at the pictures.

"Lots of memories up there," she said. She picked up the picture of her wedding day. "We were married over fifty years. We made ourselves a pretty good life."

"You have a wonderful family," he said with more honesty than she could know.

"Thank you, most days they are wonderful. That one upstairs can be a handful though," she said with a knowing smile.

Josh smiled back politely. It was true, Poppy was a lot, but that was part of what he was drawn to about her. She lived out loud, she didn't care what people thought about her, she said what she felt, and she felt things on a bigger scale than most.

"She may be a handful," he shrugged. "But she's worth it," he answered with deep honesty.

"She is indeed," she said, putting her hand on Josh's shoulder. "She's lucky to have you, I have hoped you guys would get together for a long time. But no matter what happens, you are welcome in this home anytime, young man. Do you understand?"

Josh just nodded. If he had to say actual words, he would not be able to hold it together. This kind of family is all he had ever wanted. The thought that he could get it by proxy kind of terrified him, but it was also something he wanted so badly. The desperation began creeping in, that people pleaser inside that said if he was perfect and took care of everyone around him, he would be worthy of love and would not be tossed aside. He didn't feel that way when he and Poppy were together, then he just felt lucky and in love, but here with her gran looking at the life they'd lived put everything in perspective.

She had lived this life full of heartbreak, same as him, but she had been able to fill it with so much else. So much love and family, the happiness had outweighed the sadness. Josh had the same heartbreak, but he longed for the happiness, because for him it never had outweighed the sadness.

He heard Poppy at the stairs. Gran squeezed his hand. "I'll get back to work, you two have a fun day, and don't be a stranger, Josh, you hear me?"

"Yes, ma'am," he said with a genuine smile.

He turned to see Poppy heading down the stairs. Her long dark hair was down and still wet from her shower. She had on a pair of jeans, a vintage band t-shirt with a sweater and some chuck taylors. She looked almost like she did when they were in high school, but they hadn't been in high school for a long time now. They had both lived lives parallel to one another but never crossing like they were now. He was over-come with emotion.

She smiled that kilowatt smile at him, shining the full light of Poppy on to him and he could feel it. The warmth that emanated from her was enough to make him feel it in his very soul. She cocked her head to the side. "Are you okay?" she asked.

"I'm perfect, should we get out of here?"

"Let's go."

CHAPTER 23

Poppy

"Where to first?" she asked.

"I thought we might take the table back to Bridget's, then we can swing by the theater and pick up the props that need to be returned."

"Sounds good, let's do this," she said and looked over at him with a big smile. He was pulling out of the driveway, turning around to head back past the orchard to get out to the main road. He seemed off though. She didn't really know how to describe it. He just seemed a little far away. On the surface he was happy Josh, but she couldn't help but realize that his smile didn't seem to quite reach his eyes.

"Hey, are you sure you're okay? You seem like something might be bothering you."

He looked at her and smiled a genuine smile. "No, I'm fine. Just kind of lost in my own thoughts, but I'm here." He gave her leg a quick squeeze and then returned his hands to the wheel.

"Not thoughts about how to get out of this are they? Because I hate to tell you this, but you're stuck with me."

He looked back at her, his eyes filled with earnestness. "I assure you, that thought has not crossed my mind, quite the opposite in fact," he said. Something about the pointedness of the way he spoke and the way his eyes held her in place without a word took her by surprise. Although she was quickly learning everything she found out about this man was a constant surprise.

They pulled up to Bridget's little shop and Josh popped the back gate and got the table out. Poppy shut the gate and they made their way to her shop. The little bell tinkled over their heads as they entered. Bridget stepped out from the back.

"Oh, hello dears," she said.

"I have your table fixed. I put a new leg on and put some screws in to steady the others," he said as he put the table down in the middle of the room. The store had really come together in the month or so Bridget had been renting the space. On one side of the room there were shelves filled with baskets of little crystals, little baggies of dried herbs, candles, teas, books, tarot cards, even a crystal ball. On the other side was a counter and behind the counter were shelves full with hundreds of dried herbs and oils and all kinds of little goodies Poppy would love to know more about. This place fascinated her.

"Oh good," she said. "I'm glad to have my table back, it's hard to read tarot without a table." She brought over chairs and set them around the table. She flicked a purple tablecloth with gold celestial art over the table.

"You read tarot?" Poppy asked.

"Of course, I do, lass. I'll give ye both a reading on the house since ye fixed my table."

Poppy's eyes lit up and she smiled up at Josh. "What do you say? Should we have her read our tarot cards?"

"Why not?" he said with an amiable smile.

"Ye'll not regret it, that I can promise." she said.

They all sat around the table as she shuffled her cards. "Alright let's see what the cards hold for ye."

Bridget sat down at the table with some well-worn card and gestured for Poppy and Josh to join her. Josh pulled out the chair for Poppy to sit on and then sat next to her.

"All right my dears, now clear yer mind."

Poppy closed her eyes and took a deep breath and tried to clear her mind. Having a quiet mind was never really something Poppy had ever achieved, but she tried from time to time. When she opened them, Bridget was smiling warmly at them.

"Are ye ready?" she asked.

Poppy nodded and looked over to Josh, who smiled warmly back at her.

"Okay, let's see what the cards say," Josh said in his easy going way.

Bridget laid the card before them. "The first card I turn will be representative of yer past." She flipped the card. It was the three of swords. It had a large heart against a blue background and plunged deep into the heart were three swords.

"Ahhh yes, the three of swords. I see ye've had a fair share of heartbreak in yer life. This card represents grief and sorrow. This card reminds us that pain and sorrow are a part of life, but it also reminds us that we must be allowed to feel those feelings and leave them in the past."

Well, that card wasn't wrong, both she and Josh had their fair share of pain and sorrow growing up. She was just now starting to realize just how deep Josh's pain and sorrow went. Yes, Poppy had hard things happen to her, things no child should ever have to deal with, but she was becoming more and more aware of just how lucky she was to have the family and friends she did have. She looked over at Josh who was looking at the card with an unreadable expression.

"The next card I pull represents the present." She flipped over the next card, and it showed a naked man and woman joining hands underneath an angel. "Ahhh, the lover's card. I might have known. I could see that clearly betwixt you two when ye first walked in. I think the meaning of this one is fairly self-explanatory," she said with a wink. "But ye see, this card also has a deeper meaning. It is a card of honesty and vulnerability. It is about allowing yer whole self to be seen and understood and through that finding unity and harmony."

If Poppy didn't know any better, she would swear she was blushing. She looked over at Josh who was again hard to read. She wished she knew what was going on in that handsome head of his.

"All right, dears, let's see what the future holds for ye." She flipped over the next card. There was a couple standing side by side with their arms around each other. Their arms were outstretched to a blue sky with a beautiful rainbow and ten chalices beneath the rainbow.

Poppy felt a sense of peace settle over her, she instinctively reached for Josh's hand. He took it and gave it a little squeeze.

"The ten of cups is a remarkable card to have for your future. It symbolizes love and deep contentment; it is familial love. That love that warms the heart and fills ye all yer days, and in the future position it means ye are on the right track to finding this deep contentment."

Poppy and Josh looked at one another. The moment their eyes connected the rest of the world seemed to fall away. Poppy felt in her heart what Bridget had told them. She looked at Josh and felt a deep peace and bone level contentment. It was a new feeling for Poppy. She spent her life looking for the next thing, reaching for something that always seemed out of her reach, but this feeling felt different. This felt like she had everything she needed right here. It wasn't something she was used to, but it felt incredible.

Bridget gently cleared her throat and smiled; her mischievous magic danced behind her eyes.

"What do you think my dears? Do the cards ring true?"

Poppy and Josh both sat there, mouth gaping open, trying to come to terms with what she had said. She had gotten their past right, their present right and when she spoke of the future, it was like she was painting a picture for Poppy. A picture she could see and almost feel. It was this picture of her and Josh working together in a kitchen. She didn't want to recognize the kitchen, but she did. It was the kitchen at the orchard. Poppy was busy baking and Josh was cooking right next to her. This is not something she thought she wanted, but the happiness she felt in the vision was something she desperately wanted. She looked over at Josh to find his gaze zeroed in on her, a content smile stretched across his face. The look clicked things into place for her. This was their future, she wasn't sure how or why, but that was it for them.

She waited for the dread to come. She waited for that trapped feeling that small town life always gave her. The thought of living in Mystic Falls and working at her family orchard was the life she spent her whole life thinking was a trap, but right now it felt good. She didn't quite know what to make of it.

Poppy's gaze snapped back to Bridget, she realized they had been sitting there in silence for who knows how long. "Oh yeah, that all sounds great. Are you sure we can't pay you for the reading?"

"No, my dear, I take my payment in the sturdiness of my

mended table." She looked over to Josh and tipped her head in thanks. He had yet to say anything since the reading. "I ran into yer sister at the market the other day, ye should send her in," she said to Josh.

"I'll be sure to do that, thank you for the reading," he said in his warm gentle nature.

He was the first to stand from his chair. He reached a hand down to Poppy and helped her up. "We have some other errands to run, thanks again Bridget."

"Come back and see me anytime," she said with a wave as they both headed back to Josh's SUV.

Poppy would be thinking about that vision all day. They had already visited the theater and loaded up all the props to return. In returning the props they visited the town. First, they stopped in at the market to return a leather jacket to Mr. Fipps.

"I didn't know Mr. Fipps was a leather jacket kind of guy," Poppy said to Josh as they were leaving the store.

"Oh yeah, he tells stories about riding to Woodstock on his motorcycle. Get him started talking about the Grateful Dead and he won't shut up," Josh replied very matter of factly.

"Really? Mr. Fipps at Woodstock?" She was amazed. Was it possible she knew as little about the people in her town as she knew about Josh?

"Yep. Next stop the hardware store to return all the flowerpots, then how about the diner?"

They both carried some red clay flowerpots to the hardware store. As soon as Theo saw them, he went over and took the pots out of Poppy's hands.

"Thanks for lending these to us again," said Josh.

"Of course," he said, setting them on the counter behind the register.

"And thank you for all your work on the sets. They looked amazing," added Poppy.

"I'm more than happy to help," he said with a smile. "Oh Josh, I think DeMarcus may text you later. He is working on his Eagle Scout award this weekend and installing some benches and a playset over at First Baptist, if you're free we could use another set of hands."

"Yeah, that works for me. Just text me the time."

"Will do, I'll see you two later," he said with a wave.

As they walked out Poppy couldn't really believe what was happening. She had never really experienced the town like this. No wonder Josh loved it here so much.

"Are you really helping a boy scout get his Eagle Award?" Poppy asked.

"Yeah, why?"

"Do we have any old ladies to help across the street on our way?" She joked up at him.

"Why? Do you see any? Always be on the lookout for little old ladies about to cross the street. I want to be the first to know," he said clearly joking with her. She chuckled to herself.

"Where now?" she asked.

"The diner."

"The diner? What did we borrow from the diner?"

"No, that one's for lunch, princess." he said with a smile.

After spending the day returning all the items and talking to the town Poppy was amazed. It was like she had spent her whole life here, but never taken the time to get to know anyone. Was it possible that this town has been a hidden gem and not the cage she thought it was?

They were sitting at the diner. Mae, who had run this diner since she moved to town four years ago, came to greet them. She had taken over business from her aunt who had been a staple of the community, and from what Josh had told her had helped to take care of him and his sister, like lots of people in this town had.

"What can I get for two of my favorite customers?" she asked with a smile on her face.

They ordered and not too long after Mae returned with their food. "If there's anything else I can get you guys let me know. And you know I'm nosy, but word has it around town that the two of you are a couple. Are they right?"

Poppy was caught off guard, she wasn't sure why, the rumor mill in the small town was a well-oiled machine. She looked over to Josh who was watching her, waiting for her next move.

"They're right," she said. Something about that felt official, like becoming Facebook official, but the Mystic Falls version.

"Oh, that is wonderful! You two are so good together, much better than your old girlfriend."

"Thank you for that," Josh said, giving her a look.

"Right, well, I'll let you two eat." She turned to head back to the kitchen but not before giving Josh two firm pats on his shoulder.

"What was that about?"

"Abbie." Josh said, then he took a bite from his burger.

"She's not a fan, I take it."

Josh shook his head.

"Whatever happened there? This is a small town, people generally know the goings on and I never heard why you guys call off the engagement."

Josh's brow furrowed as he finished chewing.

"It's okay if you don't want to talk about it. I understand," Poppy said.

"No, it's fine." He wiped his hands on his napkin and took a sip of his drink. "You should know. It has to do with why I got upset when you saw the video of me riding with the other girl."

Poppy watched him as he took the time to find his words.

"I met Abbie at the Lucky Saloon, so she knew what I did there. Although I had just started so I wasn't quite as good as I am now. I was starting to do some of the tricks and tandem rides like I do now. She knew and didn't have a problem with it. She knew I was doing it to earn bigger tips for the wedding she wanted. But then three months before the wedding I caught her cheating with one of her co-workers. She blamed me for it, saying that what I did was the same as cheating."

"What?" The seething rage inside of Poppy took over. It is a good thing Abbie did not live in Mystic Falls because Poppy definitely had a couple of things she needed to say to her. "She knew and was fine with it, and still used it against you."

Josh silently nodded, his face a little crestfallen.

"That's bullshit. You know that right?"

"I do know that," he said quietly.

"I would never do that. I don't see that as cheating even a little. It might make me a little jealous, but I would never do that."

"Do you want me to stop?" he asked.

She thought about it for a minute. On one hand, she didn't like to think about his body pressed up against another person's body like that, and all the sexually suggestive moves he did with them, but on the other hand she trusted him completely. That's it, full stop. She trusted him. If he liked doing it and he made good money doing it, who was she to stop him? And really riding a mechanical bull to help people unwind and have a good time, albeit in a sexual way, wasn't anything real. It was a fantasy, what existed between her and Josh was so much more.

He reached for her hand. She hadn't realize she was

making a fist until he gently took her hand and slid his inside.

"I think that's your decision. I am okay if you want to keep doing it though." She squeezed his hand. "I mean that."

"We got something pretty important happening here. I feel it." He lifted her hand to his mouth. "Do you feel it?" He pressed a small kiss to the back of her hand.

She nodded, "I do."

They took a moment, together, in the middle of town, in the middle of this diner to acknowledge what was happening between them. Poppy had never said I love you to anyone she wasn't related to. It had always been this big idea that she dreamed of but never experienced, but she was beginning to wonder if that was what she was feeling for Josh. That feeling would have implications on the direction of things, but if she was really supposed to follow her heart, Josh was where it was all leading.

She was enjoying experiencing the town this way. He was their Rory Gilmore, this perfect hometown hero who could do no wrong, and like the people of Stars Hollow would've done, they took care of him. They were his family, and she couldn't help but love them for it. And then there was the vision with her tarot cards, something was changing inside of her today, in a big way.

Josh's phone buzzed on the table. He picked it up and his eyes got big. "Hey, I gotta make a phone call. I'm gonna step outside really quick, is that okay?"

"Go, I'll be here finishing your fries," she said as she playfully took a fry off his plate.

He got up and quickly left the diner. Poppy watched as he paced outside the restaurant with a big smile on his face. Whatever it was, it was good news, and that made her happy.

He came in and sat down. "Okay, let's finish up here and then we have one more errand for the day."

"Are you going to tell me what it is?"

"Nope."

"I hate surprises," she pouted.

"No, you don't," he said as he booped her nose and went to pay the check.

He was right. She loved surprises. Patience was her only problem.

CHAPTER 24

Poppy

They walked to the center of town, which was only a few blocks away. There really was something charming and quaint about Mystic Falls, especially this time of year with the nip in the air and the color in the trees. They stopped at the driveway of the old Whitney house. It belonged to a once prominent family, but no one had lived in it for years. After the owners passed away their children stopped coming home and this property had sat empty, which was a shame because the place had character.

It was an old colonial style home, big and stately. It was white with black shutters, just like Poppy remembered it. And while it had fallen into disrepair after sitting vacant for over a decade it was still something special. Poppy used to dream about living in this house when she was a little girl. This place always seemed so magical.

She remembered when the Whitney's were in their prime, they used to go all out for holidays. This house was amazing on Halloween, they even turned their basement into a haunted house kids would enter through a creepy cellar door. For Christmas it was full of lights and beautifully picturesque.

Josh took her hand as they walked up the drive and climbed the stairs to the door. The steps were a bit rickety, and the porch was in need of some TLC, but it still had this perfect mixture of charm and being regal. Josh picked up the big brass knocker and knocked.

"What are we doing here?" Poppy asked.

"It's a surprise. Patience, princess," he said as he dropped a kiss on her lips.

Mitch Alsup opened the front door. He was a Mystic Falls local and was also the only realtor in town.

"Hello Josh. Poppy, what a pleasant surprise." He reached out and gave Josh a firm handshake. "I'm glad you could meet with me on such short notice. I know you've been looking for a place, and this one was at the top of your list, and in a delightful turn of events it is going on the market."

"You're kidding," Josh said.

Poppy looked up at Josh, his eyes were big. Was he really thinking about buying the Whitney House? Excitement bubbled inside of her.

"No, but I think we are going to need to move fast. If you want, I got permission to look around so we can have an offer ready to go as soon as the listing is live."

"Yeah, I think that sounds great."

"Ok, well I'll let you two have a look around, it definitely is a bit of a fixer upper, but it has great bones."

Mitch walked out onto the porch leaving them alone in the big house. She looked around taking it all in. The air was stale, and the carpet and paint were dingy, but it could be a remarkable place. In front of them was a grand staircase to one side, a living room with a huge fireplace and a big bay window, and on the other side a formal dining room. Behind that was a kitchen with appliances from the eighties but there was lots of light and the space was delightful. Poppy could picture herself in here with updated appliances, some marble countertops baking Christmas cookies with a small brood of children. *Where on earth did that thought come from?*

They walked up the stairs and at the top of the stairs were three smaller bedrooms and then a full bathroom, the last door upstairs was the huge master with a wall full of windows, the natural light was pouring in, and the room had almost a glow to it. Poppy looked at the master bathroom, it seemed to be the most up to date room in the house with a giant soaker tub and a glass stall shower. This place was even more amazing than she thought it would be.

She stopped in the bedroom and looked out the window. It overlooked an amazing backyard. It was all overgrown, but she could see where the flower gardens had been, a little stone path to the cutest little shed in the back and once again an image flooded Poppy's mind.

She looked down in that yard and pictured herself here in this room sitting in a rocking chair rocking a little babe in her arms while she looked out the window at Josh who was pushing this beautiful little girl on the swing, her dark hair flowing with each push, her gorgeous blue eyes, that looked just like Josh's, dancing with laughter. She was experiencing this as if it were real. She could feel it. The peace and tranquility of the moment held her frozen in place. It felt so real.

She had asked for magic, and here it was. She was overwhelmed. Taking a deep breath, she tried to push away the tears that were pooling in her eyes. Josh slipped behind her and wrapped his arms around her. Poppy quickly wiped the renegade tear that had found its way down her cheek and leaned into his embrace.

"This place is really something," she said.

"Yeah, it is."

They just sat there for a moment enjoying each other and looking into the backyard. Poppy turned in his arms, that stayed wrapped around her holding her close to him.

"You're thinking about buying this place?" she asked.

"Yeah, I've been saving up for a place like this for a long time, and if I'm honest, I was saving up for this place, but I never dreamed it would be available after sitting empty for so long."

"It's amazing," Poppy said as she turned to take the space in again.

"Yeah, I'm gonna go find Mitch and talk about the details, you keep looking around." Josh pulled her in, gave her a quick kiss, and left.

Poppy looked around. She couldn't quite put a name on what she was feeling. In a very real way, she could feel a future in this house. She could feel a future with Josh. She could see the faces of those children in her vision and feel the joy. Yet, she was feeling conflicted. She had lived her whole life trying to get out of this small town. Trying and failing, but trying to get somewhere else, anywhere else and make a name for herself. Yet here she was still living at home. Her life was on pause and she could never figure out why. It was almost like her life was waiting for her to accept this to begin, but something about that didn't sit right with Poppy.

Here she was sitting at this fork in the road. She looked down one and saw a simple life but a happy life. But on the other side was an adventure and making something of herself for herself. That was the appeal of someone like Damien St. Cloud. Yes, she knew now he was a jerk, but he represented something that Poppy had planned on her entire life. Everyone knew Poppy was just biding her time until she left. She had just decided after the whole debacle with Damien that she was going to take steps to break out on her own, but something still kept her rooted here. Maybe it was time to stop fighting it.

There was a small voice in the back of her mind coming into focus. Her best friend had lived in the city most of her life. Hannah would have helped her, but she never left. She likes to say it was out of family obligation. The business and the death of her grandfather had brought her back and anchored her here, but maybe it was something else. Something she wasn't aware of until this moment.

What should she do? It was all starting to sink in. The magic was telling her, she could feel herself falling in love with Josh, she could see an amazing life here, but so much of her identity was tied up in leaving this town and doing something bigger. Would she be letting herself down if she didn't explore that, and if she did would she ever forgive herself for losing Josh and what this life had to offer her?

She shook the feeling and turned to find Josh, maybe this existential crisis she was on the brink of was completely unwarranted. She and Josh had been dating for a few weeks, given things were going at a rapid pace, as things tend to do when you start dating someone who you have known for your entire life, but maybe Josh wasn't quite at the same place as she was. Maybe.

She walked down as Mitch and Josh were shaking hands again. "I think that's a solid offer. I'll get the paperwork ready, and we'll be sure to get it in the minute the listing goes live."

"Thank you, this place is incredible," Josh said.

"It really is, you two will be very happy here," Mitch said with a smile to Poppy. She smiled back and descended the last couple of steps.

Mitch held the front door open as Poppy and Josh left. He took her hand as they quietly walked away from the house and made their way to Josh's SUV a few blocks away. Her mind was going a million miles an hour in her head. When they got there, Josh opened the door for Poppy, and she got in. She buckled herself in as he got in himself, her mind still reeling.

"So, what did you think?" he turned to ask her.

"It's incredible, I hope you get it."

"I hope we get it." His gaze turned serious, and he took her hand again. "I'm not sure if you felt it in there or if it was just me, but I think that house could mean something special to us."

Poppy froze. She was not ready to have this conversation, she was too conflicted. She never wanted to be someone who changed her hopes and dreams for a man, but this felt like something big. This felt like it could be the starting of a new dream, but she just didn't know if she was ready to give up her old dream.

"Is everything alright?" he asked.

"Yeah, I'm fine. It's a great house, Josh." She took her hand out of his and turned and looked out the window.

"Poppy?" he asked tentatively. The apprehension in his voice knotted her stomach and she knew if she looked at his face right now his brow would be drawn, and his eyes would be concerned, and he would look like a hurt little puppy dog. She would be overcome with the urgent need to make things okay, so she just looked out the window, like a coward. Maybe she was just being selfish, maybe she was as self-obsessed as people believed her to be.

She pushed those thoughts away, she wanted to enjoy the rest of her day with Josh. She took a deep breath and turned to look at him with a smile. She was right, the look on his face gutted her. His excitement had faded, and he looked worried. She reached up and cupped his face with her hands.

"Really, I'm fine. I just have a headache all of the sudden, I think it must be from the dust. I'll be okay. Where to next?"

The tension fell from his shoulders and a gentle smile found his face, he bent his head down and gave her a kiss. "My errands are all done, Poppy. How about you pick what we do next?"

"Would it be ok if we just went back to your place and watched a movie? I think I could use some cuddle time on the couch."

"I was hoping you would say something like that, I'm ready to have you all to myself again."

He bent his head for one last kiss, this one filled with a little more passion than the last. Poppy may have some figuring out to do, but man, this guy did things to her with a simple kiss.

For the rest of the evening, they cuddled on the couch watching Bake-Off with lots of making out, but Poppy could not get out of her own head. She was conflicted.

There was a knock at the door.

"Pizza!" Josh jumped up off the couch and got the pizza. He set it down on the coffee table in front of them and went to get them plates. He handed Poppy a plate and they started eating. They continued watching the show and Poppy tried to get back the feeling she had with Josh before this all got so serious. She had been serious about him, but when it all became so real, she kind of shut down. She wanted the comfort of Josh back. She wanted him to take her back to his room and give her the best orgasm of her life again and again. But she needed to figure out her own head.

After they finished eating and the episode they were watching, Josh paused the show and turned to look at her.

"I can tell something is bothering you. If you aren't ready to talk about it yet I'm not going to push. I just want you to know I'm here. I'm here as a distraction or a listening ear. Whatever you need, Poppy, I mean that."

She cupped his face and kissed him, a sweet gentle uncomplicated kiss. "You're so sweet, I don't deserve you."

"Don't say that, Poppy. You deserve the world."

Her eyes fell to the worn blanket covering both of their laps. She ran her fingers through the yarn fringe. What was her problem?

Her phone buzzed on the coffee table next to her.

Hannah -Going into the city on Friday to finish packing up my apartment. Wanna go with me?

She had to work Friday, but she would be going to the city with Hannah. Sam could just deal with it.

Poppy- OMG, yes! That sounds amazing.

Hannah- Ok, I'll pick you up around 8. We are going to drive in and spend the night and Graham and your brother are going to be there the next day with a truck.

Poppy- Does Sam know I'm abandoning ship for 2 days?

Hannah- Nope. I left that part for you.

Poppy- Well he can just deal. I need some bestie time and some time away.

Hannah- uh oh, trouble in paradise?

Poppy- No, just confusion.

Hannah- Nothing a road trip and an old fashion sleepover won't fix.

Poppy- You read my mind.

Feeling a little bit better she turned to Josh. He was watching her intently.

"That was Hannah. She's going into the city on Friday to pack up her apartment. She asked if I wanted to go with her."

She smiled and breathed a sigh of relief, though she hadn't figured everything out but a day with Hannah in the city would probably help with that.

"Awesome. I know you missed her while she was gone. It'll be good to spend some time with her."

"It really will." She leaned over and gave him a deep kiss. When she pulled back, she smiled at the dazed look on his face.

"What was that for?" he asked.

"Just for being you. It's getting late, and I have to get up early. I wanna get some baking done tomorrow morning before I'm stuck at the register. Is it ok if I don't stay here tonight?"

"Of course! You are always welcome but never feel like you have to."

She leaned over and gave him another kiss, this time she straddled him and kept kissing him. His hands found her ass and pulled her into him.

"You're sending some mixed signals here, princess," he chuckled up at her.

"I know I just wanted to kiss you good before you drive me home, so you don't forget me."

"Not a chance." Then it was his turn to claim her mouth.

The sound of a key in the door broke their kiss. Lexi opened the door and walked in looking exhausted.

"Oh, sorry if I'm interrupting," she said as she dropped her keys on the side table.

"No, this is your house. Anyway, Josh was just about to take me home," Poppy said with a smile.

"Don't leave on my account, I'm just going to hop in the shower and go straight to bed. I'm beat after working third shift last night and then going back in for paperwork."

"No, really," Poppy said as she stood up, "I have to be up early tomorrow. We were just saying goodbye."

"When I get back, I'll make you a turkey pesto panini. Sound good?" Josh asked his sister.

"That sounds amazing. It was nice to see you, Poppy. I've heard a lot about you lately."

Josh's eyes darted to his sister.

"It was nice to see you too. I'm sure I'll see you again very soon," said Poppy.

Josh grabbed his keys, and they headed out the door. While she still had not figured anything out, she was feeling a little better, and the promise of a road trip with Hannah might be just what she needed.

CHAPTER 25

Poppy

Poppy was excited to be heading out of town with Hannah. Hannah was the perfect person to talk to about all of this for so many reasons, mainly being she was her best friend and understood the magic element in all of this. But there was also the fact that Hannah had a glamorous life in the city, one Poppy had always been low key jealous of. Hannah was from this wealthy family. She grew up on the upper east side going to prep schools and spending the summer at the farm that had been in her family since forever. It always seemed like such a dream to Poppy, but Hannah decided to give all of that up and move to Mystic Falls for good.

And while Poppy was very happy with her choice, she never really understood that appeal of small town life. But that was all changing. In fact, if she was being honest with herself, her heart was with Josh from the moment he kissed her in that prop closet. And the town was creeping into her heart as well. She was learning how magical the little town was that she had taken for granted her whole life.

Poppy was waiting by the window for Hannah to pull up. She was ready to get outta here. Sam was not taking her absence for two days well. She knew this was the busy season, but they hired someone to help with the store because business had been going well this year. So, there was someone to cover her day off, and she was taking it.

She saw Hannah's car coming down the drive and she bounded out onto the porch. Then tossed her bag in the trunk and hopped into the front seat.

"I got the best road trip playlist. Are you ready?" Poppy asked.

"Let's hear it," said Hannah. Poppy connected her phone, and the Spice Girls began to play over the speakers.

"I should've known," Hannah said, shaking her head. Poppy turned up the volume and they hit the road.

For the first part of the trip Hannah talked about her honeymoon. They had only gotten together once since she had been back, there was some catching up to do. She heard all about her trip to Scotland, how her book was going, all of that punctuated with lots of car singing and road snacks, like every good road trip should be.

"Can I ask you something, Han?" Poppy asked.

"Have you ever not asked me anything?" Hannah said.

"Fair point... How did you decide that you wanted to settle in Mystic Falls? You have the whole world open to you, you lived in the city so many people dream of living in, and you gave it all up to live in a tiny town."

"I don't really know why, but I always felt drawn to Mystic Falls. For me I think it is just a speed of life thing. I enjoy the slower pace. I enjoy the space and room. I enjoy knowing people and the community that goes with it."

Hannah said, glancing over at Poppy. "I get that it's not for everyone, but I was ready."

Poppy nodded trying to take it all in.

"Does this have anything to do with Josh?" Hannah shot her a knowing glance.

"You know it does, I always thought I wanted out of Mystic Falls. I spent my whole life planning a getaway. I even managed it once, but something always got in the way. When I did my spell, I was hoping for something big like what you got, I was hoping for this major change to let my life begin finally. But instead, I fell in love with Josh, who is the town personified. Does that mean I'm falling in love with the town? After wanting to leave my entire life?"

Hannah just watched the road and nodded listening to Poppy.

"Is it even possible to love a town? I mean Josh seems to, and he has every reason to. This town really took care of him and his sister, and it makes him happy. And I need Josh to be happy. I mean, like, it is a visceral need. My heart aches at the thought of him being upset which is crazy right? I am not in charge of anyone's happiness but my own. I've lived my life that way, but now I think maybe I've been selfish. Maybe I don't know the town and the people around me because I was too busy thinking that it was not what I wanted, when maybe it was what I wanted but I was just too stupid to realize."

Hannah interrupted her. "Okay, I'm just going to stop you for a minute. You're not selfish or stupid, but other than that I say keep going. I think you are figuring it out on your own."

"You might think so, but I'm not entirely certain. I just can't help but feel like no matter what I choose I am letting a version of myself down."

"Poppy, why did you want to leave so bad?" Hannah asked very matter-of-factly.

She thought about it, like really thought about it. Poppy had thought of the how and the what if part of things, but never fully the why.

"I guess I have always craved adventure."

"And you can't get that living in Mystic Falls?"

"I didn't think so, but this all seems to be a pretty big adventure."

"Helping me move?" Hannah grinned at her.

"No, ya weirdo! And let's be honest about that real quick, I can pack a box but we both know I'm not moving the heavy shit," Poppy said.

"Oh, I know. That's why Graham and your brother are driving up tomorrow. But in all seriousness, I think you can have adventures there. Also, if my ears did not deceive me, I did hear you say you love Josh."

Poppy took a deep breath. She did say that because if she was being honest that is how she felt. She did love him.

"Do you think Josh would let you guys live a boring life?" Hannah asked. "I haven't been close with him in years, but I do recall there never being a dull moment with him."

She thought about that for a moment, and she knew Hannah was right. Josh was a constant surprise, and she had a feeling that even after years of being together he was still the type of person that would continue to surprise her. And she knew she wanted the life, the house, and the visions she had in it. She wanted the feeling that came with it. What was holding her back?

"Okay, so clearly that magic works differently for different people, but did you ever have dreams or visions?"

Hannah glanced over at Poppy and shook her head.

"Okay, well I had a dream the night I took the tea, but then I have had other visions along the way. Like our first kiss, when we got a tarot reading, and then the ones in the house..." Poppy trailed off thinking of the vision that felt so real of her rocking a baby in the room looking down in the backyard while Josh pushed a beautiful giggling child on the swing. That felt real. It was what she had spent her whole life trying to run from but felt better than anything she could have ever dreamed.

"What house?" Hannah asked.

"The Whitney house."

"Why were you in the Whitney house?"

"Because Josh is buying the Whitney house," Poppy said.

"What? Seriously Poppy, we live in the same town. We are NEIGHBORS for crying out loud. How do I not know about all this stuff?" Hannah asked incredulously.

"It's all happening so fast I can barely keep up! But yeah, we went and looked at it the other day." said Poppy as she took a bite of the Twizzler in her hand.

"It's amazing, and here is the weird thing. When I walked into the house, I felt like I was coming home. I don't know how else to describe it. When we were in the kitchen, I had this clear image of baking in the huge, glorious kitchen with all these little children. And then when we went upstairs the master bedroom overlooked this beautiful backyard and I had this vision, but it was more than a vision. It was like I was there experiencing it and I could feel it. I was sitting in a rocking chair rocking a baby and I was looking out the window at Josh and this beautiful little child that had the best features of each of us being pushed on a swing. It was amazing."

"Yeah... that is not the kind of magic I got." Hannah said. "That's amazing. What's your dilemma? You sound pretty certain."

"I don't know. I want that with Josh. I really do, and I don't think I could fight it even if I wanted to."

"So, what's the problem?" Hannah asked.

"I have always wanted to leave and now, what? I changed

my mind because I fell in love with a guy? I'm not that girl. How do I reconcile that?" She was struggling between who she always thought she was and who she might end up being. They weren't the same, but when she was with him none of this seemed to matter.

"So, it is a pride thing?" Hannah asked with a knowing glance.

"No, it is not a pride thing!" she snapped defensively.

"Okay, have you talked to Josh about any of this?"

"No, I don't want to hurt his feelings."

"I think his feelings would be more hurt to know you are going through all of this and not talking to him about it," said Hannah.

The words Hannah said were bouncing around in Poppy's head. She should talk to Josh about it, but also that part about pride was there too. Was it pride that was stopping her from fully embracing the idea of a life in Mystic Falls with Josh? She searched her heart and maybe yeah, there might be some truth to that. The whole town knew Poppy had big dreams and wanted out, was she disappointed because she didn't want to be seen as a failure or as someone who settled? But she knew a life with Josh would never be settling. She knew she wanted a life with him more than anything, but they had never really talked about it.

"You're right," Poppy said finally. "I do need to talk to him and maybe part of the reason I'm scared is because I've gone on and on about how much I hated the town and the orchard. And now if the visions are true, I am going to marry Josh Turner, work at the orchard with him, have a handful of kids and be deliriously happy. So maybe I just need to get out of the way of happiness and live my life."

Hannah nodded and kept her eyes on the road, letting Poppy come to all this herself.

"So maybe I let go of other people's thoughts about what I

should be, including my own. Maybe I need to let go of my expectations because something I could have never expected fell right into my lap and I would be an idiot not to be happy."

Those words sunk in as they got closer to the city. Poppy was going to do this. She still needed to talk to Josh and work everything out, but if she could find the contentment in Mystic Falls with Josh, she would be a fool not to try.

In the afternoon they were finally in the city. As they walked in Hannah stopped at her mailbox to get the stray pieces that hadn't been forwarded. The door from the outside opened and Poppy dropped her bag when she looked up to see who had just walked into Hannah's building. Damien St. Cloud.

CHAPTER 26

Poppy

"Damien! What are you doing here?" Poppy asked, clearly taken aback.

"I live here. What are you doing here?" he asked.

"My friend, Hannah, is packing up her apartment. I came to help," she said.

Damien's eyes glanced over to Hannah. She held up her hand and awkwardly laughed and said "3B."

Damien gave his cool James Dean smile and said, "Nice. 2D. I'll see you around Poppy and Hannah from 3B." He winked at them and turned to head into the building while they both stood there bumbling in the foyer.

"Was that --"

"Damien St. Cloud. How in the world does he live in your building?" Poppy said in disbelief.

"That's the guy you were with before Josh? He's hot."

"I know... pity he's terrible in bed," Poppy said, shaking her head.

"What? Okay, pick your bag up and we are going upstairs to pack boxes and you're telling me all about it."

The two friends took their bags and headed upstairs, where they spent their afternoon packing and talking. Poppy shared the whole saga of Damien St. Cloud. She could clearly see now that Damien was not the guy she thought he was. Sure, he was hot, but Josh was hotter because on top of that he was one of the kindest, most thoughtful people she had ever known. And then of course there was the sex... she wasn't sure what she had been thinking with Damien.

They spent the rest of the afternoon reminiscing about their summers spent together as kids. There was a box of wine and lots of laughs between the packing of boxes.

It was around eight thirty when they finally decided to take a break and order food and take some showers. They had almost everything packed up and they would have time in the morning before the boys arrived to finish up.

"Hey Poppy, can we use your phone to order the pizza? I can't find mine," Hannah asked.

"Yeah, let me grab it." She started digging through her purse and couldn't find it. "Oh no, mine is missing too!" They both started laughing as the wine they had been drinking egged them on. They stood back and looked at all the boxes and laughed again.

"How did we both lose our phones packing all your shit up?" Poppy laughed.

"We had mine in the closet. We were listening to my playlist. Let me go look." Hannah stumbled off into the bedroom. Maybe they had been drinking a little more than they thought. Then there was a buzzing coming from the box in front of the TV.

"Hannah! I found my phone!" Poppy called out and started digging through the box. Hannah walked out her phone in her hand. She finally felt it and pulled it out. It was her phone, she looked down to see who was calling and it was Hannah.

"I found mine too. Now let's get some pizza," she slurred as she drank some more wine.

As Hannah ordered a pizza Poppy looked at her phone.

> Josh: Hey Poppy, I know you are with Hannah today, but Sam can't make it to the city. I am coming with Graham. Is that ok?

> Josh: Just checking in, we are coming tonight so we can get a jump on the morning since I work at Lucky's tomorrow night. Is that ok?

> Josh: I'm sorry to keep bothering but I don't want to just crash your girls night. Let me know.

> Josh: Ok, I hope this is ok, we are picking up Sam's truck and heading to you guys. We should be there in a couple hours. Is that ok?

Plus three missed calls.

"Ummmm Hannah, we may need more pizza."

"I know, I saw Graham's texts, you don't mind, do you?"

She thought about getting to see Josh and the giddiness that single thought gave her made her know her decision was right. She loved him and she needed to talk to him about it.

"Yeah, but I get the first shower. I don't want to be a sweaty mess when they get here."

There was a knock at the door.

"Too late." Hannah went to the door and flung it open clearly expecting her towering highlander to be on the other side. She had to stop herself quickly because instead of that it was Damien St. Cloud. What on earth did he want?

"Hello ladies, it looks like you have been busy," he said, peeking his head in the apartment and looking at all the packed boxes. "Anyway, we are having a bit of a get together and I wanted to invite you down to the party."

Hannah looked to Poppy to see what she wanted to do.

"I think we'll pass. We still have some work here to do," said Poppy.

"Suit yourself, but if you finish up early, I have a drink with your name on it, Poppy," he said with a wink.

"Thanks for the invite," said Hannah.

He turned to leave, and Hannah shut the door behind him.

"Yeah, that is not happening," Poppy said. "Now I'm going to shower."

Both of them showered, put on their pajamas and curled up on the couch together watching a romcom, drinking more wine, and waiting for the pizza, when there was a firm knock at the door.

"Wow, that pizza guy means business." Hannah got up, a little unstable on her feet and made her way over to the door with a giggle.

"Did someone order a pizza?" asked a voice in a deep Scottish brogue. Hannah squealed and jumped into Graham's arms. He barely had time to get the pizzas safely in Josh's hands before dropping either them or Hannah. "Whatever has gotten into ye, ye silly thing." She planted a big sloppy kiss on Graham's face as Josh quietly squeezed around them. He walked over to Poppy and set the pizzas on the table.

"I hope we're not intruding. When you didn't answer I wasn't sure what to do," he said with a tentative look on his face.

Poppy stood up and kissed him. "No, I'm glad you are here. I lost my phone in a box packing earlier."

"How much have ye had to drink, my love?" Graham asked Hannah with a chuckle.

"Just a little," Hannah said.

"I find that hard to believe. Let's get some food in yer belly," said Graham.

They all got some napkins and pizza and ate and chatted.

"There is quite the party going on the floor below you," said Josh.

"Oh my god! I forgot to tell you." Poppy sat up straight to turn to him. "Guess who lives in Hannah's building?"

Josh raised his eyebrows, waiting for her to tell him.

"Damien St. Cloud."

His eyebrows fell and he looked angry. "How do you know that?" he asked in almost a growl.

"Who is this fellow?' Graham asked, clearly trying to see if there was going to be trouble.

"He was the music director for our show for a bit, but he is no one," Poppy said to Graham, the last bit more for Josh's benefit.

"No one?" Josh looked up at her and asked.

Poppy took his hands in her and looked into his eyes, "No one."

"We bumped into him in the hallway, and he invited us to the party, but we declined," Hannah said.

Poppy was still looking in his eyes. She knew he wasn't a big fan of Damien's, but this seemed like a whole lot more than not a fan.

They all settled back in for the movie. Things had gotten quiet. Poppy was sitting on the floor between Josh's legs as he absent-mindedly played with her hair. She looked over at Hannah to see that she was a little preoccupied. Her and her husband were engaged in a pretty intense make out session.

"Okay, now this really is a junior high sleepover, but the kind we snuck boys into," Poppy said as she chucked a pillow at them. To her surprise, Graham caught the pillow without breaking the kiss and tossed it right back at her. Hannah laughed and broke away. She picked up her phone and squinted at the bright screen.

"It's getting late. We have to get up early and get all this stuff loaded into the truck. I think we should probably get some sleep, in that box over there is bedding, will you guys be okay out here?" Hannah asked.

"I think we can manage," Poppy told her.

Graham and Hannah got up and started for the bedroom. Josh got the blankets and pillows out of the box and started to make a bed on the floor.

"I am too old to sleep on a floor," Poppy said with a small pout.

"Do you want to sleep on the couch? I can sleep on the floor no problem," Josh said with an easy smile.

"And miss out on cuddling you? Not a chance, Turner."

"I'll make you the best, most comfortable floor bed with all the blankets and pillows I can find," he said.

Poppy reached up and kissed him. It started slow, but quickly escalated. She needed this. She had felt lost for the past few days, but now that she knew what she wanted, she needed to kiss him and feel whatever it was that existed between them. And it was there. That magic pull that made her want to be as close to him as humanly possible.

She bit at his bottom lip and then slipped her tongue in his mouth. His hand fisted into her hair and pulled her slightly giving him the access he wanted to deepen the kiss. Poppy felt her need for him intensify. She pushed herself into him and he splayed his hand over the swells of her ass and pulled her into him.

He broke the kiss. "We shouldn't do this here."

"Oh, no we should totally do this here," Poppy said as she went back in to kiss him again. "Wait, I need to talk to you."

He looked down at her and cocked his head. "What's up, princess?"

"This might not be the right time or place, but I think we need to talk about what exactly is going on between us."

"Okay," he said as he took her hand and sat on the couch. He looked at her waiting for her to start.

Poppy took a deep breath. She wasn't sure why she was so nervous. She knew what she wanted. She wanted him, and he had made it pretty clear that he felt the same way. But he deserved to know why she kind of freaked out in the house the other day, and then went radio silent the next day.

"I'm not sure if you could tell, but I kind of freaked out a little after we saw the house."

Josh nodded and put his hand on her knee. It helped to ground her and she needed it in that moment.

"So, I'm just gonna get this out. You've known me my entire life. I never planned to live in Mystic Falls this long and I was disappointed that I was still here. I think that may be why I was so easily fooled by Damien, because he represented something to me. He represented a way out, and to me you represent the town and I'm not sure how to reconcile that."

Josh's shoulders slumped and he looked away from her. His eyes glazed over.

"Fuck. I'm messing this up. I'm scared because I'm letting go of something I always thought I wanted for something that is everything I never knew I wanted."

He looked back at her with a glimpse of hope dancing behind his eyes.

"Look, I don't know if you believe in Bridget's magic or not, but I do. And when we went into the Whitney house something felt so familiar about it." His thumb started to trace small circles on her leg. "And when I was up in the bedroom, it was like I caught this glimpse of what our life would be like. It was a clear vision of me rocking a child watching you push this perfect little girl on the swing in the backyard. It made me feel such peace and joy. And then I kind of freaked out."

He gently tucked a loose strand of hair behind her ear and let her continue.

"I wasn't sure I even wanted kids and I knew that I didn't want to stay. But that day with you when we were running errands, it was almost like I was falling in love with the town just as much as I was falling in love with you." She could feel the tears welling up behind her eyes, but she just let them come. She needed to get this out.

"I mean, that's not quite true, I love you way more than I love the town, but then there's that. I'm not even sure what is going on between us, it hasn't even been two months and I am so fucking in love with you, Josh. I don't even know how you feel. If you want any of this. It's all so intense and it just feels like a lot."

He wiped her tears away and waited for her to continue.

"So yeah, I've been kind of a mess, but I know what I want. And that's you, and whatever life we can have together. And now I'm going to need you to say something because I am flailing out here."

"Don't worry, princess, I'll never let you flail by yourself." He gave her a reassuring kiss. "I have to apologize if my intentions for you were ever unclear. I am in, Poppy. I am all in. You are it for me. You've been it for me for years and now that I have you, I am never letting go." he said, tenderly stroking her cheek. "I can't believe you said I love you first. Because you must know, Poppy. I love you more than anything."

At that, his mouth found hers and pulled her close. She moved to straddle him on the couch and deepened the kiss. His hand firmly grabbed her ass and pulled her into him. She moaned and he started to kiss down her neck. She ground herself against his growing erection in his jeans, it felt delicious against her through her thin pajama pants. She reached to the hem of her shirt and went to pull it off.

He stilled her hands. "Should we do this in Hannah's living room?"

No sooner had he said that, then out then a loud crash and a thud of boxes came from her room and a moan from Hannah that then got stifled.

Poppy started to laugh. "I think they are occupied, but if it would make you feel better, we can turn off the lights and get under the covers and I will be as quiet as I can." She looked up at him with innocent eyes that made his eyes flash with hunger.

"I'll have to keep track of how noisy you are and punish you next time I get you home and you can be as loud as you want," he growled as he gave her ass a little spank.

They both got off the couch and settled down onto the makeshift bed Josh had made.

"This is surprisingly comfortable," she said, settling herself on the makeshift bed on the floor.

"I got you, princess. I'm gonna make sure you are happy and well taken care of for the rest of your life."

Poppy waited for the panic to set in, but it didn't. She loved him and she wanted a life with him.

CHAPTER 27

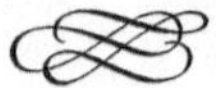

Josh

Josh gazed at Poppy lying next to him. Sometimes he still couldn't believe she was his, actually his. The fact that she chose him warmed him to his very core. She wanted a life with him, and he would happily spend his life taking care of her. He knew that for a fact.

He leaned his head down and kissed her perfect lips. He couldn't believe that he got to kiss these lips forever. These lips were his, and that thought did things to him. Things he couldn't act on right now. He and Poppy would have to talk about the dynamic they were falling into at some point but right now, he was going to make her come here right here on this makeshift bed.

He pulled the blanket over his head tenting them in, creating a perfect little sexy bubble. His hands explored her body and since she already had no bra underneath her glorious tits were there ready for his attention. He grabbed one in his hand and squeezed it and smiled at the fullness in his hand. He lowered his mouth to the other one and sucked it into his mouth, looking up at her and she bit her bottom lip to stop a moan from escaping.

She started to pull at his shirt, he swiftly pulled it off over his head while his hand roamed over her body.

"I love you, Poppy, and I intend to spend the rest of my life showing you how much." Poppy hands fumbled with the button of his jeans. Josh gave a soft laugh, "I guess my girl knows what she wants."

She kept going until she had pulled his cock out. She stroked it and Josh rested his forehead against hers and bit back a moan. He fell to the side and kicked off his pants. He wasn't much of an exhibitionist, but the idea they could be caught did add a certain scorching element to this already hot moment.

His hand slid down over the swell of her belly and beneath the loose fabric of her pajama pants. He cupped her sex and slid in a finger. She was already wet. He swirled the wetness around paying special attention to her clit. A moan started to escape her mouth. He stifled it with a kiss. He slid a finger inside of her, and then two. Then his thumb found her clit and began working slow circles. She started to grind against his hand and her breath turned into short pants. Josh could tell she was right on the edge, he dipped his head lower and adjusted the covers to make sure they were both still completely covered, then he kissed further down her body.

He kept his finger working then pressed a kiss to her clit before swirling his tongue around it. He then gently sucked the little nub into his mouth. She started to cry out, but he could hear her stifle herself with her own hand, while her other hand fisted into his hair, and she ground against his face. Her body spasmed around his fingers and he gave her all she needed.

Once she was done, he scrambled for his pants and pulled

out the condom in his wallet. He clumsily put it on, keeping them under the blankets. Then he positioned himself on top of her between her legs. He kissed her mouth as he slid in. She felt so good every time. He would never tire of this woman and her incredible body. She was so soft and full, and he loved everything about it because he loved everything about her.

He started thrusting into her. He wasn't going to take long, he slid his fingers between them and started making tight circles around her clit.

"I'm not gonna last much longer, princess. I need you to come one more time," he whispered quietly in her ear. He then sank his teeth into her earlobe and Poppy took in a ragged breath.

And as if on demand she was grinding against his hand and his dick and let a little moan escape. He picked up pace and she bit his shoulder as she lost control. Josh followed her right over the edge in an orgasm that he felt clear from the tips of his toes all the way up to his eyeballs. Then he collapsed onto her panting, forehead to sweaty forehead.

"I love you," he whispered in her ear.

"I love you too."

He pulled out and already ached to be back inside of her. He could not wait until he could do this every night.

"You bit me," he chuckled softly in her ear. He inspected his shoulder and the slight bruise already setting in around the teeth marks. Turning to her he saw a sheepish grin on her face.

"Sorry about that," she said with a smile.

"It's alright. I don't mind." He kissed her as he pulled his boxers back on. They got situated before he headed to the bathroom to clean up.

He made his way back to the bed on the floor and Poppy instantly snuggled right into his arms. He felt like he was invincible when she was with him like this. He felt like he could take anything the world had to throw at him and he would be okay. It was a feeling he could get used to.

"I think I might have to tell Hannah she needs to wash our sex blankets, huh?" Poppy said to him with a goofy smile.

"You do that, and I won't be able to look her in the eyes for months," he said with a small shake of his head.

"Ehh, it'll be okay. That's what friends are for."

"If you say so, I don't recall ever talking about sex blankets with my friends."

Giving a soft laugh, she rested her head on his chest, "So, do you think you will get the house?"

"I hope so, I love that house."

"Me too," she said. He kissed the top of her head while she traced her fingers along his chest. "Josh, have you ever thought of making your sandwiches professionally?"

"What do you mean?" he asked. His post coital brain was not following.

"Do you remember when I told you I had that vision of us in the house, well I had another one." she said, propping her head on her hand. "We were working next to each other at the orchard. We have a big kitchen there, I only use some of it with my baking, but in my vision both of us were there in this big kitchen, I was baking, and you were making those amazing sandwiches you make, and we had added a little cafe to the orchard. I think it might be nice."

He sighed contentedly. "I think that sounds perfect."

They drifted off to sleep on an uncomfortable floor perfectly happy because they were in each other's arms. Josh almost had to pinch himself. He had dreamt of being with her for so long, but he could never have imagined just how incredible it would be.

They all woke up bright and early the next morning to start getting the boxes loaded up. Hannah was still packing and cleaning the last few things while Poppy volunteered to walk a few blocks to the local donut shop to pick up breakfast for everyone. Graham and Josh were busy taking boxes downstairs.

"At least we don't have to take all the furniture," Josh said as he grabbed another box.

"Yeah, subletting a furnished apartment just made sense, so I just had to get my stuff out of here finally. I haven't lived here for over a year, its finally time," said Hannah.

"Aye, let's be done with this god forsaken city once and for all," said Graham as he came in the door wiping his brow.

"Not a fan of the city?" Josh asked him.

"Not in the least," he answered.

They both grabbed another box and headed downstairs. Once outside, they saw Poppy at the door carrying a big box of donuts and a cup carrier with four large coffees.

"Meet ya upstairs, boys," Poppy said, as she headed in and Josh moved his head to grab a kiss from her as they passed in the doorway. He was feeling pretty great after last night, he turned to watch her head up the stairs and thank his lucky stars that girl was his.

He loaded the box into the back of the truck and turned back in to get another box. Pulling his phone from his pocket, he checked the time. He was hoping they could all be on the road by nine to get back upstate that, way he could help unload before he had to go home and shower and get ready for his shift.

As he turned the corner on the stairs, he was pulled up short. He felt his heart drop completely out of his chest, his head filled with an angry buzzing, his phone slipped out of his hand clamoring to the floor. In front of him was Damien St. Cloud, his arms wrapped tightly around Poppy, kissing her.

She wriggled out of his embrace "Get off me!" she

shouted. Then she pulled back and slapped him. Not only were his dirty hands all over Poppy, but apparently without her consent. The rage bubbling inside of him hit a boiling point. Before he knew what had happened, he had Damien pinned against the wall his hands fisted in his shirt. He could vaguely hear Poppy telling him to stop, but the buzzing in his head was too loud.

"What are you going to do? Hit me again? I'll be ready for it this time." He attempted to push Josh off him, but he didn't budge.

Poppy was pulling on his arm "Come on Josh, it's okay. He's not worth it. Please don't do this."

Her pleas finally got to him, and he loosened his grip on Damien. He turned to look at Poppy. Then he felt it. A searing pain as Damien's fist made contact with his jaw. His body was flung back from the force of the blow and pushed Poppy into the railing. He turned around and quickly swung on him making contact with Damien's face.

Graham descended the stairs from the upstairs apartment in a few giant steps and separated the two men both trying to swing at each other. Josh was filled with such rage. He never let himself lose control like this, but he was seeing red.

"What the fuck is going on?" Graham bellowed, holding both men apart.

"This fucker kissed Poppy without her consent." Josh bellowed as he attempted to gain control over his emotions.

Graham turned to Damien with a terrifying glare and a low growl. Josh looked to find Poppy cowering on the floor behind him, Hannah helping her up.

"This is over," Hannah said. "You better get back in that apartment and do not come out until we are finished packing up." Hannah had a way of putting grown men in their place. Damien quietly skulked back into his apartment while Hannah helped Poppy up the stairs.

Josh could still feel his pulse pounding in his head, all the adrenaline pumping through his veins.

"Are ye alright?" Graham asked.

"Yeah, I'm fine," he said, not being entirely honest.

"Why don't you head upstairs and talk to yer lass," Graham said, giving him a pat on the chest.

"No, I need to take a walk and clear my head."

Graham gave him an understanding nod.

Josh picked up his phone and headed outside. He needed some fresh air and to walk it off until his head cleared.

Poppy

Poppy woke up that morning on Hannah's floor feeling secure in her choice. Here, with Josh's arms wrapped around her while she slept, she knew she had made the right choice. She knew he would make her happy and she would spend her life trying to do the same for him.

They were getting ready to get a jump on the day and Poppy offered to walk down to the donut shop a few blocks and get breakfast for everyone. While she was walking, she took in city life. It was seven AM in this little Brooklyn neighborhood. The city was just waking up. She passed commuters making their way to the subway and a deli that was already busy with people getting bagels. It was nice and maybe she could have been happy here, but she was happy to be getting back to her own life, now that she knew what she wanted.

She returned to the building after procuring the donuts as Josh was on his way out of the building carrying a box. He stopped and gave her a sweet kiss that warmed her heart.

She was lost in thought as she headed upstairs and wasn't watching where she was going and bumped right into someone. After steadying the coffee, she turned to apologize and then she saw Damien St. Cloud giving her a peculiar smile.

"Sorry," she said as she quickly continued upstairs.

"Why don't you come in for a while," he said and grabbed her by the arm. He smelled like he had been showered in booze.

"Are you still drunk?" she asked, still trying to maneuver out of his grasp.

Before she knew what had happened, he grabbed her by her waist and planted a sloppiest boozy kiss on her. The four cups of coffee in the carrier fell from her hand and landed, somehow upright on the floor. She pulled back and slapped him right across the face and said, "Get off me."

Before Poppy knew what was happening Josh came flying past her slamming Damien against the wall.

"Josh! Stop!" she cried. He wasn't even listening to her.

Damien sneered at him. "What are you going to do? Hit me again? I'll be ready for it this time."

Hit him again? When had he hit him the first time? This was getting out of hand. This needed to stop. She put her hand on Josh's arm. "Come on Josh, it's okay, he's not worth it. Please don't do this."

That seemed to snap him out of it. Then out of nowhere Damien sucker punched him and he flew back, pushing Poppy into the railing and then onto the floor. Her back throbbed where she hit the railing, but the horror unfolded in front of her as Josh swung back at him. She had never seen him like this before. He was usually so calm and mild mannered, but his face was filled with such rage.

Graham swooped in and split up the fight and she finally took a breath. Hannah was quickly down the stairs after Graham and was on the floor checking on her. The men were still shouting, and Poppy was fighting tears. Hannah bent down next to her.

"Are you okay?" she asked.

"Yeah, I'm fine."

Poppy watched as Hannah stood up and put the grown men in their place and Damien slinked back into his apartment.

Hannah turned and helped her up. "Come on, let's get you upstairs." Poppy's eyes blurred with tears as she watched Hannah get the Donuts and the coffees.

Once up and in the apartment, Hannah got Poppy situated on the couch and brought her some water.

"What the hell happened down there?" Hannah asked as she sat down next to Poppy with her arm around her.

"I don't know, I ran into him in the hallway, he was still drunk and tried to kiss me. The next thing I know Josh had him slammed up against the wall and it was all kind of a blur." Hannah rubbed her arm up and down trying to comfort her.

Graham came back in looking a little ruffled. Poppy waited to see Josh follow behind him, but he just closed the door behind him. No Josh.

"Where's Josh?" she asked.

"He needed to clear his head and took a walk."

Poppy nodded. She tried to understand, but right now she wanted him here with her. She had never seen him like that, and it scared her. And what did Damien mean when he said, 'Are you going to hit me *again*?' When did he hit him the first time? Poppy buried her face in her hands and let the tears flow. Getting all the stress out in a good cry can be cleansing, and she definitely needed a cleanse of some kind after all of that.

Graham continued to move the boxes down and Hannah sat with her. Poppy sat on the couch a few more minutes pulling herself together. She finally decided she was going to go into the bathroom, wash her face, and help Hannah clean the apartment a little more so they could get this over with. She was ready to head home.

Since she was in the bathroom anyway, she set to cleaning it while Hannah handled the rest of the apartment. They were making pretty good time and would probably be able to hit the road pretty quickly. After she finished giving the bathroom a final scrub she left and caught sight of Josh and Graham carrying a bookshelf downstairs. Hannah joined them soon after with a couple boxes.

The bathroom, kitchen and bedroom were good to go. There were still a handful of boxes piled up in the little dining nook, some small boxes that had all of Hannah's romance novels and her TV that still needed to get loaded up.

Poppy made her way over to Josh to see if he was okay. She looked at the redness and swelling at his jaw where Damien's punch had landed. She gently lifted her hand to caress it, but Josh brushed her hand away and made his way to the other boxes. Poppy followed behind him. She wasn't one to let things fester and she wanted to make sure he was okay.

"Josh," she said in a hushed tone. "Are you okay?"

"I'm fine." He refrained from direct eye contact and grabbed one of the boxes from the dining room and headed back downstairs. She looked over at Hannah who had been watching their interaction and gave her a weak smile.

"So, the rest of this will probably have to go in the back of my car," she said looking at the last of the boxes in the living room. "We made pretty good time, all things considered."

Josh and Graham finished the last couple trips while Hannah and Poppy checked the rooms and took out the trash. Hannah dropped her spare key on the dining room table and turned to look at her apartment.

"Well, the subletter is moving in next Monday and I am officially closing the New York chapter in my life," she said as she looked around the apartment. Graham stood beside her with his arm around her shoulder. Poppy looked over at Josh who was watching her, he gave a weak smile that didn't reach his eyes. He looked rough. Even though Poppy was still a little shaken up by the event in the hallway, her heart broke seeing him like this.

They all headed outside as Hannah locked up behind them. Hannah and Graham were driving back in Hannah's car and Josh was driving the truck back with Poppy. She was hoping she would be able to talk to him a little during the drive. They'd had such an amazing night, and now things felt all screwed up again.

The ride out of the city was quiet as they navigated all the traffic. Once they were out onto more open road Poppy was ready for some answers and hopefully Josh was ready to talk.

"Can we talk about what happened?" she asked tentatively.

"Of course," Josh said, giving her a weary smile.

"I just need you to know, he totally caught me off guard with that kiss. It meant absolutely nothing."

"I know that." He put his hand on her leg and gave a warm smile.

"Okay. Are you hurt?"

"No, I've been sucker punched before. I'll live. But more importantly, are you hurt? I'm pretty sure I elbowed you when he hit me." He shot her a quick glance with eyes full of concern.

"My back hurts a little where the railing dug into it, but I'm fine," she said.

Poppy laced her fingers with the hand that was sitting on

her leg.

"I've never seen you like that before. Honestly it was a little scary. What happened?" She asked.

He looked over at her, the expression on his face was so dejected. Poppy fought the visceral urge to comfort him and make it better. She needed to hear what happened.

"I'm so sorry I scared you. When I turned the corner and saw you kissing him my heart stopped. It made me think of Abbie all over again. But then when I saw you hit him and realized he was touching you and kissing you without your consent, I lost it. It's no excuse for my behavior. I was just so angry." He took a long deep breath. "Then Graham stopped it and I looked to see you on the floor with this terrified look on your face. The rage turned to shame, and I just needed some space."

"I get it," and she did, but she was not someone who could handle that. "But next time something like this happens please don't just walk away from me. I will give you space when you need it, but don't just disappear," she said.

He nodded and kept his eyes on the road. They sat quietly for a while.

Josh looked over at her and gave her hand a squeeze.

"I think you should probably know something about me that took me years of therapy to know about myself." Josh said with his eyes on the road. "I clearly have some abandonment issues from the way I grew up. I learned how to survive at a young age by being useful and friendly. Processing negative emotions like that can spin me out of control sometimes. I'm working on it, but the fear of losing you hit really close to a lot of triggers and then instincts just took over. It's not an excuse, but it is an explanation and that's all I got right now."

"It's okay, I understand. Can I ask you one more question?" Poppy asked.

"Anything."

"What did he mean when he said hit him again? When did you hit him the first time?"

Josh bit his lip and looked down. He glanced over at her and back at the road.

"You registered that part, huh?"

"Yeah, I did. Care to expand on that?" She asked, waiting for his answer.

"I don't really want to get into the details, but let's just say I ran into him at the inn on opening night. I overheard him say some really nasty things I won't repeat and there are sometimes jerks like Damien St. fucking Cloud just need to be punched in the face. You may disagree, my therapist will probably disagree, but I don't regret it and I would rather not talk about that," he said firmly.

"Is that why your knuckles were bruised opening night?"

He nodded.

"And I suppose you won't tell me what he said."

He shook his head.

"Okay."

"Really, you're going to drop it?" He shot her a surprised glance before returning his eyes to the road.

"Yeah, I am. I trust you," she said plainly.

Blowing out a shaky breath, he took the hand he was holding in his lap and brought it up to his mouth and pressed a kiss to it. "I really do love you, Poppy. I meant it when I said that last night."

"I love you too" She slid across the big bench seat of the truck and snuggled right into him. He pulled her close and kissed the top of her head.

"It's only nine AM and it's already been one helluva day," she said, resting her head on his shoulders They drove the rest of the way home in a comfortable silence, ready to finally be back home.

CHAPTER 29

Josh

After they got back from the city, Josh and Poppy settled into a nice rhythm. Poppy worked at the orchard, and Josh did his handyman work around town. He had pulled back on driving Uber because he and Poppy were spending their evening together. Some nights he would make her dinner, other nights they would eat with her family.

He really enjoyed those nights. The tight knit but inviting nature of the Smith family was something he had craved most of his life. He was really starting to feel like he belonged there. The whole family had been so wonderful and welcoming. This is exactly what he had dreamed of his entire life, and he had to pinch himself to make sure this all wasn't a dream. Josh had never been happier.

He was hoping to hear about the house soon. He and Poppy felt like they were kind of in a holding pattern, it was a wonderful pattern with lots of holding, but he was ready for them to take the next step. They were both adults still living in their childhood homes. It didn't really lend itself to healthy adult relationships.

While his sister was more of a roommate than anything, Josh couldn't help but feel like he would be abandoning her. She had put off so much of her life to take care of him, to make sure they had a good life. She took on so much grown up responsibility at a young age. And now, even though she was more financially stable, he worried that she would never be able to fully get out of the survival mindset.

He knew he shouldn't feel guilty about their situation. The only person who could be blamed for all of this was his father who left them to fend for themselves. The entire situation was so unfair to both of them, but he knew she took the brunt of it. He knew she did things to protect him he probably wasn't even aware of. Now he was leaving. While the thought of living with Poppy and starting their life together both thrilled him and filled him with a deep sense of peace, there was always needling guilt in the back of his mind.

Josh was on his way to his shift at the Lucky Saloon and decided he would take his sister some lunch. He had made toasted turkey with brie and cranberry relish sandwich for her.

As he was walking in, he noticed a loose floorboard on the porch and made a mental note to stop by and fix it tomorrow.

"Hello Josh, dear, I didn't know you were coming in today," said Aggie. Josh could never have guessed her age because she looked the same since he was a kid. Aggie had been cleaning rooms here ever since he could remember.

" I'm just bringing Lexi some lunch," he said, holding up a lunch tote.

"You're such a thoughtful young man. She's in her office."

Josh made his way past the front desk and gently knocked on the door.

"Come in," Lexi called.

Josh gently opened the door and peeked his head in.

"Hey Josh, what are you doing here?" she asked with a smile.

"I brought you some lunch," he said, setting the bag on her desk.

"You're the best, I'm starving." She opened the bag and took out the sandwich. "This looks so good."

Josh sat in the chair across from her. "I'm on my way to work, but I was hoping that we could spend some time together. Do you have any time off coming up?"

She looked up at him with a mouthful of sandwich and held up a finger indicating she would answer when she finished. She swallowed and took a drink of her water.

"That's so freaking good, you are a sandwich artist." He smiled at her appreciatively. "Yeah, I'm off tomorrow. I'm ready with all the doubles I've been pulling. Aren't you spending the day with Poppy?"

"Can't I just want to spend time with my sister?" He asked.

"Of course, you can. We just haven't much lately."

The guilt hit him. He knew she didn't mean anything by it, but he needed to tell her he intended to move out soon before the house finally came onto the market.

"I know, I'm sorry about that. Tomorrow it's me and you."

"You got it," she said with a smile.

"Well, I'm heading out. Gotta make the drinks for the masses," he said, preparing to leave.

"Have a good day."

"See ya when I get home." He stood to leave.

"Bye, thanks for lunch."

He made his way to work thinking about everything. About his sister, about the house and of course about Poppy. Everything seemed too perfect, he didn't want to jinx it.

It was quiet during his shift. Day shifts at Lucky's were usually quiet. They would get some people in for lunch but there was a lot of down time between lunch and dinner. After dinner they stayed pretty busy, and it became the bar part of the bar and grill. Halfway through Josh's shift he got a text.

> Mitch Alsup -Give me a call when you can.

He thought it might be about the house, so he got someone to cover the bar and stepped outside.

"Josh, hey, I got some bad news about the house."

His heart sank. They needed that house. Both him and Poppy felt so connected to it.

"What's up?" he asked.

"It looks like the owner has been working with another buyer. It is a company that turns old houses into Airbnb's. They approached them with an offer, and it looks like they might take it before it even goes to market."

"Is there anything we can do? I really want that house. Can I match the offer?" Josh asked.

"I mean maybe, I'm not sure what that number is but I will try to find out. But I thought you might be able to write a letter. I know the kids haven't lived in Mystic Falls for decades, but you might be able to appeal to their sentimental side and make some headway there."

"Yeah, I can definitely do that," said Josh.

"Okay, I will find out more about the offer and be in touch though," he said, hanging up the call.

Josh slipped his phone back into his pocket and made his way back inside. The thought that he might lose the house weighed on him. Poppy would be devastated to lose it. Hell, he would be devastated to lose it. That house meant so much to him. It meant so much to the whole town. Someone who loved the town as much as he did, who would work hard to bring back some of the town traditions around the house should live there. But if there was anyone who could write a letter about their love for this town and what that house could mean to this town again, it was him. This town had saved him more than once and returning that house to its prominent place in the community would be one of the greatest achievements in his life and doing it with Poppy by his side was beyond his wildest dreams. He could do this. He could convince the owners to let him buy the house.

THE SMELL of coffee wafted in as he sat up and stretched. He woke groggy, as he often did after working a shift at Lucky's. But with added stress of possibly losing the Whitney house, he was tossing and turning and worrying all night. If he could not get this house would Poppy still want him? She had said she had all these visions in the house, and it seemed to be a big part of why she decided to stay here with him. With the house being gone, would he be enough to make her want to stay here? That thought turned his stomach. He pushed it away and put a smile on his face. Today was about spending time with Lexi. He made his way downstairs to start their day.

"Hey little brother, are we still on for today?" asked Lexi.

Wiping the sleep from his eyes, he poured himself some coffee. "Yeah, I'm looking forward to it. What do you want to do?" He smiled at her and drank his coffee.

"What's wrong?" Her eyes narrowed and raked over him. Of course, she would be able to sense something was off. She knew him so well and was pretty intuitive when it came to this kind of thing.

"Nothing, it was just a late night at the bar. I'm gonna hop in the shower." He set his coffee down and turned and headed to the bathroom. "Then we will eat this amazing breakfast and make some plans for the day."

He went to the bathroom and tried to pull himself together. If he was going to spend the whole day with Lexi, he would need to get sorted. He also needed to tell her that he was planning on moving, but he didn't want to do that first thing.

After they ate breakfast, they decided to go take a walk around town and get some junk food for an old fashion junk food movie night. It was an old tradition their mom had started. She would buy all the junk food they never kept in the house, set it all up in the living room and watch movies all night.

They had a nice walk around town. As they turned the block with Bridget's store, Josh wanted to go in. He wasn't sure why, his sister wasn't into any of that stuff, and he wasn't sure he believed in all of it, but if she had anything to do with Poppy and him finally getting together, it couldn't be all bad.

"Have you been in here yet?" he asked motioning over to the store front.

"No, I didn't even know it was filled. It has been vacant ever since the video rental store closed years ago," Lexi said looking in the window.

"Do you want your tarot read?" Josh waggled his eyebrows at her.

"What? No." she said, eyeing him suspiciously.

"Come on, it will be fun," Josh said, egging her on.

"Since when did you get into all that stuff?"

"I wouldn't say I'm into it, but I met the woman who owns it when she moved in. She's really nice, and Poppy loves it there. Give it a try. It could be fun."

She finally gave in, and they went into the store. The bell

above tinkled as they entered and Bridget made her way out from the back room.

"Oh, Josh, hello dear, what can I do for ye?"

"She knows your name?" Lexi said under her breath looking at Josh amazed.

"Of course I know his name, he and Poppy have been in here quite a bit." she said.

"Yeah, this is my sister Lexi," he said.

"Aye, I remember ye lass, we met at the market a ways back, if ye recall," said Bridget with a warm and welcoming smile.

"I do remember that. How are you liking Mystic Falls?" Lexi asked.

"I like it quite a bit, it is a lovely little town ye all have here," said Bridget.

"I've been telling her, she should have her tarot read," Josh said as he playfully nudged his sister.

"What do ye say dear? Should I read yer cards?" she said with a magical wink.

"Why not?" resigned Lexi.

Bridget guided her way over to the table and sat on one and Lexi sat down on the other. Bridget picked up the well loved tarot deck and began to shuffle them a bit in her hands.

"All right my dear, clear yer mind for a moment," she continued to shuffle the cards. Lexi closed her eyes and took a deep breath. Bridget set the deck on the table and cut it.

"All right, let's see what the cards have to say today." She flipped the first card, Nine of Swords. The picture on this card had a person sitting in bed hiding their face in their hands with nine swords above them.

"Oh dear, this card symbolizes your past, Nine of Swords is a card of major stress and mental anguish. It seems as though ye've had some hard times. But the card is reversed which means it is time to put that past behind ye and move on. There is a time for everything, and it looks like it is yer time to heal."

Bridget turned the next card. It was the Death card. Josh couldn't stop the panic that gripped his heart at the sight of that card. He took a moment to remind himself, this was just a tarot card reading, but it did not feel good. Maybe he was starting to hold as much stock in all of this as Poppy did.

"Do not be alarmed, The Death card looks and sounds scary, but I believe it to be one of the best cards in the whole deck. It is a card of transformation. This card represents yer current situation. This card is about letting go. It means ye will shed your metaphorical skin and emerge anew. This card is not the omen people believe it to be, rather a second chance."

Well, that sounded better than Josh initially thought, he wished he could see Lexi's face. He was standing behind her and she was sitting still as stone. But if Josh knew his sister, and he did, she was skeptically taking everything in.

"Now onto the future, let's see what the cards have to say about what is to come," said Bridget. She flipped the last card and laid it next to the others. Ace of Cups. On this card was an outstretched hand with an overflowing chalice sitting in it. "Now this is interesting my dear, the Ace of Cups is a card of joy and fulfillment, this card can bring about so much healing and maybe even a new relationship if I am not mistaken."

A little bud of hope started to bloom inside him. He wanted more than anything for his sister to find happiness. She had too much put on her at such a young age. She deserved joy and happiness in her life more than anyone. Lexi had been Josh's touchstone since their mom's accident. She took care of them. It was time someone took care of her.

Josh had tried, but it seemed like the roles in their relationship were set and Lexi was stubborn. It was time for her to find happiness and let go of all the heaviness that had bogged them both down for so long.

"What do ye say? Do the cards ring true?" Bridget asked with a smile and magic dancing in her eyes.

"Here's hoping. Thank you for the reading," Lexi said, giving nothing away about how she felt about the cards.

Josh settled up with Bridget and they started to head out.

"Don't be strangers, I'm interested in seeing how yer stories pan out," Bridget said with a twinkle in her eye.

"Thanks again, Bridget," Josh said as he and Lexi made their way out the door.

After leaving the store Lexi was quiet; she seemed to be taking it all in. She had never really dated. She had always been so busy with work and surviving, now she and Josh were both in a good place and he hoped Bridget was right. His sister deserved to be happy.

They made it home and were about halfway through Goonies, because if you are gonna old school movie night then you better *old school* movie night, when his phone went off. He was hoping it was a text from Poppy, she had been pretty silent today respecting his time with his sister, but he looked, and it was another text from Mitch.

"I'll be right back." He got up and left his sister on the couch with a can of Pringles and a bag of Twizzlers.

"Josh, hey, I have some not so great news."

Crap. This was not what he needed to hear.

"The company that is interested in the Whitney house is coming in with a huge offer, I'm not sure you can match it," said Mitch

Josh collapsed on his bed. His heart started racing. This house had come to represent his and Poppy's future. He couldn't lose the house and he could not lose Poppy.

"What can we do?" he asked.

"Besides that letter to appeal to their sentimentality there isn't much. So, write the best damn letter you can, and we'll turn it in with your offer."

Josh sighed. "Alright, when do you need it?"

"The sooner the better."

"Okay, I'll get it over to you."

He hung up the phone and sat there staring at the phone in his hand. His heart was racing, and he could feel a panic attack coming on. He hadn't had a full-blown panic attack since everything happened with Abbie, but he could feel all the walls closing in on him. There was that terrible familiar tightness in his chest. He started some deep breathing, but it wasn't helping. He dropped his head in his hands and they fisted in his hair.

"Fuck! fuck fuck fuck."

Lexi appeared at his doorway, because of course she did. When she sensed something was wrong, she was like a dog with a bone. There was no hiding it.

"Okay, I thought something was off all day. What is wrong?" she asked.

He looked up at her with panic in his eyes. His heart was pounding in his head. She came and sat right next to him on the bed and took his hand.

"Hey, you're okay. Take a breath." She held his hand and modeled deep breaths for him until he was able to join her.

And then he told her, and it all came tumbling out. Everything about moving out and Poppy and the house and how scared he was if he lost the house, he would lose Poppy. She hugged him and he collapsed into her embrace, which was tricky because he was over 6'3 and she was 5'2 on a good day, but her embrace felt comforting and familiar. They had leaned on each other so heavily over the years. She wiped the tears that had escaped his eyes. He would be embarrassed if it was anyone else, but his sister had done this a million times before.

His panic attacks had started when he was in high school. She knew how to help him through. They were mostly a thing of the past after therapy, but this whole thing with the house and Poppy had thrown him. He clearly wanted and loved Poppy more than anything in life and would do anything to keep her, but he felt her slipping away as the house slipped away.

"Josh, look at me." He turned and looked at his sister. "I knew you would leave someday. I'm happy you're leaving. I'm happy that you're able to make a life for yourself and live in the house of your dreams with someone you love. Even if you guys have to get a different house, I can guarantee you Poppy will still love you, house or not. I mean, how could she not, you are one of the most lovable people on the planet."

He wished he was as sure as she was. He just could not shake the feeling if he lost the house, he would lose Poppy.

"I love you, little brother, but I think we both need this. We'll always have each other to lean on." She turned to face him. "Always." She held his gaze until he nodded. "I think you need to talk to Poppy." He nodded again.

She put his phone in his hand and gave him one more big hug. She ruffled his hair like she had so many times before and she got up and walked out of his room.

He texted her.

Josh- Are you busy?

Poppy- Nope, what's up?

Josh- Can we talk?

Poppy- Of course, do you want me to call?

Josh-Can you come over?

Poppy- On my way

He took a breath and closed his eyes. He could do this. Maybe his sister was right, maybe if he lost the house, he wouldn't lose her. He had to cling to that hope until she showed up.

CHAPTER 30

Poppy

*P*oppy pulled up outside of Josh's house. She had been surprised to get the text from him. She thought he was having a night with his sister, but she was glad to be seeing him. She couldn't wait until they would have all the time in the world to be together.

She walked up to the front door and knocked. Lexi answered the door, which was not what she was expecting.

"Hi Lexi, I hope I'm not intruding, but Josh texted me and asked me to come over," Poppy said with a polite smile.

"I know, he's having a rough night. He's in his room," Lexi said with a look on her face that Poppy didn't quite know how to read. She opened the door and let Poppy in.

"I'll just go find him then," Poppy said.

Poppy made her way up the stairs. What was wrong? She could not stand the thought of him upset. She never could, but even more so now.

She knocked quietly on his door.

"Come in," he said in a rough voice.

She opened the door and found him sitting on the edge of his bed. His eyes were red, and he looked exhausted. The sight of him looking like this broke her heart.

"Hey, what's going on?" she asked quietly as she walked into his room.

His head dropped into his hand, and she watched as his breathing increased. She went to him straight away and kneeled right between his knees on the floor, her hands firm on his knees.

"What's wrong?" she implored.

He remained quiet, his head in his hands as he took slow deliberate breaths. She stayed right there, kneeling before him, watching him. She would not rush him, but she would be here for him, because without a doubt, she knew he would be there for her. Hell, he would be there doing the same thing for anyone, but she felt a sense of honor that she got to be the one to help him.

She sat there for what felt like an eternity, hands firmly on his knees waiting for him to be able to talk to her. He finally looked up at her. His eyes were wet with tears. She moved her hand up to his face and wiped away the tears.

He took a breath and steeled himself to tell her whatever it was he needed to tell her. She took his hand and gave him time, but her heart was starting to race. He gripped her hand like he was trying to hold on to her, like she was his anchor. What on earth could have him this upset?

"I don't think I'm going to get the Whitney house."

He was so defeated when he said it. She sat there waiting for him to continue, but nothing else came.

"Is that why you are so upset?" she asked.

"Partly."

"What's the other part?"

"I know how much you wanted that house and how the vision you got in that house was a big part of the reason you decided to stay, and I just don't want you to change your mind. I'm sorry. I am such a mess," he said, collapsing back in on himself.

"Oh Josh, yes, I want the house, but it has nothing to do with how much I love you."

He released a shaky breath.

She continued, "And please don't apologize, I'm honored to be here and help you through whatever you're going through. You help everyone all the time. It feels like a gift to be here for you."

She held his face between her hands. He needed to know how she felt, because if he thought her feelings were tied to the house then he didn't understand the depth of what she felt for him.

"I love you, Josh Turner, so fucking much. I never knew it was possible to love someone as much as I love you. Not because of a house, or because of what you do for people, but because I see who you are, and I want to be with you and make you happy."

He gave her a weak smile. "I love you too."

"I know." She kissed the hands she was holding. "Now that all of that is settled, can you tell me what is going on?"

He told her. She stayed right there on the floor and listened to him. He told her about the house and how a company wanted to buy it. He told her how Mitch thought a letter could help, but his offer was under what they wanted. And Poppy listened. She listened and heard him, and her wheels were turning. When he finished, she stood up and sat down on the bed next to him.

"I think we can get the house," she said with surprising confidence.

"Are you sitting on 20k I don't know about?"

"Well, no, but there is no one more beloved in this town than you, Josh Turner. If we tell people that you're trying to buy the Whitney house, but a company is trying to outbid you, everyone will go crazy."

Josh looked at her skeptically.

"I'm serious, think about it. Is there anyone in this town you haven't helped at some point in time?" She asked.

"This town helped us as kids, and I owe so much to this town," he said.

"Perfect, we can come at it from that angle too. Do you think the town wants some company to own the house and rent it out, or do you think they want you to own it? We will reinstate all the old traditions, haunted house, holiday party, cook outs. It will be one of the centerpieces of the town like it used to be. I know this house can be ours."

She looked at him as a real smile finally found his face.

"Do you really think so?" He asked weakly.

"I really do, but you have to know this, if for some crazy reason corporate greed wins out and we lose the house," she turned her body, so she was on the bed completely facing him and took his face in her hands. "I'm not going anywhere. Do you hear me? Once I have my mind set on something I go after it, and you, Josh Turner, are it for me. This is it. Do you hear me?"

He nodded and looked into her eyes with a genuine smile. "I hear you." He closed the distance between them and kissed her. "Thank you, I love you so much."

"Now," she slapped her thighs and stood up. "Should we get to work on claiming that house?"

"No."

She looked at him surprised by his answer.

"Later. There is something else I would like to do first." He pulled her face to his and kissed her.

"I like the way you think," she said.

He wrapped his arms around her waist, pulled her back to the bed and kissed her deeply, then laid them back and kissed her more. At some point they would need to talk about everything, but right now she was more than happy to connect with him in this way. She knew she loved him, but it wasn't until tonight that she realized the depths of the love, the lasting quality of this love. This was what she wanted with her whole heart.

Poppy sat up and took her shirt off over her head and stood to start undoing her pants. "I'm gonna need you to get naked right now. Tonight, I need you, and then tomorrow we save the world."

He chuckled at her, while he took off his shirt. "Save the world? Isn't that a little dramatic?"

"Have you met me? Now, I'm naked and you still seem to have pants on. Catch up, Turner. I have plans for you."

He pulled down his sweatpants and laid down next to her. She reveled in the delicious feel of his skin against her own. She kissed him and ran her hand up his leg, stopping when she came to her intended point. She wrapped her fingers around his stiff cock, relishing the velvety steel. She gave it a stroke. He drew in a sharp breath and bit his bottom lip. She pulled back and looked at him, then started kissing her way down his body. He was dominant in the bedroom and that turned Poppy on like nothing she had ever experienced before, but tonight the tables were going to turn. It was her turn to be in control.

She positioned herself between his legs and swept her hair to one side out of the way, and made eye contact as she wrapped her lips around his cock and sucked him in.

"Fuck," he hissed as he gripped the sheets.

She started working his cock, her hand wrapped around the base as she sucked him in. She took him all in until he hit the back of her throat and he moaned. Poppy relished in the sound. She pulled back again, sucked as she did, and pulled all the way off with a pop. She looked up at him, his eyebrows furrowed but pleasure written all over his face. She gave him a stroke then sucked him back into her mouth, working him faster. She could taste the salty precum in her mouth.

"Poppy," he rasped out. "I'm going to come."

And at that she pulled all the way off and let go of his cock and left him there teetering on the edge. He glared at her, and she loved every second of it. She crawled up his body and reached over him to get a condom out of his bedside table. While she reached over him, he put his hand between her legs and stroked her. His mouth found her nipple and sucked it into his mouth, applying a small amount of pressure with his teeth. The sensation shot right to her clit which he was circling with his fingers. A surprised gasp escaped her mouth.

She ripped open the foil packet and rolled the condom down his length then she got over him and lowered herself on top of him.

"Wait," he growled out. She stilled. "I need to make you come first."

"Don't worry, I'm going to come." She was already so close after pleasuring him. Poppy took him in until he was fully sheathed inside, and she gave a little rock of her hips. The fullness sent shivers of pleasure all through her body. Then she began to move up and down. He looked up at her and bit his lip, one hand moved to her hip while the other played with her breast kneading it then gently rolling the nipple between his fingers.

She began to rock on him with a little more speed and he hissed out. Both of his hands found her hips and he began to buck beneath her. Because of her size, he didn't move her much, but he filled her so deeply she was getting so close. Her fingers found her clit and began to work little circle as he fucked her from below.

"Fuck, Poppy. You are perfect."

She cried out and came around him. His grip on her hips tightened as he slammed her down and bucked into her one last time and went rigid with his own pleasure.

Poppy climbed off and fell to his side. He disposed of the condom and then pulled her close. They both lay there in peaceful silence. This was it. They were together making their way through this crazy life as a pair, and nothing else really mattered.

CHAPTER 31

Josh

They awoke early the next day. Poppy had to work, but they talked over breakfast about what they needed to do. Josh needed to write a letter to give to the owner and Poppy was going to write a letter of her own. Then they put out a plea on social media with their intentions to buy the house and explain the problem. They asked for people in town to share their memories of the house and maybe write a letter of their own.

After work, Josh would start down his list of people who might be able to help. Today he was installing a new sliding door for Ms. Maple. On his way he stopped by the market to tell Mr. Fipps what they were up to, but he was surprised when he got there, and the news had arrived before him.

"I saw on the Facebook what Poppy posted. I think you two are doing a wonderful thing. I'll have Janet dig through our old pictures, I'm sure we have pictures of the kids at the haunted house. We are going to write a letter too," said Mr. Fipps.

Josh was not a big user of social media. He had accounts but he never really posted much and only checked them sporadically. Poppy, of course, was all over social media, but he still couldn't have guessed the response.

"Well thank you, I really appreciate that."

He kept on his way to Ms. Maple's. Writing a letter was right up her alley, he figured he would be able to count on her for a letter as well.

Adjusting his tool bag, He knocked on her door.

"Hello Josh dear. The patio door is out back."

He got to work on the door. It was a pretty easy job. He would be able to finish it by this afternoon. Before he knew it, Ms. Maple was making her way into the backroom with a glass of lemonade in one hand and a box in the other. He stopped what he was doing to chat with her. Even though he could have finished the job by this afternoon, with the way Ms. Maple loves to chat, he may be here till this evening, but he didn't mind.

"Well, it looks like you are making quick work of installing that door," said Ms. Maple.

"I'm trying," he said with a warm smile as he took the glass of lemonade from her hand.

"I must say, I think what you and Poppy are trying to do is really something special. I saw her post on the town page and we are all just a twitter trying to help you two get that house. That house needs some love, but it needs to go to two young people such as yourselves. And I must say, I am so glad the two of you got together. I just hope she makes you happy, Josh," she said, giving his hand a small pat.

"Thank you, Ms. Maple. I appreciate that. She does. She makes me very happy." He took a drink of the lemonade, and he could tell it was freshly squeezed. Sometimes this town was a little too Mayberry, but today it seemed to be the perfect amount.

"I went through my pictures and found all of these. There are some from the holiday parties, Halloween, and I even found some from when Mr. Whitney took a class of fourth graders into his study to show them his intricate model train set."

"I had forgotten all about that. It was quite a setup he had," said Josh.

"It was indeed. I know the house needs some TLC, but you are a handy fellow. I'm sure you're up to the challenge," she said with a kind smile.

"I sure hope so."

"Well, I'll let you get back to work. I just wanted to make sure I got this to you."

"Thank you." He took the box from her hands, set it next to his toolbox, and went back to getting the track of the door screwed down. He was starting to think they just might be able to pull this off, but after last night he knew no matter what he had a future with Poppy. This house would just be the icing on the cake.

When he got home after finishing up work at Ms. Maple's, Poppy's car was in the driveway. He opened the door and saw Poppy and his sister standing in the kitchen talking. There were pictures and newspaper clippings strewn over the coffee table. A model of the Whitney house made from popsicle sticks on the kitchen table next to an open laptop. Poppy's phone was next to it giving consistent dings and notifications popping up.

"What's all this?" he asked.

"You're home! Have you checked Facebook at all today?" Poppy was bouncing up and down with a huge smile spread across her face.

"Nope," he said as he looked through some of the newspaper clippings on the table.

"Well, I have to say, this town really shows up," Poppy said.

He made his way over to her and kissed her.

"Is this a popsicle stick mockup of the house?" he asked.

"Yeah, Sam actually made it in the sixth grade. I dug it out of the attic on my lunch break. I thought it might be useful," she beamed at him.

"Useful?" he asked. He wasn't sure how a model of their house fit into getting other people to write letters, but he was already aware that with Poppy sometimes it's just better to roll with the punches.

Lexi looked over at him and even she was smiling. It wasn't that she never smiled, but she was usually pretty serious, but it would appear Poppy's charm worked on his sister as well. "She's been cooking up some pretty amazing stuff over here today. I think you guys will get the house," said Lexi.

Poppy's phone started ringing and she quickly looked at the caller id. "Oh good, I'm gonna go take this. Catch him up on the plan," she said to Lexi, and she disappeared up the stairs into Josh's room.

"What's going on?" he asked again.

"So, she put out a call on Facebook for pictures of the house and letters to help you guys win over the sellers. The messages and phone calls have been pouring in all day. People want you guys to have the house and they're so happy you two are together. I think she was just planning to get some pictures and letters, but it has turned into so much more than that."

"What do you mean?" He asked.

"I think there is going to be an event in the town square this weekend. I'm not sure the specifics, but Poppy is a force of nature."

He still didn't quite know what to think, and to be honest he was feeling a bit of whiplash from the emotions of last night, to whatever this is right now. He gently opened the door as Poppy finished up her phone call.

"That would be perfect... Yes, I will be in touch... Yes, see you Saturday."

She hung up and turned around and was surprised to see Josh there.

"What is going on?" He asked her with a smile on his face.

Instead of answering she just ran straight into his arms and almost took the breath right out of him. He braced himself as she wrapped her arms around him.

"I put a call out to get pictures and letters and one thing led to another and you know how this town loves a cause, and quite frankly, loves you. I mean who wouldn't. On Saturday in the town square there is going to be a little festival where we all share our memories about the Whitney house and what it would mean to bring back some of those traditions we all grew up with," she said all in one breath.

"And to think I thought you might leave me yesterday," he said, pulling her into a big hug.

"Josh, I told you, you're it. I'm here. And I'm a go big or go home kind of girl." She reached up to kiss him. "I think it would be amazing to own the best party house in town. I mean think of the baking opportunities alone, not to mention the party planning. I love a theme." She gave him another quick kiss. "We have some planning to do. And you, sir, have a letter to write."

She was right, he did have a letter to write, and he knew exactly what he wanted to say after today. Life had hit him hard when he was younger, but he and his sister had survived together. This town helped him survive and he had spent his life trying to make it up to the people who watched out for him and his sister. And it looked like the town was about to show up and show out again. This town deserved one hell of a thank you note, and if it could put even one ounce of the gratitude in his heart for this town and for Poppy then the house would be theirs to make a lifetime of memories in. He could see it already.

CHAPTER 32

Poppy

It had been a crazy week and Poppy was busy preparing for the big event. She loved doing this, and if she was being honest, she was good at it. She had never really partaken in helping plan town events. She went to them, but she always left the planning to other people.

The orchard was going to run a booth with hot apple cider and treats Poppy was baking. She wanted donuts and muffins and all the other things she could think of. Her Gran and one of the other orchard workers were going to man that booth, so she had food and drinks taken care of.

She had been able to book a band on short notice. There would be a place for speakers to share their memories of the Whitney house and she had places to put up all the pictures people had sent her.

The pictures spanned decades: people like Mr. Fipps had given pictures of him as a child, his children, and his grand-children at what was the last Halloween party held there. She thought about what it would mean to have this space back for the town. These traditions and events she had taken for granted her whole life really were something special, and she knew that now.

She knew because Josh had opened her eyes. Now that they were open there was no going back. The realization that she was from a town that looked out for people was something that shifted the way she looked at things. Sure, a community like that had its gossip and its expectations, but it also had love and support. She had been so willing to toss it aside in hopes of something else, but not anymore.

If she was being honest with herself, she finally felt like she had found her place in all of this. Yes, she hoped to have the Whitney House where she would be able to use her newly discovered event planning skills to host some killer parties, but she also had the orchard.

The orchard had felt like a burden her whole life. It had felt like this business that was too important to her family and the town to cast aside, but it held no joy for her. But she had never used her out of the box thinking to find her place in it. Sam fit in it perfectly the way it was, he was a hard worker. He enjoyed the physical labor, which was a completely foreign concept to Poppy, but he really did seem to like working the land and researching how to best take care of the orchard. He had so many ideas for outside attractions for kids and families. He had turned the orchard into something more than it had been. Maybe she should try and do some out of the box thinking of her own and make the family business something she could be passionate about too.

She was pulling another batch of muffins out of the oven as Sam walked in. He was caked in the evidence of a hard day's work at the orchard.

"No way. Do not come into this kitchen looking that way," she scolded him.

He smiled at her and stepped outside. He took off his

jacket and hung it up, then he came in and scrubbed his hands.

"Better?" he asked.

"Slightly," Poppy said, looking a little less annoyed.

"It looks amazing in here, Poppy. How long did it take you to do all of this?"

She looked around taking stock of the kitchen. She had made over eight dozen donuts and the same with muffins. The kitchen was covered in baked goods.

"I was actually able to get this done today," she said with a new sense of pride.

"Well now that I know what you are capable of, I am tempted to make you bake like this for the orchard all the time," he said.

He smirked at her trying to get a rise out of her. That was their usual schtick. He would tease Poppy about putting her to work in the orchard and she would shoot him down, but she didn't feel like doing that anymore.

"Well, if it gets me off the register I'll bake all day," she answered back.

"Wait. Are you serious?" He asked, clearly taken back.

She was too busy taking in the kitchen. It really was filled with food. She needed to start boxing all of it up for tomorrow.

"Poppy, are you serious?" he asked again.

"About what?" she asked.

"That you could bake like this if you didn't have to work the register," he clarified.

"Yeah, I think I could. I have actually been thinking about that. I think I would like to start baking more and if that goes well, maybe we can open a little cafe."

"Who are you and what have you done with Poppy?" he joked.

She hit him in the chest. "I'm being serious. I've been thinking about this lately."

"If you are serious, Poppy, we should talk. This year has been really good for the orchard. Graham and I have been talking about building a few more features and he has some plans for his land. A bakery and a cafe would be amazing, people could spend a whole day here. Don't kid me about this," he said, looking almost gleeful.

She couldn't help but smile. Sam seemed almost giddy. He didn't get like this often but when he did, it made her happy. Generally, his role in their relationship was to keep her grounded, so when he was the one with the big dreams it made her happy. She lacked the follow through he had, it was something she had always envied. Sam would get an idea, figure out the best way to do it and then go about doing it. Poppy just could never do that. She would have an idea and do it, but she would run out of steam or get bored, whatever the reason, nothing seemed to last. But if she were to bring that same energy to the orchard, she trusted Sam would be able to keep her motivated whether she wanted to be or not.

"Also, you have to try some of Josh's sandwiches. He's kind of a sandwich artist. On our first date he made these amazing sandwiches with fresh ingredients. He's a really great cook."

"Really?" Sam asked, his brain clearly working.

"Yeah, really. It is just something to think about."

He was quiet and she could tell he was actually thinking about it. It was amazing how much had changed in her time with Josh, but it all felt right. It felt like this was how it should have been all along. Learning lessons the hard way was something Poppy had always been guilty of, and it was looking like this was no different.

"Well, I gotta start boxing all this stuff up for tomorrow. Did you need something when you came in?" she asked.

"Oh yeah, I just wanted to touch base about tomorrow," he said.

"I have a tent for you guys to set up hot cider and Gran is working the tent next to you guys with all this stuff. Just get there around one thirty to set up."

"You got it." He picked up a donut and took a bite.

"Hey! Those are for tomorrow!" she said as she tried to push him out of the kitchen.

"Alright, I'm outta here, but we are going to have to sit down and have a real discussion about this. If you want to start baking more, I think it's a great idea."

"Okay, well, let me get through tomorrow and then we can talk," said Poppy.

He paused for a moment and looked at her.

"What?" she asked.

"Nothing… I guess I'm just really happy you have found something here to make you happy. I would have supported you in anything you chose to do, but I've always hoped that we would be able to find a way to make this work together. It has always been a family business and it just feels really nice to have you be a bigger part of it."

He walked over to her and gave her a big hug. As close as Sam and Poppy were, they weren't really huggers, but Poppy didn't mind this. In fact, she found herself getting oddly emotional. She hugged him right back.

After a moment she pulled away. "As touching as this has been, I still have a lot of work to do before tomorrow. So, if you stay in this kitchen another minute, I am going to put you to work."

Sam gave her a knowing smile. "I'm proud of you, Poppy. And I'm really glad you and Josh found each other. He managed to get you to do some work around here in a matter of months and I've been trying my whole life," he said with a smirk on his face.

"Out! … and thank you, it means a lot, even if you're a pain in the ass."

"See you later, Poppy," he said as he walked out of the kitchen finishing his donut.

She smiled to herself. This may not have been her plan, but she was happy. Now, she just had to finish up planning this event and get that house, but she was feeling pretty good about their odds. Things did seem to be falling in her favor right now.

She scanned the kitchen with a sense of accomplishment, then she got to work packing up all the food. She had a house to save. But first she had a few last minute errands to run.

Poppy walked into Fipp's Market to get a final shoe box of pictures for the event she was planning. It felt good to be doing something for the town, and it pleased Poppy to be figuring out her spot in all of this. She was enjoying putting this event together and she was actually pretty good at it. If she and Josh did manage to get the Whitney House it was just the beginning of the event planning. She was starting to realize that even if they didn't get the house this was still just the beginning of the events she would help this town plan.

"Hey Mr. Fipps, I heard you had a shoe box for me," Poppy said walking into the market.

"We sure do, Janet found some real gems. Also, Katie McPhee was in earlier, she has a bunch of old newspaper clippings at the bookstore if you want those as well," he said.

"Thanks," she said as she took the shoe box.

"Some good memories in there. I'm so glad you and Josh are doing this. This little town needs people like you and Josh to bring us into the future. So many other little towns like ours are becoming ghost towns, but with people like your family and Josh taking charge I know Mystic Falls is in good hands."

"Thanks Mr. Fipps, that means a lot," she said with a smile.

"I will say though that I was pleasantly surprised. I thought you always wanted to spread your wings and fly."

"So did I, but sometimes you just need a little nudge to find out that what you were looking for was right under your nose the whole time," she said.

"Or right next to you on the bus," Mr. Fipps said with a wink.

With her interest piqued, Poppy looked at him with a cocked eyebrow.

"I pulled this picture out, I thought you might like to keep this one," he said, handing her an old photo of the big yellow school buses that were the bane of her existence at the orchard. But there on one of the little benches sat two recognizable children who looked to be about ten, one with two dark braids and one with dark hair, blue eyes, and a smile across his face as he looked at the little girl sitting next to him.

"I think Janet took this photo when she took your class to see Mr. Whitney's train set up," he said as she looked at the picture.

"I think you're right. Thank you, Mr. Fipps, this means a lot," she said with deep earnestness.

"I wish you both all the happiness in the world. Now you better get on your way, you've got a house to save, young lady," he said.

Taking one last look at the photo of her and Josh on the school bus Poppy smiled and slipped it into her purse. "I will do my best. I'm off."

"See you tomorrow," he called behind her as Poppy made her way to the door. They just might be able to pull this off.

She had one final stop before she was done. Bridget's

magic shop. Poppy thought Bridget might enjoy an update on her spell.

Opening the door, the familiar sound of the bell tinkled over her head.

"Hello dear," Bridget said with a broad smile. "I was wondering if I might be getting a visit from ye soon."

"Expecting me?" Poppy asked.

"I wouldn't say 'expecting' but yes, I thought ye might come. A happy update I hope," said Bridget.

"The happiest!" Poppy said with a grin on her face. "I must say, at first I was so confused when I thought it was Damien, then I was so frustrated when you kept telling me to follow my heart, but I must say, your spell really did help me find my true love and I just wanted to say thank you. So, thank you for your part in mine and Josh's love story. I can see a long happy life before us, and I have you to thank."

"Ye don't have me to thank for anything," Bridget said plainly.

"I really do. Your spell gave me the visions that made me realize that I am happy with Josh, and I can find true contentment here in Mystic Falls. I can't believe I could have missed out on all of this."

"Can I tell ye a little secret?" Bridget whispered leaned over the counter closer to Poppy.

"Of course," Poppy leaned in too, hungry for any little bit of magical wisdom this woman might share.

"That potion I gave ye the night of the wedding wasn't magic. I didn't play a role in yer charming love story," she said with a grin like the Cheshire Cat.

"What do you mean?" A confused look furrowed across Poppy's brow.

"There are some couples who require strong magic to find their true matches, but I have found more often than not the universe does a fairly good job of helping matches find each other."

"But the dream I had that night and all the visions, how do you explain that?" Poppy asked, trying to figure out what she meant.

"If ye think back, ye might be able to figure it out. I have found most people who have always been interested in magic have a wee bit of magic themselves, and in some cases a bit more than that. And I think ye just may be one of those cases, my dear."

"I'm not following you," she said, shaking her head.

"Yes, ye are, just trust yer intuition and ask yer questions," Bridget said with a patient smile on her face.

"Are you saying I'm magic?" Poppy asked with a sense of disbelief.

"I am," Bridget said plainly.

Poppy's mouth fell open. How could that be?

"Let me ask ye something, Poppy. When you were a small child did ye believe in magic and practice spells and make potions with the things around ye?"

Poppy shrugged. "Of course, I did. I mean what little kid didn't?"

"Have ye ever had what is referred to as Deja vu? When you have that feeling that ye've been here before?"

"Yes," Poppy said, eyes still tight with disbelief.

"Have ye ever had a gut feeling that turned out correct? Dreams that come true? A sense of danger or anticipation ye couldn't explain?"

Poppy just nodded. She was taking it all in.

"The modern world has done away with the belief in magic for the most part, but magic has not done away with the modern world. There are magical people all around us if we know what we are looking for. And you, Poppy, are a seer. Ye have the gift of sight and intuition."

Could this really be true? She wanted so badly to believe it. This was something she had always thought about herself, but you can't just go around saying stuff like this without people thinking you're delusional. But when she was little, she would have sworn she was magic, but as she grew up and the real world chipped away at her little by little, she had thought it was just a childhood imagination. Could this really be true?

"When ye were looking for signs of magic everywhere ye saw them. Ye opened yourself up to the power of yer own magic. If ye work at honing that gift I think ye could tell a couple fortunes yerself," Bridget continued.

Closing her eyes, Poppy thought back. She was someone who was always interested in magic, always drawn to stories of magic and the hard to explain coincidences in real life. She was someone people always came to for advice, and she had to admit it herself she did give great advice. And she did have a sense of intuition. She was always someone who led from the heart. Sometimes it was hard to listen to her heart when the heart wasn't always logical because society today tends to place logic above gut feelings. It was easy to lose the ability to listen to her heart. Listen to your heart... That is what she had done, Bridget had helped her to claim her own magic.

"Is that why you told me to follow my heart? So, I would be able to tap into my own magic?"

"I told ye to follow your heart because that is what ye needed to do. Ye needed to get out of your head and out of yer own way. There is no spell that can do that. Ye finding yer own magic was just a happy coincidence, but I stopped believing in coincidences a long time ago," Bridget said with a wink. "Besides, it didn't take magic to see just how in love with ye Josh was, ye just needed to figure out how much ye love him too."

A sigh of deep contentment filled Poppy. She really did

love Josh, and sometimes she could kick herself for taking this long to realize it. But everything happens in its own time at its own pace. Now she just needed to get the house so they could both start living their lives.

"Thanks for everything, Bridget. Really." She reached across the counter and squeezed her hands. Her mind was still reeling from the news that had just been shared, but as out there as it sounded it made sense to her. All the pieces of herself she could never explain, this explained them. This was not what she was expecting when she asked her for a spell at the wedding, it was even better. Her current state was beyond anything she could have imagined, and now finding out she had a little bit of magic was just the cherry on top of a truly magical few months.

"Ye're welcome my dear. Come see me after ye save yer house and we will have a long chat about magic," said Bridget.

"I am going to take you up on that! You are going to wish you never told me," she said with her kilowatt smile lighting her face up. "But I do need to get going. See you soon!"

CHAPTER 33

Poppy

By the time Saturday morning rolled around Poppy was amped up. She had thrown herself into this event and was working hard to get it off without a hitch. She knew she wanted this house for her and for Josh, but she also wanted it for the town. Poppy may not be getting in-laws, but in some weird way she felt like the town would serve as that role. She had been told by more of them than she cared to think about not to hurt him, and she didn't intend to. This was it. This was home, even if the Whitney house wasn't theirs, Mystic Falls was.

The only person happier than Josh about her change of heart involving the town was Sam. He loved this town, and he loved their orchard, the two things Poppy had spent a good portion of her life trying, but failing, to get away from. Now those two things felt like a complete gift. After she and Sam had that talk in the kitchen, she was picturing things more and more. She would bake and help her Gran make all the jellies, and Josh would make his amazing sandwiches. She thought this would work out great. With all the improvements Sam and Graham had been working on at the orchard they had the best season yet, and a cafe would be a perfect fit.

"Where are we setting up shop?" Sam asked, carrying a crate full of gallon jugs of the orchard's apple cider.

"That tent next to the gazebo." She pointed him over to set up the food and cider from the orchard.

She knew they were pushing there luck with the weather planning an outdoor event in November, but luckily it was a gorgeous day. The leaves had already dropped, of course; they had been gone for over a month now. It was sunny and warm for November, but warm for November still isn't warm, so hot cider from the orchard would be perfect.

She had just finished setting up the galleries. There were collages of all the pictures the town people had given her and in the middle of that was the popsicle stick replica. Some of the town people had volunteered to share their stories and Josh wanted to speak. She was looking forward to that, knowing he would speak from the heart.

Josh stepped up behind her and rubbed her arms to warm her up and then slipped his arms around her waist. She could feel the heat radiating off of him warming her.

"Things are really shaping up. I can't believe you did all of this," he said.

"WE did all of this." Poppy leaned back into him and set her hand on his. She looked around from the art hung, to the vendors setting up, to the band setting up at the gazebo. This was going to be a great event.

She could just kick herself for the years she spent trying to find her dream and it had been right under her nose the whole time. And honestly, it just kept getting better. She was reminded of that when Hannah and Graham, the newest members of town, approached. She smiled at Poppy and gave her a hug.

"This is quite the shindig," Hannah said.

"Yeah, hopefully it will work," said Poppy.

The band started to play, and people filtered in. Everyone came from Ms. Maple to Theo and Vivian Williams, and of course, the mayor. Person after person got up and shared their memories of the Whitney house. It was an amazing afternoon. The only person missing was Mitch Alsup.

The sun was starting to set and soon it would be time to start getting packed up. Josh was the last one to speak. Poppy didn't know what he was going to say, but she knew he would make everyone happy. That is just how he was. He had a way of making you think about things but also making you feel comfortable. That is probably the reason he was so beloved by every single person in this town.

She watched in awe as he stepped on the stage and smiled a genuine smile warmly out to the crowd.

"I've known most of you my whole life," he started. "I have seen you at festivals and town events just like this over the years. I have fixed some of your doors." He smiled at Ms. Maple. "I have probably bagged all of your groceries." He smiled at Mr. Fipps. "I've given some of you Uber rides, mowed your lawn, fixed your bikes, raked your yard and all the other little ventures I have had over the years. I can honestly say Mystic Falls has saved my life. The kindness you have all shown to me and my sister has helped us more than you will ever know, and I am forever grateful.

All your support has put me in a place where I am able to do something for the town. Poppy and I are hoping to restore the Whitney house to what it used to be. Make it the heart of the city where we gather for parties and holidays and all the other milestones we share. We have all shared many milestones over the years, and I am hoping to share one more tonight. As most of you know, Poppy has been putting this whole thing together. And let's face it, her unstoppable energy is what got this event thrown together so quickly, but we put this together because we hope to buy this house together. Poppy, can you come up here with me?"

Her heart started to pound in her chest and her knees shook a bit as she made her way up the stage. She didn't know why she felt so nervous, she had been performing in front of these people in one way or another her whole life. He reached out and took her trembling hand and helped her up the stairs. She wasn't sure how, but she made it up. Everything but him fell away as she watched him drop to one knee in front of her. Her hand flew up to her mouth and tears pooled in her eyes as she watched him reach inside his coat pocket.

"Poppy, we may not have been together long, but I have been in love with you since I sat beside you on the bus in the fourth grade. So, in a way I have been in love with you most of my life. That is how I know for certain, without a shadow of a doubt, I want to spend the rest of my life with you. Will you, Poppy Smith, do me the honor of marrying me?"

She nodded her head at a fevered pace. "Of course, I will marry you!" she shouted. She was only mildly aware of the cheering of the entire town as he stood up and wrapped her in an embrace and kissed her.

He leaned his forehead to hers. "I've got you now, Princess."

She smiled up at him, hoping he really would get her tonight, especially when he called her princess. Poppy was pulled out of the moment by someone tapping on Josh's shoulder. Mitch whispered something in Josh's ear with a smile on his face.

His arms fell away and he turned to face him fully. "Are you serious?" he asked.

"It's yours. Meet me at my office tomorrow to start the paperwork."

Josh pulled his realtor into a giant bear hug. Then he turned with the biggest grin on his face she had ever seen.

"We got it," he said to Poppy, shock still in his eyes

"What?" Poppy's brain was still trying to catch up to the life altering events of the last few seconds.

"We got the house!" he yelled, and the microphone carried the news to the whole town.

Poppy squealed as he pulled her into the biggest hug. He kissed her and she melted.

"This is only the beginning. I cannot wait to see where we go next. I love you," he said.

"I love you too." She kissed him again.

The Cheering finally started to register in her mind. She looked out at the whole town. She could see Hannah and Graham, and her family. Josh's sister was smiling up at them bigger than anyone else. The center of attention was something Poppy had sought out since a young age, but it never felt like this. She had never felt this sense of love and belonging before, but she had a feeling starting a life with Josh would only be the beginning to this feeling. She only hoped he felt it too.

EPILOGUE

ALMOST ONE YEAR LATER

Poppy

"Hey Josh, I'm just about finished up here for the day. Gran invited us over for dinner. I think she put in a roast. Sam and Jackson are going to be there. Do you want to go?" she asked as she washed her hands.

"Of course. You know I'm always up for a family dinner," Josh called from the dining area of their little cafe. He had just finished wiping down the tables and setting the chairs for the night.

She did know that. They were married at the orchard in spring when the apple trees were in bloom. It was Poppy's favorite time of year, when the orchard was full of flowers. Sam was glad they picked then as well because the workload wasn't as heavy for an orchard in the spring. Even though they got married only six months after they started dating, it all felt right. Plus, Poppy wasn't one to wait once she set her mind to something.

Poppy finished wiping down the table in the kitchen and checked the list of things she was baking in the morning. She really had found her place here. She enjoyed baking and although it was still midseason the cafe had been a hit. The orchard business was booming, and she got to spend her days with Josh.

He had been able to quit Uber and didn't do much handyman work anymore. He still did a couple shifts at the bar, mainly because Poppy loved watching him ride. He worked most of his days here with her and sometimes Sam would steal him to help with some of the other work on the orchard. Josh seemed really happy, he fit in perfectly with her family. She knew how important it was to him to have that.

Poppy was drying her hands as Josh came through the door.

"Are you ready?" He asked.

"Yep, let me just grab my jacket and we'll head over."

He helped her slip on her jacket and locked up the kitchen and the store. On the way over to the house he held her hand. Sometimes she had to pinch herself because she fell a little bit more in love with him every day.

They walked in the door, and she heard her gran in the kitchen.

"Is that you Poppy?"

"Yeah, it's me. Do you need any help?"

"Is Josh with you?" asked Gran.

"Of course, he is."

She walked out of the kitchen wiping her hands on her apron. "Oh good," she walked over and gave him a hug.

"Nice to see you too, Gran," Poppy said, pretending to be offended.

"Josh, if you go to the top of the attic stairs you will find a box of Halloween decorations I set aside. Poppy told me you both are getting ready for a haunted house in your cellar. I just love that," said Gran.

"Wonderful, I'll go grab them. Thank you for setting them aside for us," Josh said.

"Of course."

The back door opened as Gran and Poppy both headed into the kitchen. Jackson came in and hung up his jacket. "Sam is on his way. He wanted to stop by the house and clean up before dinner."

"Wonderful, will you two set the table?" Gran asked.

Poppy and Jackson got to work setting the table while Gran finished up the dinner.

Sam and her dad came in talking numbers. "This is the best year we have had yet. We may have to add on another field trip day. I had to turn away a group yesterday because we didn't have any more space this season," her dad said.

"That's definitely something to think about," Sam answered back as he hung his jacket up.

"No," Poppy groaned. "No more field trips."

They both ignored her. Everyone found a seat around the table, but Josh wasn't there yet. Poppy decided to go find him to see what was taking so long. She found him in the living room standing over by the piano.

"What are you doing?" she asked as she walked over to him.

He was there looking at the picture on the piano. He picked up a frame examining it. As she got to him, she rubbed his back. He was looking at their wedding photo. He looked so handsome in his suit and Poppy wore a flowing white gown with a hair braided and flowers tucked in, and they stood among the flowering apple trees in the orchard. Setting the picture down with all the other photos, he turned to her and gave her a tight hug. When she pulled away, she looked into his eyes and saw they seemed a bit misty.

"Are you okay?" She asked.

"Yeah, I am. I'm really happy, Poppy," he said, bending his head to give her a kiss.

"Me too." They stood there for a moment longer looking at the pictures on the piano.

"Are you guys coming or what?" Sam called from the kitchen.

"You ready?" she asked.

"We're coming," Josh answered back.

Poppy turned to walk away. Josh smacked her ass and she stopped. "I have some plans for you when we get home, princess," he whispered in her ear as he walked by.

She still got the flutters when he called her princess in that low raspy voice.

She walked into the kitchen as everyone was sitting down. And she had to admit, she was happy too. Things may not have turned out like she had expected them too, but they were better than she could have ever dreamed.

25 years later

Josh

JOSH STOOD outside the event center on a beautiful fall day. On the other side of this building was a field full of people waiting for him to walk his daughter down the aisle. He couldn't believe this day was finally upon them. He looked over and saw his wife walking towards him. She was still as beautiful as the day she married him, although some grays had found her hair and her eyes were bracketed by the tell-tale lines of a life full of laughter.

"You look beautiful, Poppy. I would marry you again today if I could," he said, reaching out his hand for hers. She reached back for him, and he pulled her close to him and kissed her. Even after all these years the pull was still there, that magic that existed between them still just as strong as it was when he kissed her in the prop room all those years ago.

"They're on their way down. I think we're just about ready to get started," she said.

"You may be ready, but I'm not. I'm not ready to give up my little girl."

"She's not going anywhere, and you are gaining a son, growing the family bigger. You love that," she said with a knowing smile.

"You're right, I do, but where did all the time go? It seems like just yesterday I was pushing her on the swing in the backyard and here she is today getting married."

The string quartet started playing as he spotted his daughter and her two best friends coming out of the house. She looked beautiful in her dress with her dark beautiful hair flowing and her blue eyes smiling. He felt the tears already pooling in his eyes. He took a deep breath and blinked them away.

"I need to go, I'll see you down there," Poppy whispered in her ear and gave him a quick kiss. He watched her walk away and smiled at the way her wide hips swayed as she walked. He was still just as attracted to her as he had ever been, much to the chagrin of their children who were constantly groaning at his and Poppy's frequent displays of affection.

His daughter joined him there on the steps. She smiled up at him. She had Poppy's big smile that lit up any room she was in. The tears he had been fighting won the battle and streamed down his face.

"Don't cry, dad. You're going to make me cry."

"I can't help it, sweetheart. I'm a crier, you know that" he said, dabbing his eyes with the handkerchief he had thought to put in his pocket.

"I do." She wrapped her arms around his neck and kissed him on his cheek. "I love you, daddy."

"I love you too."

The bridesmaids were making their journey down the aisle. "Are you ready, sweetheart? It's not too late to run." He whispered in her ear. He looked at her and saw that it was in fact too late. Her eyes had already connected with her groom who stood up handsomely under the arch of flowers, his red hair shining in the sun, wearing a MacNeil tartan kilt.

The crowd around them stood as he walked her down the aisle. All the friendly faces smiled at her, but her eyes only connected with her groom. He wiped a tear away from his eye and looked at her with awe as she came down the aisle. Josh knew that feeling, he had felt the same way on his own wedding day.

It seemed right that his and Poppy's daughter would marry Hannah and Graham's son. They had been raised together. Even though they didn't get together until they both went away to college and realized they missed each other a little too much.

Now here they were both working at the orchard. As happy as he was, he thought Sam might be happier than anyone here. He had good hands to leave the orchard in if he ever decided to leave it. The orchard was an incredible business now. Yes, there was still the orchard, but it had become a whole business. They grew blueberries, a petting farm, horseback riding, massive playgrounds, and of course the restaurant and the bakery he and Poppy oversaw.

He looked around at the people smiling at him, and he had to wipe another tear away. For someone who had spent a large part of his early life wanting a bigger family, here it was. All these people here from the Smith family and the Glenn family he counted as his family. And of course, the town was here, probably the whole town as he looked around. There were new faces and old faces, but they were all smiling faces today.

They made it down the aisle somehow and the love between these two wonderful people was written all over their faces. As much as it was bittersweet having his daughter get married, he was so happy it was to someone who loved her almost as much as he did.

Being a father was wonderful, it had helped to heal some of his old scars. His family was his purpose, his heart. He could never understand how his own father could have just left him and his sister. He had made a promise the day their daughter was born to be a better father than he'd had, and he had succeeded. He had a wife he was still head over heels in love with, three remarkable children, and enough love and laughter to make up for the years when he wasn't sure if that was in the cards for him.

He heard the officiant say something, but he was too lost in his own thoughts to take it in. His daughter gave him a gentle nudge and he realized he had just asked "Who gives this woman to be wed?"

"Her mother and I do," he said weakly through the tightness in his throat and pushed away another tear. A tall handsome Scotsman reached out and took her hand, and he fought the urge to yank her back into his arms.

He went to join Poppy at his seat and noticed she was openly crying and handed her a tissue from his jacket pocket.

"Thank you. She looks so beautiful," she whispered in his ear.

He nodded and squeezed her hand. "So do you," he said, bringing her hand up to kiss it.

And he looked around once again at the people around him, basking in the love that he was lucky enough to have his life filled with. He had hit most of life's major milestones with Poppy and today they checked off another, walking his daughter down the aisle. He knew life had so much more in store for them, and he was looking forward to all of it. Even though it got off to a bit of a rocky start, he had created a truly remarkable life and he could not have asked for more. He often thought he could never be happier, but then days like this would happen and that bar would raise higher. He was a lucky man, and it was all because he and this woman next to him had created this truly magical life.

He couldn't wait to see what the future would bring.

Coming out soon

Keep and eye out for what's happening next in Mystic Falls.

Lexie Turner has lived her life on autopilot, working hard every single day and taking care of her brother. It is time someone came to sweep her off her feet and turn her carefully guarded world upside down in the best way possible.

Lexie Lets Go

Coming this summer!

ACKNOWLEDGMENTS

There are so many people who have helped me along the way with this book. I am so grateful for each and everyone of them. It would take me forever to thank all of them, so if you helped me, just know how very much I appreciate it.

First I always have to thank Will, my amazing partner. He always has my back and makes life easier. I could not do life without him.

I also need to acknowledge the supportive online community that keeps me inspired. From the authors who help me stay sane, to the fat activists who keep me inspired, and the readers who remind me of my why and how important representation is.

Also, this one is a little out there, but I have to thank Mrs. B, my high school drama teacher. I remember the Poppy in me who longed for more adventure and to see her name in lights. In my graduation card Mrs. B wrote that sometimes dreams grow and change and we can't be afraid to grow and change with them. Those words have been right there whenever I needed them. My dreams have grown and changed a millions times over by this point in my life, and I am thankful for each iteration of them.

And of course, I have to thank Leni Kauffman. Her cover arts bring my characters to life in the most beautiful and inspiring way possible.

Also I have to thank Lexi at Morally Gray Author Services. They have been an amazing editor and support to work with.

And my beta readers, your early feedback is crucial. It helps me to craft a better story and I look forward to doing it again very soon.

Stay tuned there is much more coming from Mystic Falls and the universe it exists in.

ABOUT THE AUTHOR

Mary Warren lives in Illinois with her family. When she's not writing stories of fat women, she's reading them and advocating for better fat representation. Mary founded Fat Girls in Fiction, pointing out positive fat representation for women, femmes, and non-binary people in books. This project became a community and is something she is immensely proud of and happy to be working on.